BY B. J. CHUTE

THE
GOOD
WOMAN

by
B. J. Chute

AUTHOR OF

GREENWILLOW

ETC.

THE VANGUARD PRESS
NEW YORK

Library of Congress Cataloging-in-Publication Data
Chute, B. J. (Beatrice Joy), 1913–
The good woman.
I. Title.
PS3505.H99G6   1986   813'.52   85-32297
ISBN 0-8149-0920-5

Designer: Tom Bevans

Jacket design by Hank Blaustein

Manufactured in the United States of America.

Dedicated to any wayfarer

"... If they looked behind them, ther was
ye mighty ocean which they had passed, and
was now as a maine barr & goulfe to seperate
them from all ye civill parts of the world."
—WILLIAM BRADFORD
History of Plymouth Plantation

CONTENTS

I
THE PRISON

1

A golden lance from the west struck through the windowpane, through the slanted blinds and the pale curtains. Gold leaped from the tinder of dark cherry wood, licked at the corner of an armchair, and blazed for an instant only on a small clock, fake-gold, ticking quietly.

A cloud shut down the sunset and took the fire with it. Twilight cornered the room, and it was twilight that woke the woman on the bed. Her last breath in sleep was a sigh, and she put the back of her hand across her eyes before she opened them.

When she did open them, the room, of course, was there. It was always there, morning after morning, evening after evening, day after day. I sleep too much, she thought, but in sleep it was all right not to be anywhere and there was no need to respond to anything.

She turned her head and looked at the clock. It showed nothing but time, its delicate hands as impassive as if there had never been sun or anything else alive in the room at all. "I don't care," the woman said out loud. "I really just don't care." Then, of course, the telephone rang.

Thursday, Millicent; after-five, evening rates. It would go on ringing until it was answered, as if, out of her own stubbornness, Millicent could somehow force her mother to be home, even if she were out.

Well, Millicent's mother thought, I am home. She got up from the bed and switched on the table lamp, since, when the sun left this bedroom, it left it completely, sliding down the walls, having only one aperture to come through. Aperture, opening, wall has openings. What she really wanted to do was to lie down again and go back to sleep.

But the telephone would split its throat. She stood by the bed, smoothing her hands down the sides of her dress, wondering why she was wearing the best (better) gray one when she was not going anywhere. It was not very important. Out there in Michigan, Millicent could not see her to say Oh-Mother-it's-all-creased. But she smoothed her hands down her sides anyway before she picked up the telephone and said "Hello?" with a question mark.

"Mother?"

Who else?

Millicent's bright reproachful voice, saying where had she been? the phone rang so long.... "I just got in," her mother said, and wished that Millicent would learn to say a simple "hello" and go on with her Thursday-evening conversation.

"Where *were* you?" said Millicent.

Lying on the bed, my dear daughter, being nothing at all. Leave me alone. "I went shopping," Mother said.

"At this hour?"

"Some of the stores stay open, evenings are less crowded."

"What were you buying?"

I was buying a nightmare. She had again the feeling she had so often, of not really being in any place at all, and of wishing that people would not expect her to respond. She drew a deep breath, reached for a plausible lie, and came up with a satisfactory one. "I was looking at baby things."

"Oh, but darling, it's three months yet!" Millicent would be glowing modestly, holding the telephone to her ear. (Millicent, who had rather large ears, though nicely shaped, sounded a little girlish for her thirty years, somewhat cowlike and somewhat girlish, Millicent would make the perfect mother.) Of course, I love my daughter, but I don't want to answer anything she asks me. I don't want to answer anything anyone asks me. I feel crooked inside my head. Not crooked; lame. "We don't even know if it's going to be a boy or a girl, darling," Millicent was saying. "You can't choose colors before we know."

"I won't," said her mother.

Suddenly suspicious. "Mother, is everything all right?"

She put on the brightest voice in the world for responding. "Everything's lovely. The weather's lovely, it's been clear all day, it's been..." Perfect lovely, echo mocked.

"Have you had your supper?"

"Not— Yes, of course, I have."

"That means you haven't."

"Soup. And toast, and some raisins." The raisins gave an authentic touch to that meal she had not eaten, no one would invent raisins with soup.

"You don't eat enough," said faraway Millicent. "And you don't get out enough."

"Yes, I do," her mother said. "I told you, I just came in!" Then she put her hand partly over the receiver and whispered, "Go away."

"What?"

"I said yes, I do eat enough, I do get out enough." I have to go, she thought frantically, go before I stop answering altogether, fade out attached to a telephone cord. I have to go, dear, she thought inside her head, looking for an excuse to go because she was born polite and had been raised polite and would die polite, always thoughtful of other people's feelings. I have to go, dear, the raisins are boiling over.

"Well, I worry about you," Millicent said with satisfaction.

She took her cue. "Worry about yourself," she said, "and the baby. How is Gerry?"

"Gerry's fine. Busy."

"Give him my love."

"I will.

"Yes, do." The telephone had become an extension of her arm. She looked at her hand and saw the cord growing out of her fingers, but it was not profoundly interesting. Her eyelids closed down over her eyes, very smoothly. "Yes, do," she said again.

"I will, of course. —Mother, you sound tired, you're doing too much. Your voice sounds so—" She hesitated. "Flat."

Not flat, flat had edges. Dull, perhaps. She summoned up something that would sound better. "I'm sleepy," she said, just as bright as could be. "It's my own fault. I watched the movie on the Late Show last night. I shouldn't have stayed up so late."

"You and your TV movies," Millicent said indulgently. "Go to bed early, and *do* eat something beside raisins. Really, you have no sense."

That was it—no sense. No sense of anything. Not dull, not flat. Numb, perhaps?

"Mother!"

"Yes, she said. "That's what I'll be. I mean, that's what I'll do. I'll have something more to eat, and then I'll go to bed. Take care, dear."

"What was the movie?"

"What movie?"

"The one last night, on TV. Really, Mother darling—"

"It was an old one," she said, sounding firm for the first time. "Very old. And dull. It was dull, too. Good night, dear, take care." She hung up her hand, and the instrument with it. Somewhere she heard Millicent saying something, Good, night, Mother, dear, take, care.

If she lay down on the bed now, she would fall asleep at once. Her gray dress would wake creased in the morning, her head might ache, which would reassure her that her head was there. What is the matter with me? she thought languidly.

She turned back toward the bed, meaning to lie down on it only for a moment. Then she would get up and really think about what was the matter. Only for a moment, only the eyelids coming down over the eyes....

For a New York street, it was a quiet one. Thin traffic sounds; something scraping on something, like a fiddle or a cricket; a brawl voice from somewhere skipping like a stone on water.

The street light slowed the dark at the window, half open in early mild September. Black was half closed like her eyelids. There was nothing to be gained by opening them except to get up and get ready to undress and go to bed or to read a book or to walk to the corner and buy the Daily News or the New York Post, both of which she detested—had used to detest, rather, because she had not felt that kind of energy for a long time now.

I suppose you're ill, she told herself, making an effort to appear interested. In a nice apartment, with kind doormen called Joe and Ernest and Albert, with a daughter in Michigan, with a son-in-law who has a good job in a good law firm, with a grandchild coming, you are so very lucky, not like those bodies that lay in graveyards not able to feel anything any more. Not half-ghosts like me, not quite dead but floating so near to it. How pleasant if her eyes, shut now, never opened again. Pleasant? Alarming, surely? Frightening. To drift off like a wave sliding onto the sand from the sea, not obliged to go back into deep waters. Horrifying, of course.

Horrifying, but very pleasant. She nodded silent approval and let the dark come down.

The morning was better. She even felt faint embarrassment, but there was no one she had to explain this to. Sometime after midnight, she had wakened suddenly, the husk of her, and had prepared for bed as one should. Nightgown, robe, slippers, toothbrush, cleansing cream, as orderly as the alphabet. Once waked, she could no longer sleep, so that when this morning came she got up calmly, being awake already, and the alphabets resumed. It was harder to slide off the rim of day. The spring of some tiny motor in her head was wound tight enough to last till sundown. If the sun stayed up forever ... No, it would be the same. And, no, she was not ill. Her health, as she knew very well, was excellent. She had nothing to use it for, but it was excellent. Like time, it had no forward or backward any more. It was just there.

In spite of the excellent health, she had noticed recently the extreme heaviness of things. Perhaps today would be different, and she would feel something, want to do something, weigh something light or heavy in her hand or in her head. Perhaps, after all, she was very ill? something subterranean, so she could do nothing for a long, lone time.

She was doing that anyway. And, no, she was not ill.

With an enormous effort, she summoned herself. She would have instant coffee, instant orange juice, instant toast. She would put on her second-best suit, a healthy suit, navy blue and geometric, and she would go out on the New York street and find something to do with her day, which stretched ahead of her shining and new and unendurable. She drank her coffee slowly and told herself she had everything a person could wish for, and that if the telephone rang now and someone asked her to lunch or a matinee or dinner or an orgy (that was funny for a moment but she couldn't hold the moment) she would say yes, thank you, and she would GO. She could see the GO as a green light in the street, to be driven through rapidly, waved on by approving police officers.

This was all very silly. She tried some toast, because Millicent was right. Mother didn't eat enough. Toast, butter and plum jam, and drink your orange juice. She did so, successfully, while the policemen applauded.

When the telephone rang, she found herself sitting with her hands in her lap, her coffee cold in the cup, and her toast cold too but buttered and stickily spread. She wiped her hands on her linen napkin—she would not use paper napkins—and went to answer the phone in its bedroom.

Not unpredictably, it was Janet. Many many years ago, long before her marriage, long before all the fulfillment that had befallen her, she had thought of Janet as best-friend. When she answered the phone now, she merely hoped Janet would not hear in her voice the resentment at being called at all.

Yes, dear, how lovely to hear from you so early. She glanced at the small gold clock, and it was not so early after all, it was nearly eleven and no one knew how long she might have been sitting with her hands in her lap. Well—yes, dear, anyway. Of course. Lunch would be lovely, that new place on Madison Avenue, just a few blocks from the library—the Library, the one with the two lions. Janet thinks I'll get lost, people keep worrying about me lately. I must tell them, she thought, that I don't worry about myself at all, not in the least. I'm very contented. I'm very...Oh, God!

She screamed silently. Inside her head. Outside her head, where contact between ear and telephone was so precise, she went on listening to Janet's voice. It sounded rather like Mil-

9

licent's, and she noticed, in the muffled space after the scream, that her own fingers were so tight about the phone that the veins stood up on the back of her hand like an old, old woman's.

Fifty-two, last May. Fancy that! The dear old thing.

"I'll see you at one-thirty then," she said to Janet quite brightly. "We'll miss the crowd."

She put the telephone down and whispered "see-you" to it. If she managed not to think at all, she could perhaps manage to get through the day.

2

The best thing to do with Janet, across the tablecloth, over the silverplate spoons and forks and knives, above the white china cups, was to nod in reply to everything. The soup had been pleasant, faintly pink, faintly aromatic, faintly warm. There were two crackers apiece in cellophane wrappers, and, when Janet said a little crossly that they were very small and one would think they would give you at least four, nodding was a perfectly adequate response.

The chicken Tetrazzini had been adequate too, served with rolls and butter, and, if one ate well now, one would not have to prepare anything at home later. Would she have ice cream or a cup of coffee? She would have ice cream, Janet could choose the flavor. She would have preferred tea because she had already drunk cold coffee at breakfast time, but Janet was ordering coffee. Better not to interrupt Janet, who ran on like a river and accepted a nod as a reply.

"Black?" said the waitress.

Janet said, "Cream, please, for both of us," and, when

the waitress had gone at last (a mothering, smothering waitress, "Is everything all right, dear?") she said, "I'll drink both
our creams. I know you don't take any." Her brow clouded,
she could be seen to be thinking about her hips. "You're the
one who ought to be having cream, Florence," she went on
accusingly. "You're getting thin. Are you all right? You don't
look all right."

She nodded, accepting question and criticism. The basket
of rolls was still on the table, so she took out another and
buttered it to forestall more reproofs. The waitress slid a dish
of ice cream neatly under the hand that was holding the roll,
and she now had the buttered roll and the ice cream and two
very dry-looking cookies besides.

"You won't want that," Janet said, and took the roll away
from her. Janet smiled, and she had a very pretty, healthy
smile. *I want the roll back from you. Janet,* she thought, but there
was no point saying it aloud. There could not be, in so pleasant
and lukewarm a restaurant, two women, both in their early
fifties, struggling for possession of a buttered roll.

"You'd have to give it back to me, if I asked," she said,
aloud this time but not loud enough to be heard because of
what happened afterwards whenever one said anything; you
were supposed to listen and respond and then to listen and
respond again, and it was too much to do even on the good
days. And how long had it been since there was a good day?

Janet said, "What?"

"I said I'd had a good day." She was being very clever.
"Having lunch with you and everything." It was a mammoth
effort, she need not talk again for a long time, surely.

"Nice," Janet said comfortably. "Aren't you going to eat
your cookies? Oh, I shouldn't have taken your roll away from
you." She looked around for the roll, but it had already gone
with the waitress, quite silently. "How bad of me!" She had a

11

pretty, healthy chuckle too, exactly like the smile. "What shall we do after lunch? We could walk up Fifth Avenue and look at the windows. I really ought to think about buying a fall suit, but it's always so difficult. Maybe, if you were with me..."

Oh, no, no. No, no, no. She could feel her shoulders shrinking against the back of the chair. It all crowded in on her, just how it would be—the suits on the racks, the salesladies hovering, the little coops for trying things on, the saying Oh, that's lovely, yes, Janet, no, Janet, that's not really your kind of...Oh, no, no, no, no, no.

She drank the little black puddle of coffee quickly and put her napkin down on the table. "You go alone. I have to go somewhere, I promised..." The great stone lions outside the Library, the lions that had been the waymarkers for this restaurant, shouldered their way into her mind. "I have to go to the Library, to look something up. I promised Millicent. It's something Gerald couldn't find in their local library, and I said I would try..."

"I'll go with you," Janet said, and then, escape almost blocked, shook her head and smiled her smile and said, "Oh, no, I won't. I'll be a good girl and try to find a present for little Stevie. I can't even remember what three-year-olds like any more, not that it matters. When's yours?" she said suddenly.

"Three months yet."

"A grandchild will be good for you, Florence," her friendly, serious, kind friend said, wanting only what was good for her, wishing her nothing but the best.

The waitress put the check between them. They would divide it exactly, agreeing on the tip, coins and bills exchanging hands with a minimum of fuss. They had known each other since the age of fourteen, and that made it easier to divide the check.

The waitress thanked them, they thanked the waitress, the girl at the cash register thanked them both, and they both thanked her. It began to feel like an earache. They walked together to Fifth Avenue, where they stood on the sidewalk and touched cheeks, and one of them said good-bye and one said thank-you. Then one went north, and one went south toward the lions.

3

The broad marble steps were littered with sunlight, bodies, and pigeons. She climbed up toward the columns slowly, wondering what to do when she had gone through the great doors and into the dark calm. Look at the glass-case exhibits in the lobby? letters of everybody dead, very interesting. Once, she had been truly interested; centuries ago, she had been an English major in college.... In college? She had gone to *college?*

She had gone to college. Now, the steps of this Library were littered with young college bodies, jeans crossed at knees, sneakers crossed at ankles, arms crossed behind heads.

Not all young, of course. Old age sat on the benches and drowsed in the sun. Hands crossed on canes. The bottles were whiskey, she supposed, and the cans were Cokes, and some of the drinking straws had carousel stripes like party favors for tots. She would soon have a tot of her own, a grandchild, her very own grandchild. She would have to respond to it, ga ga goo goo.

She would have to respond in a moment to someone at a desk in the Library. Did they still have people at the desks, or computers? She had not been here in a long time—in fact, she did not belong here, not wanting to ask, not wanting to answer. She turned away and started back down the wide steps, saying *Sorry* under her breath when her foot encountered anything firm and not meaning it in any possible way. She was not sorry. She might hate them, if she had the energy, but she was not sorry.

A man with a brown briefcase had been leaning against the north lion's pedestal, and as she neared him he moved away briskly. The space around the space he had occupied was so clearly outlined that she stepped into it at once. The pedestal gave her a wall against her back. Her shoulders pressed tight against it, she let herself slide down, holding her handbag carefully, her knees bending like hinges until she was sitting on the step, beneath the north lion, with his pedestal at her back.

She was very relieved. Somehow she had managed to get into this space inside the space that the man had left for her, and she need not even say thank-you to him because he had already gone. The relief was quite extraordinary, she had not felt such relief for a long time, almost like pleasure. She remembered pleasure, a long time ago too.

From her fortress, she looked out and down to the sidewalk, where people went by as streams—waves of marsh grass, currents, eddies of color. A boy—teen-age perhaps—detached himself and marched smartly up the steps toward her. She dropped her eyes and shrank away, but he went on past and up. He did not seem to care that a well-dressed woman in her well-made fifties should be sitting below a marble lion, and so she continued to sit there, unnoticed and unrebuked, eyelids half shut against the sun and half open against intrusion.

When the intruder came, it was as a shadow, though whether cast by the sun or from its own existence there was no way of saying. First, it was above her, and then, like a great black glob of melting wax, it was at her shoulder, on her level, before she could pull away. The shadow sighed. In puppet response to the sigh, jerked on its strings, not wanting to see, she turned and looked.

The black glob of melting wax was wrapped inside a heavy black coat, and, as it settled, it spread, settled further, sighed again, became lumpy, became massive, had soft parts and solid parts. When one of the solid parts—a shoe, an ankle—hit her, she said "Excuse me" to it as if the fault were hers. What she should have done, possibly, was to get up and move away. Instead, she sat there and shivered a little, until she stopped shivering and realized what she was next to. Not the Angel of Death, not a murderer, not even an intruder. She knew what it was by name, because she had read about them in the newspapers, back in the days when she had read anything.

The glob was nothing more than one of New York's bag women. Or were they properly called bag ladies? She had seen them sometimes lying in doorways with their shopping bags gathered around them like ugly sheep, staring or breathing or sleeping, to be stepped past quickly, not to be looked at if possible. Shipwrecks, no visible home, no visible means of support, no shape, no reality. She was, however, sitting next to one.

For no reason, she said "Excuse me" again. Nothing of the black heap turned toward her, or even moved. Dead, undoubtedly. Or, and how wonderful, completely non-responding. She said rather too loudly, as if she were lecturing, "I said, Excuse me."

The bag lady, beneath the black coat, spread her knees. One could see the hillocks of them parting, making not so much a lap of the heavy black cloth as a basket or a mad cradle. From somewhere inside endless folds, a bright green—Irish green—shopping bag emerged like a horned toad, and

15

from somewhere else the two hands that belonged to the coat sleeves came out of them and began to dig in it. The mumbling seemed to come from the hands.

Clutching her own neat leather handbag and reminding herself of who she was (as by name, Florence Butler; as by residence; as by telephone number; as by her own handbag), she felt herself getting up and moving away hastily, felt herself boarding a bus, depositing her fare, sitting down....

She had not moved. She was chained to the bag lady. If she tipped her head back against the lion's wall and half-closed her eyes again, looking out and beyond at nothing, she could still see the bag lady quite clearly, peripherally but clearly.

The woman was not, after all, merely black coat, groping hands, and shopping bag. She had a head, wound in layers of black cloth stuff, encircling the ears, the hair, the forehead, and then going down to strangle the neck in blackness. In between was a small face, eyebrowed, mouthed, a nose that was too large, and no eyelashes at all, though these might have been plucked up into the sun. The head poked out like a tortoise's and, now, when it leaned suddenly into the Irish-green shopping bag, it disappeared altogether and there was nothing human left behind (supposing that the head was human) except the hands. The hands, and a magazine that had come out of its tunnel, and a wedge of dirty foam rubber.

The marvelous thing was that the bag lady existed only as melted black wax. She did not speak, nor respond, nor move beyond her own black area, nor really exist. She had made her ultimate escape into a night island. unregarding and unregarded.

It had been a long time since the neat woman sitting next to that night island had felt anything as strong as envy. She felt it now, although it took a little while to identify it. The envy flowered, it might turn into anger if left to spread like

16

a weed, or even into hate. Finally, when she knew she would
have to move away or suffocate in a smother of emotion, she
managed to get to her feet. She had been holding her handbag
so desperately tight that her knuckles ached, and she swayed
a little because her heart was knocking inside her chest and
she was not used to any feeling from it except sluggishness.
She stared down at the top of the black heap which was a bag
lady and saw only black wax which need not move or testify
to life or answer any questions or look up or sideways or down.

She stared too long. She began to feel herself becoming
wax—wax in her bones, her blood changing to smoke, her
nerves disintegrating. If she stayed, she would barter her
bloodstream for the life of the heap below her, she would
collapse. They would not have to come and dispose of her,
because she would be gone already, like haze. On a meadow.

She thought lucidly, Not a meadow, not with lions in it,
and her own reasonableness jolted her free. She was back into
what and where she was, a person on the steps of a library
building, quite calm, not trembling any more, her fingers
unlocking from their grip on her handbag, her heartbeat
coming back to rhythm. The lion pushed her away gravely,
and she was at last able to believe that she could move and,
of her own free will, leave the black heap on the white steps.

She did go. She did board the right bus, pay the right
fare. She did put the key into the lock, did lie on the bed,
and did—with the back of her wrist cushioned against her
forehead—say in quite a loud voice, "I would like that, to be
like her," before she fell into a sleep as dark and formless as
the black mass itself on the Library steps.

17

4

When she woke the next morning, she was businesslike, alert, rational, and possessed. Not self-possessed, but seized. She must—at once!—be on the Library steps, below the northern lion, under his great paws, as she had been yesterday. She must wear the same suit, the same shoes, even the same underwear, carry the same handbag. If she did, the bag lady would come again and settle next to her.

She could not have been calmer, but she had no memory of any time between. She was sitting on the stone steps, under the lion. The sky was grayer than yesterday's sky, and a small wind fingered the paper cups and the plastic straws. At any moment, the black island would come and sink down beside her. She pulled her feet up, wrapped her arms around her knees, and made herself small. It seemed that people were staring at her, sitting there so, and she wished she had brought a book with her so she could retire respectably behind its open pages and not be noticed, or, rather, have an excuse for being there at all. A newspaper would have been better yet, she could have sheltered behind the Times all day.

No one came, or if they did come they were not what she was waiting for. She had no idea what time it was, past noon perhaps because she felt a little hungry. —Had she eaten breakfast? There was a way to find out how much time had escaped her, and she looked at her wristwatch and it was not there. She had forgotten to put it on. She felt exposed without it and vaguely troubled, but not enough to move. Waiting was now her entire existence, even if the sun shifted from the lion's great paws and the shadows raced across the wide steps and it was night again. She could sleep here.

She did not want to have to go home. She did not want to have to go anywhere. There were trash baskets to put her into, dustbins, potter's fields. I'm not feeling well, she thought, I should have had breakfast. Millicent will be so angry, and I will have to explain to Millicent why I am here, and she will ask and ask and ask. There was a sound inside her head like a snowfall, and she jerked her chin up. Her handbag slid off her knees, she snatched at it mindlessly, felt it being taken from her, wanted to cry out.

A hand put the bag back on her lap. A voice said, "You all right, miss?" A woman's voice, a nice woman's voice, a woman's nice voice. She looked up and, behind the voice, was a young woman, pretty, sleek-haired, long sleek hair like a city mermaid. She said, "Thank you, oh, stupid of me" to the mermaid, and then "Thank you very much" in order to sound grateful and to cut off the conversation.

"Okay, then." The face between the long straight strands was ivory and oval. "I thought maybe—Okay, then." The mermaid left her, gone away lightly, up the stone steps. Gone away. Thank God. No more to be said.

She put the handbag into her lap, curled herself down around it, so that *that* couldn't happen again, and began once more to wait. What time it was when the black mass of the bag lady came up the steps toward her she could not possibly know. If she looked to see where the sun was, to tell the time of day, she would have to look both up and out, which was now too high a price to pay. It was a terrible disappointment when the bag lady, hoisting herself along, heavy foot by heavy foot, trudged toward the other lion, the south lion. How could she have not foreseen this would happen? How could she have waited stupidly in the same place?

But, at once, everything became wonderfully simple. She got up, hung her bag over her arm neatly, brushed off her skirt like any ordinary woman, and crossed the space between the two great beasts.

The mass of black wax was already spread, but there was room for someone next to it. And no one need ask, no one need answer, no one need move close or pull away.

She sat down silent, drawn in, motionless, a captive or a victim. Her whole being was focused on the Irish-green shopping bag. The woman's hands were inside it already, dragging things out and spreading them around her as if they were wares for display. Rags, torn newspapers, a huge brown comb with broken teeth, a piece of plastic folded and refolded but with a memory for all its creases. There was string. There was something smashed and dripping that was suddenly thrust into the mouth, into the face around the mouth, between the black stuff of the coat and the black stuff of the headdress. Her watcher could see the jaws moving, a cud-chewing black cow in an Irish-green meadow, dark fodder in a dark barn. Something jingled—a cow bell?—but it was only a little cart on the sidewalk that was so far below, a little man selling little things. Looking back quickly and then away, she almost escaped the other woman's eyes, but she was a moment too late and they looked into hers.

The other eyes could have been mirrors. Better never to get caught by them again, and she turned away, leaning sideways and looking down, trying to see what else was in the bag. Its owner pulled away from her, shoulder jerking like a peevish child's. The mouth stopped chewing long enough to say something in syllables with the sound of mud.

"I'm Florence," Florence said, quite madly. "Florence Butler. I'm a widow, no, that's not quite true. I divorced my husband a long time ago, no, not really a long time ago. I have a daughter and a son-in-law, and I'm going to have a baby again. That is, my *daughter* is going to have a baby...." What was she doing here, chattering like a magpie, next to this sick black raven? Oh God, Oh dear God, make her go on sitting there! She doesn't have to listen even, just let me tell her everything without her telling *me* everything. Let me stay next to her, don't let her move away. Make her stay! God? Dear God?

The bag lady did not move away. She was putting everything back into the green horned toad but she was not moving, only pulling all her blackness around her now and drawing in her small tortoise head and closing her mirror eyes. She was not listening, she was arranging for sleep, swathed in dark cloth and blankness, turning the steps into a bog, turning herself back into a lump of wax, a graven image. Marsh-silent, stone-silent, not having to speak, not having to answer.

"It's not that I want to trouble you," her companion said timidly. "It's only that I want to know—I mean, can someone else—? I mean, is it hard?"

The graven image drew its deep breath, and everything around it fell into folds and crevasses and heaps.

"I mean," said her companion, "do you think *I* could do it?"

Unanswered, she remained beside the black lump for quite a long time. When at last she got to her feet, a little dizzily (it was true that one ought to eat breakfast, one ought to eat lunch, one ought to watch one's health, to live sensibly and respectably, one certainly ought to), she knew she had arrived at a perfectly clear obsession.

5

In the thrift shop, the piles were staggering. Women who were dressed as neatly as herself combed their way through the heaped-up tables—wools and cottons and linens, sequinned scarves and lace collars, gloves, mittens, shoes, books, handbags, handbags endlessly. Enormous damask napkins, chunks of jewelry, pants, jackets, babies' clothes, toddlers' clothes, clothes for boys, girls, ladies, men. Old men, old women. Bag ladies. Bag ladies' clothes.

She wanted something black, like her exemplar, but nothing that was black was large enough. She tugged at cloth-stuff from the deepest piles, dredging like a fisherwoman for what lay below. When she found it, it was gray but it was enormous—a circular cape cut out by a mindless cookie cutter, with deep armholes and a great gray button under the chin, and the look of having been used as a tent. It was perfectly the color of soot, not easy soft soot sifting down on streets but heavy soot, grime. It was the color of grime, and she bundled its folds together and put them under her arm. It was so aggressively ugly that it must be waterproof, sunproof, proof against people's eyes. One could settle down into it on the steps of a great city library; one could conceal shopping bags; one could...

She stopped thinking "one" and thought "I". I can hide a shopping bag under it, she thought. I can hide myself.

She had shopping bags at home saved from all the nice New York department stores where she bought her clothes, when she had bought clothes, which was a long time ago lately. Millicent was always urging her to buy something new and nice—you look so nice in blue, Mother, why don't you wear blue more? or whatever color Millicent's mind happened to have seized upon. You look so nice in soot-gray, Mother. Grime is your color.

I shall need shoes, she thought, escaping Millicent. With the gray cape wadded under the arm, she circled the attic-like store until she located the shoe counters, and found herself standing on one foot with one shoe off, like everyone else near her, trying on sizes. They all hurt. She could never walk as she would have to walk (because one could not stay forever on the steps of the Library) in any of these shoes, but neither could she wear her own. She glanced down at her feet, rather narrow, correctly shod, in good taste, something called Easy Walkers, she believed, or E-Z Walkers, which was the kind of grating cuteness she particularly disliked. Her shoes for the future would have to be big and shapeless, but they would also have to be comfortable. Narrow inside, wide outside, there was no such thing made.

She picked up a pair of cloddy black oxfords, tied together by their black laces, flat-heeled, elephant-footed. Awkwardly, cape under arm, shoe in hand, she managed to bend over and get the left shoe on. The right shoe clunked down on the floor alongside. Too large, but wonderfully anonymous. She looked at the foot as it lay next to the other, one so neat, one so—not grotesque, not formidable, but used-up, used up by trudging and more trudging.

She took the shoe off, put on her own, wrapped both shoes inside the cape's bulk. She looked around. Something for her head, so no one could see her face. Perhaps she could find heavy dark glasses, but she could not ever remember seeing a bag lady in heavy dark glasses, which would be for a film lady, a night-club lady, a night lady.

Walking heavily, as if she were already wearing the old

23

shoes on her old feet, she hunted the store for hats. There were people to ask, ladies in polite pink smocks, volunteers from the Charities that would benefit from the Sales, the sales of old capes and dead shoes. But she did not want to ask or to be answered, and she made her way steadily through the narrow aisles. There were not many hats, however, and such as there were offered no shelter. One with a floppy brim was white straw, which would be ridiculous; another was too tight, hurting her headache.

It was true that she had a headache. It had come on in the night while she slept, and her need to get to the thrift shop had pushed it away, but now it was back again and circled her head. She picked up a yellow plastic rainhat, a silly-style copy of the kind children wore with little yellow sou'westers, with side-flaps that met and tied under the chin. Yellow, bright yellow. She could not go about in a bright yellow hat, advertising herself like a sunshine biscuit.

She put the shoes and cape down on the floor, holding them between her feet firmly along with her own handbag, and then she took the yellow plastic hat into both hands and jammed it down over her hair. It was too big and it came below her eyebrows, the yellow flaps and ties dangling on either side. She could only see things below the counter level— floor, feet, ankles, legs, skirts and pants, waists, hands pulling and pushing things about. She would be obliged to hold her chin quite high if she wished to see the upper half of the world. She pulled the yellow hat off, and now her hair was disheveled. Everyone would be staring at her.

She lowered her eyes against their stares. She put the yellow hat back on the counter, very reluctantly. It had been comforting somehow to look at half a world from under the yellow eaves of the yellow hat, and she reached for it again and then pulled her hand back quickly. Not yellow, noisy as a dandelion, calling attention to itself, calling attention to her when all she wanted to do was to disappear. The yellow hat would be a target.

She picked up a gray hat next to the yellow one, but it was a man's hat. She could not wear a man's hat, although this one was well-worn, with a smudgy top and a drooping brim. Next to it was a brown hat marked with a tag that said 65¢, sexless with age. Once, it might have been a respectable fedora, or a floppy felt, or a trucker's hat held up by large ears. After a moment, she put it on, and like the yellow hat it encompassed her.

She was invisible.

She became invisible with such certainty that she could walk out of this thrift shop with the hat on her head, the cape and shoes under her arm, to be arrested at the door, held as a thief, Millicent called by the authorities.... No, no, no! Stop there. All she needed to do was to take her purchases respectably to the cash register, pay for them, have them bagged, and go out with no one knowing she had even been there.

Holding everything stiffly in her arms, she pushed her way between racks and people and counters (were thrift shops always so crowded?) to the cash register, and it *was* a cash register, old-fashioned with a money drawer and money taken out by hand in plain sight, pale sums showing behind its pale window, and a bell that went *ping* at each accounting. *Ping* for the gray cape, *ping* for the black shoes, *ping* for the brown hat.

It all came to seven dollars and seventy-eight cents. She had a ten-dollar bill in her purse, but, for some reason, she searched further until she had found a five-dollar bill, two one-dollar bills, three quarters, and three pennies. The woman at the cash register waited patiently and pleasantly, very nicely indeed, it was a very nice store, and when she had found the last three pennies, she heard herself saying idiotically, "It's the material I want, of course, the shoes are for my cleaning woman, she has trouble with her feet." Why did she have to explain everything? No one believed her.

But no one was listening. The pleasant lady handed her a receipt, a paper bag with her purchases inside it, a dismissing, patient, pleasant thank-you.

She would get home as quickly as possible, and there she would be able to find out whether a hat could block out half a world or if she was, again, only under an illusion of escape.

6

There were more problems than there was hope, but now that she had a single aim in her world the problems could be solved. In her own apartment, with her door double-bolted in broad daylight, she set about the process of creating her new self.

First, the shoes. She had known they were too large, her narrow feet shuffled inside them. She tried wedging in her bedroom slippers, but then the shoes became stubbornly small and would not admit her feet. She tried wads of absorbent cotton stuck in at the toes, and it was immediately clear that the stuff would turn into unendurable lumps. She tried crumpled newspaper, but, even in careful walking about the apartment, the shoes slipped and began to hurt meanly. If she was to escape into a bag lady, she could not be thinking all the time about her feet.

She went to her closet and looked at her other shoes, and none of them would serve her needs at all. She walked over to the bed and sat down on it, pulled off the thrift-shop shoes and stared at her stockinged feet, maddeningly patrician in their narrowness and to be hated. Foam rubber might fill without packing, but where did one get foam rubber? She looked around the room, and then she stood up quickly and took a flat cushion off the small rocking chair by the window. With a pair of scissors, she cut it open as if it were nothing at all (and she had chosen the cushion with special care, *You have very nice taste, Mother,* Millicent sang), and inside was not foam rubber but something stiff and expensive. She threw it back on the chair, and it lay there with the scissor-slits gaping.

Heavy socks might help, but she had no heavy socks. There had been heavy socks on counters at the thrift shop, men's socks with big feet, her late husband had owned such socks. Not her late husband, her *divorced* husband, the husband who had left her for no reason—

No! She had *told* him to go, she had divorced him, it had been her wish to erase James. She had erased him; very well, then. James's socks had been large-footed, and some of them had been thick, and the thrift shop had been full of thick socks which she had not thought to buy. She must go and buy them now, instantly, no time to waste, or else she would not be on the Library steps tomorrow morning.

She put on her own shoes, she found her handbag. "Going out again so soon, Mrs. Butler?" the doorman said, and she said, "No, thank you," refusing the taxi he had not offered. Between that door and the door of the thrift shop, she remembered nothing. The men's socks were limitless on the counters, and she spent something between ten minutes and an hour making her choice, matching them for size because each pair would have to be larger than the pair under it, layers on layers of socks, a Chinese puzzle-box in wool. Wool that had walked with the large feet of large men, which was just what James had been. But he had not left any socks behind him, he had not left anything.

The volunteer at the cash register apparently did not

remember her. Part of her resented that, part of her felt safer. When she got back to her apartment building, the doorman greeted her all over again, and she wished he would be less attentive, would be as unremembering as the cash register. How was she going to get past him when she was dressed like a bag lady? Would he look clean through her disguise and say Good-morning-Mrs-Butler and then turn away, wondering vaguely why the tenant in 7-A was so oddly dressed? Or would he not recognize her at all and challenge her presence in the building? Could she claim to be Mrs. Butler's new cleaning woman? —Oh God, she would never get past him, never reach the Library steps, never take her place among those enviable women who had found a way to disappear.

She stood in the middle of her living room, forcing herself to think in a line straight enough to go from here to there. If she took the shoes and the cape and the hat with her in a big bag, in a shopping bag which she would have to have anyway, and wearing her own daily clothes —Then, tomorrow morning, she could leave the building openly and all she would need to do would be to find a place to change—a ladies' room. Saks Fifth Avenue had a ladies' room, and so did other stores, even closer to the Library. And so, of course, did the Library itself.

She sighed, not with relief but with acceptance. All she needed to do now was to select the shopping bag. She went to the front closet and chose the ideal one immediately— sturdy brown paper with no lettering, sturdy string handles— sometimes on a hook, sometimes fallen to the floor, always in her way in that orderly closet but kept from some vague now-rewarded thriftiness. It would hold everything, her old leather handbag with a purse deep inside and money in the purse (she would not need money, surely, just to sit like any citizen on the Library steps, the *Public* Library?), a precautionary small package of Kleenex, her reading glasses (what would she need those for? the books were inside the building) and perhaps something to eat? She could do without lunch, or she could buy food at a grocery store. She would be free of tables and tablemats and silverware, which she always laid out precisely in order to keep herself from becoming slack, a hermit. Once, a gym teacher in high school had told her, right in front of the class, not to slump her shoulders, and she remembered wanting to shout back that *slump* was not a transitive verb. But nobody cared that she was very good at grammar, and nobody dared to shout at a teacher.

With the bag packed as neatly as she would have packed her suitcase to take with her to the taxi, to the airport, to be met by Millicent and to be reproved for putting too much into it ("It's too heavy for you, Mother, I'm only thinking of you, no, I don't mind carrying it, of course not.... I'm going to have a baby, I am all woman." Well, I had *you*, Millicent.) —She turned her mind off. It was getting easier all the time to turn her mind off.

She opened the door of her bedroom closet and pushed it wide so she could look into the long mirror, and then she began to dress herself, in rehearsal. First, her plainest dress, navy blue, with straight skirt, long sleeves, and decorous neckline. Next, her shoes, lined with the socks. It only took one pair after all, maroon-color wool, very thick and bulky, and the shoes became feet and could be walked upon. Then the cape, colored grime, closing around her and canceling her out, all but her head. The cape's open front betrayed her and revealed the dress underneath, hopelessly respectable. She found three large safety pins, as assertive as pieces of machinery, and they closed the front of the cape completely and still gave her room inside its ample, wonderfully dreary folds.

Finally, she pulled on the hat which had conferred invisibility on her in the thrift-shop aisle, pulled it down hard over her neat hair, over her eyebrows, over her ears, her nice ears. The spell worked. She vanished from the mirror, at least everything that could identify her vanished. She was now, in her own mirror, nothing but her lower half—the gray skirt of the gray cape, safety-pinned against disclosure, the feet that were not feet but only large black awkward shoes, the brown-paper shopping bag on the floor beside her.

She picked up the shopping bag, and in the mirror it was still visible, hanging below waist level, but the top of everything else had vanished. There were no pictures on the walls, no lampshades, the bureau was nothing but its bottom drawer. Floor was there and two rugs that were blue like the hems of the curtains, there were baseboards and a wastebasket, and there was the lower half of what had been Florence Butler. To see more, she would have to raise her chin and look up. She need not do so.

Tomorrow she would put her costume and her mask into the shopping bag. The heavy cape over her arm, she would leave the apartment as Mrs. Butler in 7-A, known as such to neighbors, doormen, and familiars of all kinds. She would go to the ladies' room in the Library, and there she would leave Mrs. Butler behind her, and she would become, on the Library steps, this new anonymous person of whom all that she could see in the long mirror was what might have been anyone. Or anything.

She unlocked the safety pins, removed the clumsy cape from her shoulders, and let it fall to the floor. She bent over, untied her shoes, took them off, peeled away the ugly wool socks. Then she closed her eyes and pulled off the hat and opened her eyes again. She was there once more, in her mirror's full length, her unwanted self, in stockinged feet, holding a shapeless brown hat in her hand.

30

She put the hat on the bedside table. Once, in the night, when she woke out of a vague thin dream, she reached for it, pulled it to the pillow beside her, and then slept again. Dimly, she supposed that everyone who knew her would believe she had gone mad, and the thought gave her a kind of contentment. She slept without any more dreams, and, when she woke, her reason was inside her and outside her, narrow and sharp and cold, like a steel file.

Even without the hat on her head, the closing of her world had already begun.

II
THE
PASSAGEWAY

1

She was delayed by a call from Janet, and she escaped by
saying that it was such a lovely day and she was visiting a
friend out in the country, Connecticut, actually, and the friend
was picking her up in her car and she didn't have time to talk.
Not a line in the lie but came easily to her tongue. What was
the name of the friend? Where in Connecticut? Wasn't it very
sudden? Janet had not asked, but if she had, all the answers
would have come, quick and ready. The answers were wooden
shutters; the sooner they slammed down on Janet (out *there*),
the sooner she could be at the Library steps.

Mortal necessity.

She noticed a very slight tremor in her hands as she
dressed—the navy blue wool, fastened high at the neckline;
no belt; her flimsiest shoes because they would have to be
stowed away in the shopping bag. Assembled, she stood for
a moment looking around her apartment, and then she went
out rapidly and double-locked the door behind her. Throwing
what she believed was called the dead bolt. Shutting out, so
they said, all the city dangers.

The doorman did not seem surprised by the large brown
shopping bag, so packed and fat, and when, on sudden ex-
travagant impulse, she asked for a taxi, he got one with infinite
ease. She did not know the morning doorman's name, usually
she went out after lunch, if she remembered to have lunch,

but he was nimble with taxis, and he held her shopping bag as he handed her in. She thought of giving him a tip, but that would start a needless tradition and she would be tipping him forever. Anyway, she never tipped the right amount, always too little or too much. "They come to *expect* it," someone had told her once, quite angrily. At that time, she had always wanted very much to do the right thing as if Millicent were watching, and her son-in-law, and James, and indeed all the people who had ever watched her, so persistent and so close.

When she got out at the Library, she gave the taxi driver too much, jarring the squat silent man into wishing her a good day—Haveagoodday—and she should have answered, "You, too," but did not remember the simple phrase until she was halfway up the great steps between the great lions, halfway down the corridor and at the elevator.

There was, she knew, a ladies' room in the basement, as well as the one on the third floor. Should she have chosen the basement room, associated in her mind with cheap basement goods? She would go in as her well-dressed self and she would come out as a shopping-bag lady, and at some point she would be the wrong person for either ladies' room.

Suddenly, she was struck with fear. It was none of it going to be possible. She would be recognized in some ill-fated encounter with an acquaintance. She would be arrested for impersonating, she would be... But then the elevator came and its door opened, and she stepped into it with her bulging bag, only one of a handful of ordinary people ascending upward into information, knowledge, wisdom.

On the third floor she turned the wrong way and it was several minutes before she found the ladies' room, and that seemed to her a bad omen. She gripped the leather handle of her handbag and the string handle of her shopping bag even more tightly, pushed open the right door, and walked in.

The ladies' room was larger than she had remembered it, but no one was making use of its space. She entered a cubicle (her mind evaded genteelly what could certainly not be called a bathroom) and, as slow now as she had been fast before, she began to perform her transformation.

It was astonishingly simple. The seat became a neat little table on which to put everything out of her shopping bag. She took off her shoes first and pulled the thick maroon socks on over her stockings. She put the black clod shoes onto her feet and tied the laces carefully, put the narrow shoes into the shopping bag, her handbag next to them. Then, still very careful, she shook out the cape, color of grime, and put it around her shoulders. She had forgotten the safety pins.... No, she had not forgotten the safety pins, she had fastened them inside the rim of the shopping bag the night before, forgotten she had been so forehanded, remembered it after a moment. The omens were becoming favorable. The cape covered her from shoulders to ankles, the safety pins locked her inside it as the dead bolt locked her apartment. She pushed her hair behind her ears, picked up the hat and put it on.

It snuffed her out, like a candle. All that she could see inside the cubicle was her own lower half—the cape, the heavy feet, the open space under the door, and, of course, the cover of the (again the delicate evasion) bathroom seat.

Bathroom cubicles were very private. She stood for a moment, leaning against the door, listening, in case someone was outside, but there were no revealing sounds of running water or of walking or of voices. She pulled back the bolt, pushed open the door, and stepped out, in disguise.

There was someone there, after all—a woman at the far end, standing by the row of wash basins. Half a woman, because from below the hat everything else was only basin-high. Light tan shoes, sandals with straps and high heels, very pretty, legs in stockings, very pretty, tan skirt. Above that, invisible.

Nothing to talk to, no one to see.

In her own black heavy shoes, she crossed the tile floor and was vaguely pleased to find that her movement was all heaviness. The shoes weighed her down, turning her from Florence Butler into a bag lady. A lumberer, a trudger, an old cow.

She moved toward the basins, prepared to wash her hands, a health measure. Did you wash your hands, Flo? her mother had always said. She stood on heavy flat feet next to the light tan shoes and the long legs and the tan skirt, put her shopping bag down on the floor beside her, and reached out to the faucets. Her hands, protruding from the long sleeves of her dark dress, alarmed her. They were too white, too slender, too delicate, belonging to a stranger. They would betray her at once. She pulled them back hastily, hid them in the folds of her cape, picked up the shopping bag so that it hung inside those folds and her hands could not be seen. *Had the woman next to her noticed anything?*

She could wait until the woman had gone and there was no one there at all (though someone else might come in?), or she could leave without washing her hands and then what would her mother say? She could still hear herself, answering, Yes, Mother, yes, I did, I washed them carefully. It was the first lie that she remembered from a very small age. She had been in such a child's hurry to go somewhere, to do something very important, back all those years ago when things were important and she did hurry to do them, had been eager to do them quickly.

"Yes, Mother, I did," she said now under her breath. "I did wash them." She turned, and her shoes trudged her out of the room. The woman in the high heels must be doing her hair or making up her face or something to keep her there such a long time, so quietly employed. But, under the covenant of the hat, there was no reason to look high enough to see.

When she came to the wide stairs leading off the wide corridor, she decided to take them instead of the elevator, walking slowly and leaning against the handrail. She would have liked to hold onto it because the skirt of her cape was trailing on the steps, but there were her hands again. She thought worriedly that she must go back to the thrift shop and buy gloves—dirty wool gloves to match the cape, clumsy gloves. She would do it tomorrow morning before she came down again to the Library.

So she was committed for tomorrow, then. Tomorrow she would be able to put a clumsy gloved hand solidly on the rail and descend securely, lodged between steps and hat brim. She kept her eyes fixed on the step ahead; if anyone approached her coming up or passed her coming down, she would not be able to see them. What she could not see was not there.

She achieved the last step, crossed the floor level, reached the wide double door, where—and she realized it now, too late—there was a man who checked to see if books were being stolen. He would search her. She would be discovered. She had not foreseen this at all.

Numbly, she huddled into her cape, pulling it around her to show how thin she was inside its folds, concealing nothing—no books, no manuscripts, no precious documents. Numbly, she held out her shopping bag to the man, holding it from the bottom like a tray, hiding her white hands, her too slender wrists, under its tough brown paper. The shoes were on top, their toes pointing up mutely. She did not raise her head under the hat. The brim was pulled so low that she would have to raise her chin to see upward at all, and she would not raise her chin no matter what happened. Because it was not safe to see upward. She knew that already, had known it at once when she had first jammed the hat down over her eyes in the thrift shop.

She had no way now of knowing whether the man at the door (neat trousers, well-polished shoes, a credit to his calling and he would do his job very efficiently, he would find her out) had looked into her bag, fingered the heels of the shoes, peered downward, or whether he had merely made a judgment with his eyes. After all, he was paid to make such judgments, trusted for it, a trustee. She heard him say "M'mm" meaninglessly, and she took it for acquittal. Mutely, she withdrew the bag; moved on, mutely. No one called after her. For the moment, she was safe. Tomorrow she would wrap something soft around her handbag, camouflaging it, anything so it would not look or feel like a book.

Books were a part of another century in her life. She was through the great door now, outside in open air, could see the giant columns, and beyond them the people sitting on the steps. Because they were below her, she saw them whole, in spite of the hat, and she reached instantly for the handrail. The place was a forest of handrails, and she attached herself to this one, ignoring the whiteness of her hands. It was a risk, it was a risk, but better than going down with eyes half closed so as not to see people whole.

She edged her way down with terrible caution until at last she came to the pedestals and the shelter and bulk of one of the two great lions. There was space there, and, as she had done before (yesterday? last week? last month?), she moved into the space and sat down.

Under the hat, enveloped in the cape, her bag pressing against her knee like a dark dog, her ugly shoes planted below the hem of her skirt, she sat, blind, deaf, and dumb. An island cut off from the mainland, without communications, without

40

people, a place where—if one did not wish to—one need not even go on breathing. She saw herself blessedly able to withhold air on command, her lungs collapsing to her will. She saw herself toppling forward, human but non-breathing, bumping down the wide steps, lodging at the bottom against a pedestrian foot, a bus-stop sign, a peddler's cart.

She held her breath, experimentally. *In a moment, in a moment,* she said, hushing herself. If she stopped breathing, she would not have to worry about tomorrow, about getting past the man at the Library's door, who might ask questions to be answered in words. She needed only to clutch and trap her breath, inside her.

Her gasp was involuntary, she breathed without her own permission. It was not going to be that simple. She would have to find another way to make herself disappear.

She had an illusion that she was thinking very clearly, on her island. Slowly, in her thoughts, the woman who was inside the cape, the woman who was wearing a respectable dark dress, impeccable underthings (her mother had taught her that, but she had never not wanted to), the woman who had bought a hat and shoes and a cape at a thrift shop—that woman began to recede. She was now becoming the cape itself, the hat itself, the shoes themselves. She was wide and heavy and blessedly deaf and mute and almost blind in the half-world with the shutters over her eyes and the blankness in her mind that had, freely, by choice, left everything behind. She had not felt so secure, so—she groped for the word—so cozy in all her lifetime, lullabied in this cradle in the shelter of a lion. She was not only unseeing, she was unseen.

She would stay here as long as they would let her stay.

Time passed. The street traffic roared, whimpered, whined, and she did not hear it. There was a shuttle of people

before her somewhere on the steps and on the sidewalk, beyond her lion-cradle, but she never saw them. She was in the
circumference of nothing but herself, and her mind was a
bog into which the beginning of every thought disappeared
before she thought it. The sun rose toward noon, still a summer's sun, lingered, fell away, all beyond her attention or
interest. The total emptiness was almost as good as not breathing at all. Perhaps, later, the non-breathing would come of
its own accord and everything would be solved. Solved quietly.
She did not want to make a fuss.

When she felt too warm, it was more like a fever than
sun, but she kept all of herself covered, especially her hands,
which would give her away until she could hide them in gloves,
heavy and grime-gray like the rest of her. Except the black
shoes. And, of course, the hat, which was brown. In all her
blankness, the only thing that stirred emotion was the hat. It
forgave everything, kept her from seeing. Best of all, it kept
her from being seen.

It was hunger that finally roused her. It came first as a
hollow inside her own hollow, and she nudged it away, lit-
erally, pushing elbow into flesh at the place under her breastbone which was complaining in a voice as still and small and
peremptory as conscience. When there was a growl from the
voice, she roused sharply from the safe blankness that had
been surrounding her and felt her cheeks burn with shame.
One did not, one simply did not, it was unbecoming for a nice
little girl...But it brought her around, and she raised her
chin a fraction to see if anyone had heard.

For the moment, there was no one to hear her. She ought
to get up and go home and find something to eat, and then
she could lie down on her bed without unsuitable noises coming from unsuitable areas. There were the gloves to be bought
too, but first she would have to go back into the Library and

go up to the ladies' room and change her clothes, and then she would have to come back past the man at the door (who would be a different man, if it was as late as it might be), and she could not possibly go through all that again. She could not hold out her bag to that man, he would see who was inside it.

What was inside it, she told herself sternly, catching up her own words inside her head. She began to think about the gloves, and she could see their non-color plainly in her mind's eye. It seemed to her very likely that she already had just such a pair put away against winter. She *must* have them on before she held out the bag again under the eyes of any man at any door who would suspect her because of the wrong hands showing. Like her underwear, her hands did not match.

Rescue came. She thought of the department store across the street. She did not have a charge account there, because it was a store that catered to large sizes and she was not a large size, but it would have a ladies' room and there would not be anyone at the door demanding to see which books she had stolen from its shelves.

It was the hunger first, and then the urgency to see if her memory of the winter gloves was accurate, and then suddenly it was a more immediate urgency, and she thought like a child *I need the bathroom.*

She got up more quickly than she meant to, forgetting the long skirt of the cape and the grip of the large safety pins, and she almost fell headlong, would have hurtled down the steps this time really, and the breathing instead of stopping first would stop afterwards when her headlong head and body struck whatever it was they would strike. But she caught herself on the edge of the abyss and, though she had to reach out with one of those betraying hands (her wrist pale and narrow to her own eyes from under the hat), she was either not seen or was ignored. She was able to go down the steps sideways, crablike and heavy, holding her bag under the cape and holding up the cape so she would not trip, and so, slowly, arriving at the sidewalk. Because of the bathroom, and because of the gloves.

Her heavy shoes carried her to the corner and across the street. She went inside the store whose name she could not remember, and she found the ladies' room number on the sign by the elevator, which was low enough for her to see from under the hat. In the ladies' room were bodies from the waist down, skirts, slacks, blue jeans, but all she wanted was the cubicle.

Inside it, once *that* was over (the relief was like the relief of being under the hat), she bent and took off her shoes and took her real shoes (were they?) out of the bag and put them on. Then the safety pins to be unfastened, the cape to be pulled off. Then bundle everything inside the bag. Then, take off the hat.

She did not want to take off the hat, but she would have to because it was a part of that other world where Millicent's mother and Janet's friend and James's wife who had divorced him and her dead mother's daughter all lived so warily in a single shell. If the hat moved into that world as nothing more than a dingy hat she had chosen to wear on a September afternoon, it would not be any more what it was: the excluder, the protector, the keeper from violation.

She wrenched it off and stuffed it mercilessly down into the bag, under the shoes and the cape, before it could cry out against her. Then she walked out of the room and out of the elevator and out of the store, as she might walk out of any store, as if she had been making a purchase, neatly dressed and respectable Mrs. Florence Butler. But she felt naked without the hat, everyone looking at her, and she must hurry home.

"Good evening," said the doorman at the apartment building, touching his cap. The building had standards in doormen, this one was Donald or David or Dennis. She would remember him suitably at Christmas.

She said, "Good evening." So it was that late, later than four o'clock anyway, because the doormen changed at four and Donald or Whatever-his-name probably started to say good-evening as soon as he came on.

After that, it was uneventful. There was no one in the elevator to whom she need say another good-evening. There was no one in the apartment except herself.

She went at once to her bureau and pulled out the middle drawer, and the gloves were there, just where she had remembered them. Winter gloves, black wool, a bargain pair and warm but not nicely knit or shaped, and she had never worn them. They were too clean but, day after day, in the city, next to the great lion at the Library, in her own place, they would begin to learn grime. Now that she had remembered department stores and had found her gloves, there were not going to be any more problems. She would be able to sit on the steps, below the lion, for long stretches of time, inside the envelope of her clothes—not answering, not asking, more and more silent, more and more safe.

Now she would have a thin supper and go to bed, and to sleep where there was silence, too.

2

The alarm clock thundered, and she jerked into wakefulness. She always set it for seven-thirty in the morning, which was unnecessary because she had nothing to get up for, but some bored Puritan in her brain instructed her to get up anyway. There had been a time when eight o'clock was important to her, so that she could watch (without admitting it, even to herself) a children's program on television. Captain Kangaroo had held her hand for many months now, years perhaps— anyway, ever since the time she had begun to feel everything slide away. Lately she had not turned him on and perhaps he was no longer there, no longer inside that television show not meant for adults at all. Once, she had watched soap operas, eyes glazed with daytime sleeplessness, but one day she had not turned on the only one she had thought she liked, and after that she had not turned on anything at all.

Now, she lay flat on her bed and looked up at the ceiling and realized that there was no actual Captain Kangaroo, so she had entrusted her hand to someone who was not there.

It would be better to put on her woolen gloves and leave the apartment again. When it dropped your hand, the television set became more an enemy than a friend; it had been there only to keep her thoughts from circling, and now they had become too dim even to circle. She could get up and dress as she had yesterday and take her shopping bag and go back to the lion, she could cling to that marble ship as if she were a mindless barnacle. She had a moment to wonder whether it was safer to have no mind at all than to have one that thought of barnacles, but the telephone rang and she had to switch her thoughts and lie wondering if she should answer it.

The Puritan reached out a hand to take the phone from the bedside table and say "Yes?" Not "Hello." Hello was a response, even if it was a response to silent air.

"Florence?" It was Janet, stirring the silent air with apologies for calling so early. "I called you yesterday afternoon, but you weren't back yet from Connecticut. Did you have a nice time?"

"I was out." Her head was swimming with the sounds, first the shrilling of the clock and then the telephone as strident as a siren, but the Puritan had been raised polite as well as obedient. "Oh, yes, lovely," she said, and then said again, "I was out."

"I know. —Are you all right?" Janet said. "You don't sound like yourself. Oh, I woke you! I know I woke you! You were sleeping late!" On no answer, she said "Florence?"

It was a matter of summoning up every possible reserve, mobilizing every possible force, to respond. If only I never had to answer anyone's voice again, she thought. She answered, "I'm always up at seven," severely. "I forgot to put the alarm on for this morning, no, I didn't put it on because when I went to bed I had a headache...." You see? Answer at all and you answer too much. *Don't answer.*

"Are you feeling all right now? I'm so *sorry.*"

She held the phone in her hand and stared at the wall opposite. Once she had been unable to decide whether that wall should be pale yellow or rich cream, not because it mattered very much but because, when she had had to start to live alone, (after *then;* after her husband had died—no, he had not died, he had left her; no, he had not left her, she had told him to go)—After she had become a divorced woman and he was, once again, inexcusably, a married man...It would have all been so much easier if she had been widowed, though one could not, of course, say that out loud. "When I started to live alone," she said very distinctly into the phone.

"What?" said Janet.

"Nothing. I forget what I was gong to say." She should not have said even that much. Janet would press her about forgetting, she would not say it was a bad sign but she would say one should not live alone. If one responded, Janet would, as forever, press her conviction that they, the two women, one divorced, one decently widowed—that they should live together, share an apartment. Share the rent, because the cost of living was rising so rapidly that it was no longer practical, and because We get along so well together, don't we? We always have.

If she said nothing, Janet would have to say something. "Anyway," said Janet, "I called to ask about lunch."

There was room for only one person in the lion's shadow. "Not today, please, not today. I just want to stay quiet, I don't think I—I know you understand." Always, she answered too much.

Janet said, of course she understood, dear, we'll make it another time, take care, get a good rest. She hung up.

If she lived with Janet, she would be forever understood, told to take care, to rest. Janet was her best friend, closest, loyalest, dearest. Almost her only friend now? She laid the phone back into its cradle (like the lion's cradling), took her fingers away from it slowly. She would have to eat enough breakfast to see her through the day, but she would also put something into her shopping bag in case she stayed longer than usual (it was only the one time, but it had already become the *usual*)—raisins, to displease Millicent? a bar of chocolate? Somewhere she had a package of granola bars, bought for no reason and never opened. They would be gray with age. Like the shopping-bag lady sleeping inside her, who must now wake and go out.

At last, "Good morning," she said to the doorman. She

could not be expected to remember his name, because she was already at the lion, she was already cradled.

"Good morning," he said. She supposed he could not remember her name either. She nodded to herself faintly, not caring, rehearsing the moves she had to make: the taxi, the department store, the ladies' room, the enveloping cape, shoes, gloves. Most of all, the hat, erasing the world. And then, the lion.

When she did reach the lion, it was like coming home.

It went on so, for six days. On the seventh day, when the Lion had finished His work and found it good, a fog came down over the city.

She huddled her way through that morning, but there was no sun and the cape was not as warm as it had promised, and inside it her body felt as heavy as a sack of stones. If she did not get to her feet and go somewhere, she would become waterlogged since it was surely going to rain, the fog turning from damp to wet. She cleared her throat, out of fear that she was getting pneumonia, not because she cared about it but because she might be taken off somewhere and put into a hospital and so lose this safe place, which so far no other bag lady had tried to take from her. She had thought about that often, sometimes at night, about coming to the lion's shadow and finding a copy of herself hunched in her place. If she had pneumonia and could not come back at the hour she had appointed to herself, it would somehow, she knew, all go wrong.

So she sat there, turning damp in the fog and thinking, more intensely than she was used to thinking now, about getting to her feet. She was no longer her own weight inside her clothes; she was as heavy as the clothes.

"Better get under a roof, lady," said a slurry voice.

She opened her eyes, which she had not known were closed, and saw feet wrapped in dirty rags, as if they were bandaged, and shiny black trousers. The feet were dancing a little, mocking the Library's steps with slipper arabesques. "Want a joint, sweetheart?" said the voice, and a hand pushed something that looked like a badly made cigarette in under the brim of her hat.

She reared back, outraged by the invasion, and the outrage woke her enough to make it possible to struggle to her feet. She did not look beyond the hat, and, in danger of seeing upwards, she pulled the brim further down over her eyes. "Friendly," said the voice, "my little friendly bag lady, ah, ah, ahh." Then, aggrieved, "I was on'y being nice."

Part of her knew all about him. Part of her knew that the Library steps and the Library plaza and the park behind the Library were home and harbor for puffing and snorting (like a drugged dragon) of all the drugs that had so many names, evil flowers in an evil garden. The odd thing was that she ought to be afraid, and she was not afraid at all, merely indignant.

She heard herself saying hoarsely, "Go away," and she said it at least three times before she realized that she was not the one who was saying it but the figure standing over her, retorting, telling *her* to go away, not talking any more about being friendly. She shut herself tight against him and struggled to get up, hands unwinding the cape, hands reaching for the bag, hands wanting to push away the dirty rags he carried for his feet, which seemed both revolting and familiar. "*You* go away," she said.

He crowed like a rooster, cackled like a hen, and backed off. From under her hat, she saw the dirty rags retreating into the day's fog, but now she was standing and no longer in danger of him or of pneumonia. She could go home and take off her wet clothes and have a nice hot bath and lie down on her bed and go to sleep.

And that, of course, was where everything turned false, because she was not really a bag lady at all. She could leave her lion and her disguise any moment she wanted to, and be safe inside that civilized apartment in which there was no safety whatever and from which she had thought herself to be, safely, escaping. I will have to do it all the time, she thought confusedly, or I will never know, not so long as I can go back and lie down on that bed among those walls of which I am now afraid. But why afraid? Why not just go back there and lie down and be indifferent, senseless, sensationless, until she fell off the edge of the world and that was it?

The fog was thickening into rain. She would go home. The man with the ragged feet would go to his evil flower garden, and she would go to her bed. They would be children again, tucked up for the night. If she really had no place to go, she would have to lie down like him wherever he lay, and she would not have to think about the world that she was supposed to think about. (Mother, you don't take care of yourself properly. Florence, did you have a decent breakfast? Good morning, Mrs. Butler, do you want a taxi? Dear Friend of Children, will you send a check? Dear Reader, will you please give your attention to our screaming headlines? Dear TV Viewer, will you buy, buy, buy?) Bye-bye, she thought, suddenly anxious. Bye baby bunting daddy's gone a-hunting, I must get home, tomorrow I will think about what I will do today. Tomorrow I will start to be what I am now. I will be a bag lady twenty-four hours a day, then I will know, I will really *know*. . . .

She started home, started to walk the block to catch the bus to take her home to lie on her bed, when she remembered just in time that her present self would not be allowed into her apartment building. First she must go to the ladies' room, change into respectability, then go home, then lie on the bed, then...

It did not take so long after all, she was getting quick at it. She was home within a bearable time ("Aft'noon, Mrs. Butler"), she was turning on the television set (a rags-to-riches show, instant money, everybody shrieking), turning it off. She was lying on her bed, on top of the counterpane, hands crossed, like a knight waiting for the drug dragon, a damsel enchained, a bag lady lying on Mrs. Butler's bed in Mrs. Butler's clothes.

Mrs. Florence Butler, born Florence Munday, resident of New York City, mother, ex-wife, grandmother-to-be, Mrs. Blank of Blind Alley. Close to the end of a very short tether, she thought, but she thought it without resentment or malice or even dismay, because outside now was the bag lady and she could become that, not for just a few hours at a time but for weeks, months, years, perhaps forever.... Bye, baby bunting. Tomorrow she would arrange everything. Tonight she would sleep.

3

It was another day, and it was almost noon, and she woke quietly. Her pillow was cool enough, but too soft to be the lion's marble pedestal, and she suffered for the fraction of a second a wave of infinite longing. It passed because by the end of the day she would be with the lion whenever she wished to be, not coming home at night (if this place could any longer be called home). She would be wrapped in her cape like a shroud, peaceful, beyond boundaries.

Between future freedom and present bondage, there lay

only a series of devices, arrangements, explanations—the undoing of all the tiny vicious claws that hooked her into yesterday. She did not want to plan, but she would have to or she could never buy that unplanned time of complete withdrawal.

She would have to call Millicent, and what would she say to Millicent? I am leaving home, Millicent dear daughter. When? At once. For how long? A week or a lifetime. Where? Somewhere; first, one somewhere, and then another somewhere. Mother, how can you do this to me? Easily.

She turned on her back and lay there, looking down the length of herself. Like a tree trunk, she thought complacently, felled. In the woods I shall not be noticed at all. Perhaps the best way would be simply to walk out of the apartment, lock the door behind her, give the key to the doorman, Eddie-I-shan't-be-back-maybe-never. Yes, Mrs. Butler, the usual tip at Christmas time, right? After weeks had gone, they would begin to wonder. Millicent would be raging at the superintendent, calling the police, rousing the F.B.I., a mother-to-be whose own mother had disappeared and what would one's friends say?

She sighed, laid her arms alongside the felled trunk of her body, bare arms lying on light summer blanket in this warm and mild and golden September. She regarded them as an abstraction, arms that would have to be accounted for to Millicent, to Janet, to friends, acquaintances, doormen, when all she wanted to do was go out the door and slide into that other lifestream which was so secure and so mindless. She did not wish to use her mind now, all that explaining it would have to do. She was, after so much sleeping, excruciatingly tired. She could not even lift up her mind....

There crossed, over that mind, a shadow of fury. She, who wanted nothing, must not now be stopped from finding

53

nothing. She lay rigid on the bed, foxlike, a vixen protecting her own escape.

She threw the sheet aside, and the light summer blanket, and she got out of bed, pulling on her light summer robe. She thrust her narrow feet into her light summer slippers, urged herself to take up the telephone, dialed the area code, the digit-numbers that belonged to Millicent exclusively, then stood waiting with a kind of docile impatience while the phone rang and rang and rang. Millicent in her garden? in the basement? in the garage? at a neighbor's?

"Yes?" said Millicent, impatient but not docile.

"Darling," said her mother automatically.

"Oh, it's you." Then, "I was going to call you this evening."

Evening rates, of course. She dragged her voice up and out from wherever it had gone, brightened it like a toothy smile, dazzling. "I wanted to tell you right away," she said, pushing urgency into the vowels, the consonants. "I'll be leaving town for a week or two, I'm so excited." She managed to keep her voice from trailing away, managed to reveal the effort.

"Leaving town? Leaving New York?"

Millicent had a way of picking up what was said and dangling it in the air, like a— Like a dead mouse, she thought but not resentfully, because that was what Millicent did and she was accustomed to it. "For a week or two," she said again, "for a sort of holiday." Too breathless, she who was never breathless. It was important for Millicent not to suspect anything, the door to escape might somehow close. She pulled a name out of memory and hurried on. "Liz Endicott called me—just a little while ago. You remember my talking about Liz Endicott, don't you? We went to college together."

"No," said Millicent, "I don't remember."

"That's the baby coming," her mother said cleverly. "I

forgot all kinds of things when *you* were on the way. It's only natural, darling." She went on even more rapidly to take advantage of the silence which seemed to have a different tone—more respectful? "Anyway, Liz and Doug—that's Liz's husband—are planning a week at the Island, they generally close their house but the weather's been so beautiful, and she wants me to go there and spend it with them—lovely house, so much room, I'll have my own bathroom."

"The *Island?*"

"Of course. Easthampton. So lovely. I'm almost packed, and they're picking me up in an hour."

"But it's so sudden, Mother! Why couldn't they have let you know earlier, not that I don't think it's splendid, but it's so—" There was a pause for sensible thinking. "Perhaps they asked somebody else, and it fell through."

Thank you, she thought in one last ironic flare before she snuffed her candle of feeling and walked out of her daughter's life and out of her own life. Thank you very much indeed. "I knew you'd be pleased," said the vixen fox, quite pleasantly.

"Where will I be able to reach you?" Millicent said.

She put her hand to the bridge of her nose as if it ached, because she had not anticipated the question, and then she said, "It's a box number, darling, everybody in the Hamptons has box numbers. I'll write it to you when I get there. I've got the phone number right here—" She paused as if she were pushing things about on the telephone table, in her known-to-be incompetent way, gave a little laugh. "It's right here somewhere, I'll send it to you, dear." She added brilliantly, "It's not a listed number," and then added, even more brilliantly, "Of course."

The *of course* had its desired effect. Millicent would not admit that she had not realized the Endicotts were the kind of people who did not list their number. She said dubiously, "Well, it all sounds quite wonderful, Mother. I hope the weather stays nice."

So do I, thought her mother, the bag lady who would not be carrying an umbrella or a suitcase or an electric heating pad. "I'll be in touch," she said swiftly, and added, choosing to be the well-wisher, "Have a good time while I'm gone, and take care."

"Yes, of course, but, Mother—"

"I have to run, dear. They'll be calling from downstairs.— Darling, I mustn't keep them any longer." As if they were calling already, as if their chauffeur was calling, pacing up and down the lobby, in full livery.

"Well," said Millicent quickly, "I must go too." Duties, baby calling her though not yet born, as much in demand as her mother. "Blessings."

"Blessings," her mother said. She had not heard that since Millicent was a very little girl, and something triggered wrong so that she almost slammed the telephone back into its cradle. The cradle of the telephone, the cradle of the lion again, how odd. She managed to put the instrument softly into place, befitting the mannerly mother hastening to be the mannerly guest. There was that chauffeur waiting.

She stood looking around the room, planning exactly what she would have to do in the next hour. Call Janet and repeat her story. Pack her handbag and her shopping bag. Pack folding money into a wallet, coins into a coin purse. See that there was nothing in the refrigerator that would spoil before she came back, *if* she came back. Put the philodendron into a bowl of water so it would live, or die, she thought indifferently. Say good-bye to the room, good-bye to the door-man. . . . No, not say good-bye to anyone, just take her shopping bag with the old clothes inside it, the clothes that would transform her. Walk out the door. Not say good-bye, not say farewell.

It all seemed so clear in that moment that it was as if it had been done already. Finished. She need not go at all.

Almost she did not go, but then, underwater, she began to move, and as she moved the water currents began to take her over and she found herself hurrying, but with an extraordinary forgotten deftness as if she had done it all before.

III
THE CITY

1

It was not until evening that there was any difference. When the Library behind her closed its great door, she was still sitting with her back to the pedestal, the marble building crouched behind the marble lion. Her eyes and ears were shut. One of her clumsy black-wool hands lay limply on her dingy voluminous lap, the other held limply to the brown shopping bag against her knee. Nothing happened, nothing moved in her world; knowingly or unknowingly, no one looked at her; she was as still as a gravestone, and waiting.

When the sun fell from the sky, she had her signal. First she must eat and then she must sleep, although *eat* did not mean a restaurant and *sleep* did not mean a bed.

She got to her feet, heavily because of the clumsy clothes but not stiffly because—as an acquaintance had once remarked icily—"Really, Florence, your health is excellent," only because that same Florence, coddled in such excellent health, had been rubbing her forehead against the threat of a headache. She had not known how to respond, but she had been swept by a wave of resentment. Now, however, that excellent health, which had not permitted her to die when she wanted to, was giving her these uselessly supple joints. Deep down inside her disguise, she moved freely. Outside, she was an old peasant woman, fumbling at her shopping bag, furtively seeking out a dollar bill. It was crisp, she could almost hear its crisp greenness, and it should have been crumpled and soft, smelling of age and poverty. She crushed it in the palm of her right glove, and finally she rolled it into a ball and stuffed it into the left one.

Inside the gloves were the slender white hands. Inside the clods of boots were the narrow white feet. Inside the grime-gray folds of the cape was the body of a well-nourished fifty-two-year-old female in prime condition. The outside would have to move, the inside to plan, and she did not want it to be that way, the inside wanting only to retreat. If she set the heavy shoes to walk, they would take her somewhere, would they not? The old bag lady she had created must move on an unknown current, drift independently toward food and sleep, find things out for herself without guides. If she had wanted to control, lead, plan, instruct, she might as well have stayed home in that apartment whose walls had enclosed her.

Her feet took her down the steps, out onto the sidewalk, and she kept her head so low that all she could see under the hat brim was her own feet and other feet. Her own turned her west, in some obscure knowledge of New York's geography because of the sun and the shadows, or merely by instinct. She was totally indifferent. Let this outer scarecrow take her where it wished. The thing inside, the person who wanted to escape into non-existence, could lie there like an animal, nose between forepaws, eyes shut, passive, not even needing to think.

She sighed with relief and walked, as mindless as a puppet. Her skirt hampered her, the brown shopping bag dragged at her hand, but nobody bumped into her as they did so often in real life (real life?) and perhaps this was because she was so wide, a puddle to be stepped around. The engulfing hat made her bag-lady vision focus on feet and legs, sidewalk and curb, and street. No green or red lights at the corners, they were too high up—just move when other people move. Someday she might get hit, a truck or a motorcycle doing for her what no one else would do, but she would not look ahead to that singular event. She would not even look ahead to food or to night, only to go where she was taken by this other woman. She went on walking, for how long or in which direction or why she neither knew nor cared.

When at last, from under the brim of her hat, she saw the bottom part of a bright window set in white tiles, she raised her head enough to see into it, enough to see a sign that said *Sandwiches, Hot Coffee.* She gripped her bag tighter in her right hand, curled her left hand around the dollar bill, and went inside.

The stool at the counter was white and high, and it took an effort to clamber her wrapped self (a mummy, really, not a scarecrow) onto it. Under her downward eyes, a black hand swiped a gray cloth across a white counter. "What'll it be?" said a black voice.

"Soup," she told him—unless the black hand was a woman's. No, it was a man's.

"What kinda soup?"

"Bean," she said.

The soup was thick as a stagnant pond, but it nourished. The gloves made her awkward, and she grasped the handle of the spoon the way a child would grasp it, making a fist. She swallowed slowly, following the heat and the taste down her gullet. When the black hand (she need never know what the face looked like) pushed a glassine packet of crackers toward her, she accepted it, but the slippery thing resisted opening and, after a moment of struggle, she pushed it away. The black hand took the packet, opened it, set the thin crackers down in front of her, as if this was what it had been doing for years. What she should say, as she chewed down the crack-

ers, was "Thank you," and she would not. She did not wish
to.

She ate wordlessly, finished the soup, put her hands down
under the counter to extract the dollar bill without being seen,
and laid it on the counter. When, in a moment, the change
was pushed back, she stared at it. Decades of taxi drivers,
waiters, doormen rose accusingly before her. How much should
she tip? In front on her were two quarters, one dime. One
dime was not a tip, it was an insult, but surely from an old
bag lady...

It was the bag lady, the scarecrow, the mummy, who
smiled a wintry smile to herself and took all three coins off
the counter. There were no problems, there would not be any
problems. She was at home in this sea. She had not been found
out, had simply been accepted as a derelict with a dollar bill.
The man probably assumed that she was a mad old thing,
possibly even a wealthy one, an eccentric. All the city's folktales
would support that theory. Or he thought she was really poor
and old and someone to tolerate. Or, in this part of whatever
part of New York she was now in, no one expected tips.

No matter. He was a pair of black hands and nothing
more, and she did not have to respond to him or even to
admit his existence. She shuffled out the door, perhaps a little
elaborately but she was not yet entirely used to the total detachment of the waves and the seaweed and the caverns. In
time she would be able to respond only to herself, and then
only if she wished to. Sustained by the soup, she listened to
her nearest necessity—a place to sleep.

It was warm enough to stay outdoors, even in the open
drafts of the streets, without danger of pneumonia, although
she could shrug at danger anyway since it made no difference
whether she woke up or not the next morning. She did, however, want to sleep now, and it was a desire so intense that it
muffled every other sound in her head.

For a while, she walked, sometimes in the light of street lamps and sometimes in darkness, armored in indifference, her head swelling with the need to lay it down somewhere. Her cape dragged at her, the shopping bag was as dead a weight as the bulk of her own body. When the doorway presented itself, she merely accepted it.

Like the lion, it was a shelter. It had a back to it, someone's door. It had sides, and a broad stoop. It was out of the wind's way if the wind came, and it was out of reach of the fingers of street lights. If she sealed her eyelids down in this place, she would be beyond all prying.

Turning, she backed into the doorway, her shoulders against the door, sliding down it in a kind of slow luxury, melting onto the stoop. Her head was against the corner angle, her hat was a cushion. Her body slumped and her knees spread, making a lap of the cape. Her feet in the square black shoes pawed at the sidewalk until they fit it. She leaned her shopping bag against her projecting hip, leaned her cheek against the rough wall. There was no tomorrow. The telephone would not ring here, voices would not insist, no one would demand answers. She could come, she could go. She would, perhaps, be beckoned, and go entirely.

In this holy reassurance, she sighed briefly, flickered, and slept.

2

Daylight had fingered at her long before she woke. The street was dingy, the morning light was pearl. A man passed her, staggering, and did not see her because he scarcely saw the sidewalk. There were sparrows in the street, self-confident and busy, and two pigeons circled her, with splayed feet and red eyes. Nothing was very dirty, nothing was very clean. The sleeper was an accepted piece of the landscape.

When she finally moved, stirring slowly as if she were in her own bed in her own bedroom, she dislodged a bottle lying next to her elbow. It rolled away, across the sidewalk, down into the gutter, cracking in the street. She was already on the edge of waking, and so she woke.

Not having dreamed, she knew at once where she was, as if her mind had prepared her, as if it was the bag lady who woke and not the woman inside. Was it then possible that she could lose altogether that woman inside, the dreary thinker, the one who even now wanted to turn her head and sleep again? No, it was not possible. The call of nature, she thought resignedly without any humor at all. And on what door could she knock?

Before she got to her feet, she pulled her hat down well over her eyes. The hat was her badge of immunity, and since it did not let in the sky, it could be believed there was no sky and therefore no day. Her body still moved itself quite comfortably, even after a night in dark air and a dawn in dark light, and she picked up the bag and shrugged her shoulders deeper into the cape.

But who would take her in? This was going to be a continual problem, but, since nature for the moment was being less insistent, she started to walk in the direction in which she was facing, moving her feet under orders that she had nothing to do with. In her half world, everything cut off midway, she thought she would see only what she wanted to see, and so she was not prepared for the dog coming toward her. She could see the whole of its ugly body, and it was large and scrawny and grimy like her cape. She drew back sharply, and it gave her a look as if she was not a bone and went its way, big-footed and loping. She shut her eyes for a moment against the unwanted truth that she could not avoid seeing some things whole, and she would have to accept it. Once, she had liked dogs.

She had more important things to think of. In the subway there would be a ladies' room, it was required by Law. She plowed on down the street, determined that in the city of subways there would be an entrance, and she came to one within a bearable time. Its stairs were littered with cans and paper trash, and she went down them, clutching her cape high around her, not to keep it clean but to keep from tripping on the hem and sprawling headlong. Nothing was going on inside the dim vault at the bottom of the steps, and she stopped on the last one to dig out another dollar bill and then stood still, uncertain and confused.

It was a long time since she had been in a subway. No one she knew used it at all if they could possibly avoid its known dangers, except people like her cleaning woman Nina who came Wednesdays and who was small and dark and as irritating as a summer fly. Small dark women fitted into subways, so did large black ones. She herself did not fit, and she felt an instant's insult that she should be here. Then she looked down at her wide drab front, and she remembered who she was now, too concealed even to guess her color, her face perhaps not showing at all under its safe hat. She found herself whispering, "I could be black, Millicent, your mother could be black," and then she trudged up to the change booth, its half-moon opening for money just under her hat-brim eyes.

She pushed her dollar through the hole. A large white hand, dimpled across the knuckles, took it and shoved a token at her. She snatched it up and moved away, there was already someone behind her, and then she pushed the token into the slot of the turnstile and pushed herself through, hearing the token as it dropped.

She found the ladies' room, reluctantly raising her eyes enough to see WOMEN, to see OPEN 9 TO 5 on a dangling cardboard sign, to see the padlock and the chain. Her hand, raised to push the door open, dropped to her side. She would have to wait, she could wait. She had great self-control, and even as a child she had been easy to take on long shopping trips, but the padlock and the chain outraged her. She had paid her way into this subway hole only because there would be a bathroom.

Now she would have to go back up all the stairs again, climb over the edge of the upstairs world, and find another place. Poorer by the cost of that token, and no further along.

She could, she supposed, sit down in some corner of this drafty subway room in the company of that white female in the change booth, in the company of the strangers coming down the stairs. She could sit or lie where no one would notice her, and she could go to sleep again. People and trains would go past. A train was coming now, she could hear it roar in the distance and then roar going by and beyond, and, because she changed the level of her vision too slowly, it was gone before she realized that it was on the middle track and roaring off in the opposite direction. It must be an express train, which meant she was not at an express stop, but it made no difference since she was, specifically, at limbo.

She would have to sit down and wait until nine o'clock when the bathroom opened, but no clock ticked and she had no way of knowing the time. Time was one of the things she had left behind in the apartment.

The subway noise came again, not in such a roar as before, and she went to the edge of the platform and stared along the track. Train lights were coming at her. When the train stopped, it opened a door in front of her, and the light inside was brighter than the platform light but the space inside was smaller and so more welcoming. She stepped into the car mindlessly. By the time she got out of it, some door of some ladies' room would have been opened.

She found a corner seat where she could lean against the wall, and she sank into it and looked out carefully from under her hat. Across the aisle were six people—six pairs of shoes, five pairs of pants, one skirt. The skirt was tight with a slit in it almost up to the knee, the shoes were spike-heeled, the ankles thick, the calves bulging. She pressed her lips together disapprovingly and went on to the pants. Four were men's, she could tell because of the shoes (how flat men's feet were! she had forgotten), but the first pair was sneakers which everyone seemed to wear nowadays, and they were sexless because, she thought distastefully, young women's feet were getting so large. Even Millicent's feet were too large, although Millicent did not wear sneakers. She wore tennis shoes. *Tennis shoes for tennis, she plays tennis for exercise, or did before the baby started.* Millicent and Millicent's baby drifted in and out of her mind like a fog. They did not interest her.

Foolishly, the Florence Butler inside the grimy cape darted a glance upward into the very world the hat was meant to shield her from, and then dropped her eyes quickly. The sneakers belonged to a black girl, with a stylish nose but thick lips (they intermarried all the time, there was no telling where it would end). The thick ankles belonged to a stout woman with brassy hair, eyes starred with mascara like black daisies, and a look on her red, red mouth that said "come" and "go" at the same time. To the late Mr. Butler, it would have said "come."

She had thought that too quickly to stop herself, and it was not, of course, the *late* Mr. Butler. James Butler had married again. He was still alive, somewhere. It had been a mistake to let Florence Butler look out from under the bag lady's hat. She would not let it happen again. She did not wish to see the women with come-and-go mouths, the blacks who intermarried—all the threats to everybody's sense of—order? decorum? threats to everybody anyway. Her own Nina, who came Wednesdays, who cleaned the apartment, believed that people should stay inside their own races. Nina's husband was a Hispanic. A Hispanic? or was it *an* Hispanic? Did Nina have a husband at all? She had children certainly, no, no, her sister had children, she looked after her sister's children, that was it.

I don't care, she thought, which was certainly true of Nina's children, since even Millicent's coming baby had been dismissed from—from what? From Florence Butler's head, or from the bag lady's? Confused, she closed her eyes, then opened them. The train was slowing down, she could feel it, and she must get off at whatever station they were coming to. Surely, by now, the ladies' room at whatever station would be unlocked. She needed it, urgently.

It was the bag lady who hoisted herself to her feet and

moved toward the door. When it sighed open, she got out and walked along the platform, watching the feet around her. There were a good many, which must mean that the working day had started. If the working day had started, there would be no lock and chain on the door of the ladies' room.

And, when she found it, there was none, and she was at last triumphant over her needs in a cubicle that must once have been white and was now splattered with graffiti which she would not read. Her sigh of relief was wholehearted, the sigh of a bag lady. Millicent's mother, Janet's friend, would never have indicated such feeling, not even alone and in a cubicle.

She walked out, comfortable, and when the next train, moving to nowhere, came along the track, she moved into it. It was again possible to secure a corner seat, which might mean that it was not yet rush hour and that this station opened its bathrooms early.

Toilets, said the pulled-down hat and the gritty cape, the black shoes and gloves, and the shopping bag.

She was so affronted that she could feel her shoulders draw together, but the outside woman was not affronted and it was the outside woman who would be taking her wherever they would be going. She had better let her alone. Very well.

The hat, cape, shoes, gloves, bag were reality. She would take no responsibility for thinking. She moved more intimately into her corner, which was like the corner under the lion but without sun or shadow. When the train lurched, a beer can rolled toward her feet and pulled away. There was a piece of wet newspaper sticking to the floor and something small and dark that moved and was a cockroach until it disappeared under a man's shoe and reappeared as nothing more than a bit of dust.

She liked the sound of the train and the way it swayed

and the voices that had, so beautifully, no faces. She liked
being a blur, it was easy. After a while, she dozed off, waking
fitfully and dozing again, riding free because she was going
nowhere and her first trip had been paid for a long time ago.
After a while, she would have to think about eating, but sleep
had been the path to her escape and for so long now that she
slid into it again without any guilt. ("Mother, you don't get
out enough." "You're getting too thin, Florence, you should
eat more.") Very faintly, in her sleep, she smiled.

But when she woke finally, the dog that she had seen
outside on the street was already chewing at her brain. She
had known all along that it was there, because *once* (as she
had remembered) she had liked dogs.

She would have to think about the dog. She had no choice.

3

She could not get its image out of her mind, where it had
relentlessly reconstructed itself. The head had been so large
and the body so gaunt that there was no reason why it should
have reminded her of any dogs from the past. When had she
stopped liking dogs? *Had* she stopped liking them? Wherever
you went in New York there were dogs, and, in the excellent
neighborhood from which she was now running away, most
of the dogs were leashed and as polite as their owners would
let them be. One met them constantly in the elevator: Yorkies
with topknot bows, poodles up on their hind legs and pawing
in the air, whippets all bone and style, foolish puppies, old-
gentlemen dogs with graying mutton-chops, dogs called Pixie
and Buck and Precious. When she had first come to New
York, they had fascinated her. It was only when she stopped

wanting to respond to anything, as she wanted now not to respond—No, it was not the dogs. It was the people who owned the dogs. Shake hands with Mrs. Butler, Pixie-pet. Get down, Buck, Mrs. Butler doesn't want, oh, I'm so sorry. She could hear them inside her head, click, click, click, people interfering with her dark cocoon. When the people began to interfere, she had stopped liking the dogs.

The dog on the street had offended her by looking so lonely—lonely and draggled and lantern-jawed, demanding that she have some feeling toward it. But she had left her feelings behind in her unfeeling apartment, or at least she had left behind any obligation to appear to have feelings. Here she could be a blank, here on this train going-into-night and no telephone ringing in her ears. Telephones insisted, reproached, solicited. She was escaping them, she was going down a long tunnel, away from Baskerville....

Just sliding off the edge of consciousness, she was jerked awake again. What had put Baskerville into her brain?

"The footprints of a gigantic hound..." A child of ten was lost inside a book, shoulders and toes curled in an ecstasy of horror, the gigantic hound loping toward her from the pages of Sherlock Holmes. Horror was pure delight when suffered in perfect safety, and that child had been safe. She could feel now, deep inside her, the armchair nest with pillows stuffed all around to make it smaller because it was wide enough for Father. For Daddy. She had called him Daddy until she went to high school, and then he had become Dad under the watchful eyes of her peers. When had Mother become Mom, that round apple-pie name which had turned itself into an epithet? She could remember telling Millicent not to call her Mom—that was back in the time when she cared what Millicent called her, before the sliding-off time, the no-feeling time, the dead time, the time she was still locked into.—Witness this body sitting in a subway train, a sack of mortal perishables except for the click, click, click of the voices of unwanted people and unwanted dogs, inside her head.

She returned to the Baskervilles in order to arrest the clicking. It was a long time since she had read anything but the headlines of the morning Times, not even looking at the rest of it, safe from it really. Whatever happened to the city or the nation or the world, she could still lie, lie still, on her bed, quite safe and asleep. She could sleep now, if she wished. The train would go to the end of the line and then go back again, like a shuttling needle until, sometime but no way of knowing when, it would go at last into its cradle....

Station. It would go into its station and officials would march through it and they would order anyone off who had been riding all day long on one endless fare, drifting in and out of no door except sleep's.

Baskervilles; being called Mom; reading, not reading. In the past years she had been dutiful about reading, remembering how she had once lived by it. She had gone to the branch library and brought home books. She had put them on her living-room table and left them there unopened until they were due. She had returned them on the due date exactly. But then, somehow, they had begun to pile up, and finally there was the day Janet came and found them and said "Oh, Florence!" in the way she had, pulling one back from the very brink. Janet had, most kindly, returned all the overdue books to the library, but afterwards she had telephoned one a little more often, asked one out to little lunches, gone with one to the neighborhood movie. Art films, usually, which could be slept through with an erect body and wide-open eyes.

She came back to the Baskervilles without wanting to, drawn there by the ten-year-old and the looming hound.

She found herself wishing she had never grown up, never

started the irreversible process leading to ruin. She opened her eyes briefly and looked down at her lap, draped like that statue of Grief someone had done, it was in Washington. She had encountered it first through a novel, had later been astonished to find that it was real. Someone had done it, some sculptor with a French name. She shook her head, closing her eyes, but the image of herself as a ruined object persisted. Not ruined perhaps, but as if Saint-Gaudens' statue of Grief had been cracked and mutilated—

That was it. That was the lost name of the sculptor. Saint-Gaudens. At one time, she had been interested in art as she had been interested in books. In college, she had taken a course in Art Appreciation, she had even given thought to Art as her major instead of Literature. It was odd that Saint-Gaudens should have surfaced now in her mind. She made a vague effort to remember the name of the novel as well, but it was a listless try and she went back to the child who had read in the arms of the armchair, before all this long dying. Children never knew about time, or, if they did, they stopped it.

Her concealing hat became Daddy's pillow at the back of her head, the wall her corner of the armchair, her drowsiness the child's reading of some drowsy book, not the Hound but some perfect fairy tale that would begin once-upon-a-time and end happily-ever-after. You could curl into a fairy tale, a *good* fairy tale, a Cinderella tale, a Snow Queen tale where everything melted except the Snow Queen's heart of ice. She had not really liked that story very much, and she stirred uneasily even now, remembering the frost and the cold and the splinters of the magic mirror.

I don't want to think about it, she thought now. I did not come all this way to think, and I will not think. I will sleep.

Sleep avoided her. The train kept jerking, making sudden

stops and starts. Someone stepped on her feet, and, when she opened her eyes, the other feet, the ones stepping on her, were gigantic, like twin animals on a leash, black polished beasts. Someone grunted "Sorry," and she raised her eyes resentfully but then stopped the danger of seeing much except dark-blue trousers. She shook her shoulders, deepening her own den, and closed her eyes once more. This will to sleep was passionate; the ability was gone.

I'm hungry, she thought, just at the moment she also thought, That was a policeman who stepped on me, black shoes, dark-blue trousers. He was still standing in front of her, and she studied as much as she could see, without emotion. Bag ladies had a right to be on subway trains. She felt nothing but indifference toward the Law, which had—rightly— apologized. She could see, beneath her hat, the edge of the blue tunic and the bulge at the hip. People got shot on subway platforms sometimes. What would it feel like to be shot on a subway platform?

What would it feel like to be ended, she who could not even end her own wakefulness now? Perhaps she should never have left her apartment, her room, her bed, her secret silence. Clear as a bell in her ear, the bag lady announced that she was hungry, and it made sense because sometimes, at the apartment, when she could not escape instantly into sleep (and she was afraid of the pills the doctor had prescribed because they brought dreams with them), she had, after a long time of thinking tiredly about moving, roused herself and sought out a cracker or a glass of milk, or best of all a chocolate to nibble on.

People were always bringing her chocolates to nibble on. People were very kind to her, which was perhaps why she had come to dislike them so. Not dislike really, that was too strong a word, but they would not leave her alone, although if one of them would give her the chocolate now...

Her stomach growled. She opened her eyes in sudden alarm, in case the policeman had heard, but he was quiet, his large feet were quiet.

Not stomach. Intestines. I have an intestinal problem. That was a decorum that came from her childhood. She had had intestines when she was a little girl, her "little insides" they were, and sometimes they got upset and worried her father. Her mother had said she would grow out of it, and it was true. She had gone on growing, and in time had acquired what her friends referred to as her disgusting health. When her stomach growled again, she ignored it.

She had no idea where she was in the world of subway, and if she got off right now she might come up anywhere, a thousand miles from food. Besides, she did not want to move. She wanted to stay here, in this her apartment, in her own bed, with food nearby in the refrigerator....

It was the hands of the bag lady that reached for the forgotten granola bar, one of the several she had thought of so cleverly when she planned her escape. The hand, the black wool glove, found it by groping, and when the bag bumped against the policeman's knee, he said "Sorry" again and moved away just slightly. In the space in the bag between his knees and the bag lady's, she found one of the bars guaranteed to be full of health and nutrition, sop for the little daughter's little insides.

She ate it. When a small piece broke off and fell into her lap, she wet her black wool finger with her tongue and picked it up, savoring in the crumb the taste of wool and granola. She ate methodically and well, but the bag lady wanted something more, a cup of coffee perhaps. It seemed likely that the outer woman was going to make demands on the inner one, not emotional but physical, and there would have to be some kind of agreement between the two. Negotiation.

She crumpled the paper the bar had been wrapped in

and put it tidily into her shopping bag. This was a victory for herself, because the bag lady would have thrown it on the floor of the subway train, but she did not want victories. She wanted to go back to that armchair where Daddy used to sit, she wanted to go to sleep in the armchair, not lie awake thinking about a cup of hot black coffee. —Negotiate? Why should she negotiate with this bag lady's body?

Stubbornly, she closed her eyes. Steam curled from the cup of coffee, and the armchair had gone. She opened them again, and the policeman had gone too, melted into steam. *Let her have her way.* Trudge with her into some eating place. Drink her coffee. Shut her up.

We'll get out at the next station, she said, and she almost said it aloud, not noticing that she had used the plural pronoun. If there were going to be negotiations, all the old problems would come back. She would find herself responding, reacting. The bag lady would become Millicent, would become Janet, would become James where negotiations had been so intolerably...

Anything was better than James. Grimly, she refused to think about James. She pulled her shoulders up high inside the cape, pulled the brim of her hat even further down over her eyes, pulled the shopping bag onto her lap, and pulled herself to her feet. Everything pulled, but it was the bag lady's doing, and she herself had no part in it. Give her her cup of coffee. If life was going to become a trade-off between the two of them, so be it—the bag lady eating, the bag lady mollified, the bag lady letting her escape into dreams. Not dreams, memories. She did not dream.

She was on her feet, but what she was wearing had suddenly become the whole of her body, and she could no longer balance it. The train lurched and she lurched with it, and a very strong hand grasped her elbow. "Steady," said a policeman voice ending in blue trousers and shiny black shoes. She thought he had gone, and, though she had no wish to be lying flat in the aisle, she felt aggrieved and she tugged her elbow out of his grip. He let her go.

The train came into its station. She lurched toward the door, and it would have been embarrassing (all eyes upon her?) but she was not the one who was lurching. Well, the old thing had earned its cup of coffee! There was not going to be any need for negotiation. She would take the old thing along on its leash; it would tell her when it needed a bone or to be taken to the curb.

That was almost funny, except that it was the kind of crude thought only a bag lady would think of, and she did not intend to let herself be taken over by someone else's thinking. Lurch, eat, drink, snore. Etcetera. (Etcetera is *my* way of saying it, Millicent.)

She was outside now and on the platform, and someone bumped her from behind and said an inadmissible four-letter word. She muttered, of all things, "Mind your manners," which was the first reproof from childhood she had ever really remembered.

The person who had bumped into her was long since gone, and there were stairs ahead. She clambered them, holding the rail and getting used to being bumped because everyone except herself was in a hurry. She was not in any hurry at all, because the mind-your-manners voice from the past had taken over the entire stairway, had even exorcised the bag lady and her insistent cup of coffee.

The voice had been the voice of an aunt, and the occasion had been the niece's sixth birthday. It was piled high in her mind with packages and a cake with pink frosting and six pink candles and a gathering of relatives, including the aunt's husband who was also, of course, the birthday child's uncle, a jolly man of pockets and cigar smoke. The aunt was Aunt Belle, her mother's sister, plain as a weed and usually most doting of her good little niece.

Something must have happened to change the doting to reproof. *Mind your manners. Mind your manners, young lady* was what the doting aunt had really said, but even the elevation to young ladyhood had not compensated for the sudden sharpness. The six-year-old had run sobbing to her mother's knees, clinging to the comfort of her skirt, balling the soft cotton material between fists that had become sweaty with instant rage. She remembered burrowing, the party spoiled, the pink cake uneatable, the unopened packages no longer exciting. She remembered sobbing, then hiccoughing, then quiet, face buried in skirt. She remembered relatives gathering around, patting, soothing, Aunt Belle saying that she was only joking. Flo, dear, Flo dear, look at Auntie Belle. She remembered her mother prying her fists open, kneeling to get onto childhood's level, taking her daughter's face between her hands and kissing her emotionally on the brow. Saying "There, there," saying coo. She remembered herself being so comforted that she was able to turn triumphantly to Aunt Belle and give her the kiss that was being begged for. Someone said "How sweet," someone said "Fuss over nothing." Surely not her father. Her uncle perhaps. She remembered now, she remembered perfectly that it had been her uncle. She remembered too the packages afterwards, the tiny flaxen-haired doll she kept playing with and losing and finding again, and, most of all, she remembered that the sixth birthday had been very happy indeed for everybody, except possibly Aunt Belle, who was not made for happiness but who did have Uncle Edgar for the rest of her lifetime, dying before he did and justified.

Uncle Edgar, as a widower, had been much less pocketed

and certainly less jolly, but his niece remembered him all her growing-up years until she was in her teens, when he moved to San Diego and died at such a distance that his niece (by then a married woman with a child) missed his birthday and Christmas presents to her rather more than she missed him.

The bag lady tripped on the top step, grunted, righted herself, and moved steadily toward some unknown place that would have coffee and real food, not granola bars.

Surely she was not right about the way she remembered her uncle's death? She had not mourned greatly, but he would not have wanted her to mourn, would he? Her mother had mourned, stoically; Uncle Edgar was a favorite. *When* had Aunt Belle died? It ought to be easy to date that event, because it should have been cause for much greater mourning for her mother, though Aunt Belle was ten years her senior and there were two other sisters and a brother, who did not come to family parties because they lived in different states, and anyway the brother was not a family man.

She came up into fresh air at the head of the stairs with no idea of where she was and an equal indifference. Under the hat which already cut off so much of the world, her head was down and she almost walked into a mailbox, although it was in her range of vision. Automobile wheels were going past her on the right, feet on the left. She moved away from the curb in order to be near the storefronts, a desire for coffee and something substantial to eat filled her horizon. She stared into the bottom halves of plate-glass windows—a drugstore, a florist shop, a bank sign coaxing depositors with a come-to-the-Golden-Throne offer of tomorrow and tomorrow's security. A man named Anderson looked after her own investments, he was a large person ruddy and reassuring, he explained things. She was well taken care of, she reminded herself hastily, she was well taken care of! That was something she need not think about. Money. Except to buy a stack of griddlecakes, a dish of spaghetti...How odd of her to be thinking so much about food. Distasteful, almost, but the bag lady was in charge for the moment, all but rubbing her black-woolen gloves together in vulgar anticipation.

I think I feel sick, she thought. I need to lie down. This was what she had been doing at home, in her own apartment, feeling sick without being sick in the least and then lying down because she had a need to lie down. A coffee shop interrupted her explanation of herself, but it was really an ice-cream shop with a poster in the window that showed a drooling chocolate cone. If she went in and bought an ice-cream cone, instead of coffee/griddlecakes/eggs-and-bacon/spaghetti/T-bone-steak, she would have to decide on a flavor. She stood there at the window, reading the list of flavors over and over, just under the brim of her hat as if it had been put there on purpose to make it impossible, not wanting an ice-cream cone at all but driven to make a decision. Someone was always expecting her to make decisions.

Strawberry ice cream would be the exact color of that six-year-old's birthday. What had she done to make Aunt Belle say Mind your manners, young lady? There must have been something. Had she, feeling so charming, been pert? Thinking back now, it was Aunt Belle herself who had given her the tiny doll. She had not meant to be pert, if that was it, and the terrible thing had been not knowing what she had done wrong, not knowing why she had lost Aunt Belle's approval.

Until now, she had not wanted it.

If she could just, feeling sick, lie down on her own bed. But, of course, the telephone would ring and she would be tethered again at the black end of the black cord....

Strawberry ice cream, said the bag lady peremptorily. Thank God, someone was making the decision at last. It was as good as a bed.

She went through the ice-cream door. There were no customers at the low white counter, and behind the counter only half of a person in what appeared to be a white shirt with a belt that had a tin-gold buckle and a voice that said "Yes?"

She dug first to find another of her dollar bills, not knowing how much a cone would cost, and as always it was hard to reach and everyone was watching or would have been if there had been anyone there. She said "Strawberry" in a loud mumble, and went on digging. "Cone or cup?" said the white shirt and the belt wearily.

"Cone." She had never seen a bag lady eating an ice-cream cone—did they? should they? But she had found the dollar bill and was pushing it greedily across the counter in the bag lady's grasp, and the white-shirt voice was already saying "Double scoop?" with the same mechanical fatigue.

She nodded. The cone was put into her hands, and danger was an imminent earthquake. She could not possibly manage this bulging two-decker thing *and* the change *and* the voluminous cape *and* the getting out of the door again, but, before the despair could become total, the change was in the bag lady's hand and had been dropped quite casually into the bottom of the shopping bag, the bag-lady paws had already seized the cone, and she was outside and on the sidewalk. Licking. Slurping, like a dog. Her tongue encountered a frozen strawberry, and she let it ride there. The September sun was melting-warm, and she moved into the shade of something—an awning. It was above her head, and since she could not see above her head, she accepted it as if it was a cloud in the sky. Pink strawberry ice cream, pink birthday-frosting cake, but the bag lady was not dainty. *What* had she done to affront Aunt Belle?

Forgive us our trespasses as we forgive our Aunt Belles. Really, she must not let herself think that kind of thought, there were days when she was almost blasphemous. Aunt Belle was so plain that she had been obliged to talk constantly in order to be heard—Was it possible that, on the pink cloud of being six years old, the birthday child had interrupted her? That was it, certainly. A child's eagerness on Her Own Day, bursting with good news, running over with excitement. One could include Aunt Belle and the child in the same absolution, dismiss them in the same nod. Had she ever really *liked* Aunt Belle?

The strawberry ice cream was dribbling down her chin in the sun and onto the front of her cape. She had been walking, the bag lady had been walking, without any heed for anything, and the ice cream was almost all lapped up out of the cone, and the cone itself was coming to pieces. She crammed the whole end of it into her mouth messily, no one would notice how an old bag lady ate ice-cream cones, and then she rubbed her chin with the back of her glove and spread pink onto that too.

She was not answerable to anybody, not now, not any longer. The person who was answerable had telephoned her daughter and her best friend and had told them she was going to the Island. What island did not matter. The bag lady was no longer clamoring for a cup of coffee; the cone had done its appeasing work. What she wished to do now was to sit down somewhere, inside the cape and under the hat, and to sleep upright as she would have slept horizontal on her bed. Like a knight on a tomb, hands long and slenderly pressed together in prayer, if one prayed when one was already dead.

Tennyson had befallen her like an archangel. She must have been thirteen when it happened. Later, she would learn to think of Tennyson as not really very good, and, later still, as merely musical, and even later (best of all) as mildly amusing. The hot breath of peer culture had struck her in her senior year of high school, and she had given up Tennyson without a pang. Forever, of course.

So they rowed, and there we landed.
O venusta Sirmio!
There beneath the Roman ruins where the purple
flowers grow...

Loveliest of Roman poets, nineteen hundred years ago ...something, something...Ave atque vale, something about Lydian laughter, and then sweet Catallus' all-but-island, olive-silvery Sirmio. Wherever Sirmio was, but she was astonished to find what a long tail the Tennyson cat had. *I* remembered that, not you, she reminded the bag lady, but her thick companion was glutted with pink sweets and was now occupying herself, quite contentedly, with putting one clumping foot in front of the other. Nobody knew where she was, nobody cared. Somewhere they would find a bench to sit on, to lie on. They would make a chapel of their prayerful hands and lie on the knight-tomb. Full military honors. The conceit might have troubled her, back there in the apartment, but here she could think whatever she chose. She could pick up the past and lay it down without explaining. She could...

She could do nothing. The dusk was stealing up her backbone, and she must sit still so she could drift out, let the tide come in to comfort her, not responding, not listening.

When a new subway entrance presented its stairs, she went down them like a rabbit into its warren. The railing was painted egg-yellow, and she held it until the last step, where she stopped to open her shopping bag and find money or a token or whatever it was she needed next. She must learn to put loose change into her pockets, but she had no pockets, why had she come out without pockets?

85

A hurtling body struck her from behind and spun her around, and she grabbed atavistically at her bag, the way a caveman would have grabbed at his club. As she spun, thrown against the wall, she clung all the more desperately.

Hands caught her. A voice screamed, "Jesus! what you want to stand there right in the way Jesus you old fool stand up can't you!"

Clinging to the shopping bag, she found the yellow rail again just below her eyes, and she clung to that. Drowning. She ought to look up and see who was killing her, but her hat was jammed down so hard over her forehead (as she meant it to be, as it must be or the knight would not sleep, hands in prayer, on the tomb) that she could see nothing but yellow rail and wall.

"Jesus!" said the same voice.

She did not like people who said "Jesus" as an obscenity, although some of her friends did it, quite old enough to know better, had picked it up from their young in the dangerous days of the 60s. Millicent had been a very docile student, thank God, not a hippie (horrid word).

She clung to the wall and wondered if *Thank God* was really all that different from *Jesus* as an expletive. It was an expletive, she had always been very good at grammar. . . . Get on with it! said the bag lady, it's nothing more than a shake-up. Jesus! said the bag lady. Get *on* with it!

Whoever had hit her from behind was long since gone. A subway train had gone too. She had heard it in the back of her head roaring down its rails while her mind had shot through a few decades and the bag lady's mind had given itself a shake and was already lusting after another seat in another subway train.

She leaned her forehead against the stairway wall for a moment, thinking it would be cool like a cool hand. The hat, of course, got in the way, but it was the hat that gave her immediate confidence. *Because of the hat, no one could have seen anything.* In fact, while she stood there, shoulders and hips and feet had been pushing past her, in a hurry, as if they were waves going around a rock. A rock in a gray cape. They had rounded the Cape of Good Rock—

She let go of the railing, telling herself that she was being silly. Don't be a silly! Daddy had said sometimes, hurting her little feelings (which were sensitive like her little insides) because she knew she was too bright to be called silly. She had always been very bright, but it was the impatient bag lady who, remembering all about the last transaction, had already stalked to the token booth.

There was a new set of stairs in front of her, which was wrong because she had already come down one set of stairs and was inside the subway walls. If she kept on going down stairs, what lower depths would lie ahead of her? Tolstoi had written about the Lower Depths; she remembered encountering all the Russians in Lit. XII, had never liked them particularly except for Anna—Anna—Anna Karenina. She would think about Anna Karenina, instead of thinking about the man—the woman? the body that had hit her and spun her around clutching the yellow rail.

No, she would not think about Anna, who had died under the wheels of a train.

The bag lady was not interested in any of it. She was already scuttling to find herself a place inside this rabbit warren. Moles, not rabbits. She was plowing down the stairs, the new stairs, into the Lower Depths, and there was a terrible sound of a wild wind rushing and panting and then of doors opening, and then the whole problem became perfectly clear in one burst of intelligence. So! she was not a little silly at all. The new stairs had simply led downstairs, down to the Express platform, and the train just in was an Express, and the name of the writer was not Tolstoi, it was Gorki.

The bag lady dragged her on board and headed for the corner that was already her favorite, two sides to a box, where she could rest her head.

There was someone inside it already, and the bag lady promptly jammed her knees into the knees of the someone— blue jeans, young blue jeans, get up, get up, all of you who made all that trouble in the 60s, and you'd make it again if you had your way. The knees straightened as the body stood up, the hands that were hanging down were pale and soft. Girls were nicer than boys, women were nicer than men. Sometimes.

She burrowed into the box-space, hugged it around her. It was an Express, it might go on forever. She could sleep forever, hands wrapped around her shopping bag, little insides wrapped around a strawberry ice-cream cone, pink as a dream. Aren't you going to eat your cookies? said Janet, smiling at her, smiling at the waitress. Janet would have smiled at the girl in the jeans, would have said thank-you-my-dear-oh-so-nicely.

She raised her shoulders up, pulled her head down into them, arranged her cape so it covered the shopping bag. Sleep, the safe sleep, encompassed her like a fog. Her black-wool hands dropped into her lap. Her fingers twitched indifferently. In the tunnels, under the City of New York, she could sleep forever.

4

There was a worm in the dream. It shifted and coiled and unrolled its black-green fluorescent length in shudders and smoothness. She woke four times and got off the worm and found another, but she was no more awake than the worm was. She was willing to be drugged by the dream, and the dream drugged her. She remembered only once seeing the outside of the worm, painted in flashing psychedelic graffiti—greens and reds and a purple as deep as a king's. There were slashings of gold in it too, the Excalibur sword plunged into the waters of the lake, and the last time (that is, the last time she saw the sword) she came out of the fog and the crisis long enough to remember that the worm had courtiers and the courtiers painted graffiti, and the effort of reaching the graffiti (a Romany-gypsy word) smothered her brain, so that she fell back into sleep again with the worm and the cape coiled tightly around her shoulders. But nothing seemed dangerous.

Once when she woke there was no one in sight, no feet visible from beneath the hat brim, and she thought she was being taken somewhere she could never return from, but even that did not seem dangerous. After a while she heard voices, so she was not alone after all, and they were raised and angry but not coming at her. Nothing to be answered. She blinked her eyes against a borrowing of brightness, closed her eyelids on half-dark, then closed them tightly on blackness. It was not new in her to like blackness; she had lain on her bed at home (home? she had called it that?) and let blackness come in to all the corners, peacefully, welcomed.

Down here, with the worm, there was not a telephone or

a doorbell or a doorman or a friend or a daughter. Nothing dangerous at all, so she had no reason to be afraid. She knew, behind the black eyelid dark, that sooner or later the bag lady would want something of her, drag her off the worm and put her somewhere else, but that would be at some other time and the voices she was hearing now were not her responsibility.

The bag lady was not her responsibility either, she thought suddenly, and she opened her eyes on the thought and then closed them again. She was the bag lady's responsibility. Carefully, her eyes still closed, she put one black-wool hand on top of the other, so that each of the two who sat inside the worm under the same low-brimmed hat—each of them would be holding the other's hand. One could not ask for more reassurance than that.

The joined hands raised themselves from her lap, the string handle of the bag between them, and then they dropped. She remembered the hand that held Excalibur rising from the lake, the dripping arm clothed in white....Clothed in white—white, white, some kind of white. The two locked hands raised themselves to brush her forehead, which was tired from trying to think of the white, the white, the white.

Oh, she did not want to think! That was not what she was here for. She had been told to come here and to sleep safely, and now she was being told to move inside her head as well as inside the worm. Clothed in white, white—*samite*. Her breath escaped her mouth in pure relief. The word had returned, everything was safe. The eyes of the bag lady can now be closed; the woman named Florence has received absolution; the lost syllables have been retrieved. Everything has been moved safely back into the passive tense. I was always good at grammar. When I am awake, grammar will be something to think about. If I am ever awake again.

But not waking was no danger at all. The worm would take care of everything.

5

When her mind did stagger awake, it was because the bag lady wished, peremptorily, to scratch her right leg, just below the knee. She wished to hike up her long cape and then the skirt underneath it and to scratch it luxuriously in an exact spot. Her hand was already clutching at the cloth when Florence stopped her. The mind that was so good at grammar recognized that the pulled-up skirt would reveal nylon stockings, unsuitabilities, unmaskings. The fear she had not felt about the worm suddenly made her throat thick.

She said *No* out loud because the bag lady's hand had to be stopped, and the bag lady mumbled *Yes*. The itch below her knee turned into an agony of pain, so that for a moment she became Millicent about to have the baby, but no, she thought, no, Millicent has nice wide hips, the baby will be a boy which was what James wanted and *I* was the one who had all the pain. I suffered terribly, the doctor patted my hand and told me I was a brave girl, he was a nice man very strong and he spoke to my husband about my being sensitive to pain, although he had not said sensitive, he had said...He had said.

Her mind turned to glass, abruptly, very beautiful glass like a silent lake where everything was reflected. The passive lake brought back the samite and the grammar. She remembered as early as age seven being pleased with the fitting together of words. She might have been a writer.

"It itches," said the bag lady, sounding angry but not loud, which showed who was in control. It was necessary to be in control, not just now but at all times, order being Heaven's first law. (That was from a poet, too.) "Keep your hands off," she said between her teeth, and she covered the bag lady's creeping hand with her own hand, keeping them both off. If the skirt was pulled up and the nylon stockings were revealed (passive voice), They would put them both off the train (active voice). Active voice was to be dreaded, and, under the beautiful glass, staring through it, the bag lady gave up. The itch subsided. It was a triumph, and now They would know who was master.

Mistress. It was always better to win. She had known that, even when she was very little, but she had always done it nicely, not just ladylike, *nice*.

There had been the playmate named Edna, small and wiry and dark and not at all pretty. Edna had a passion for animals, they came to her on the streets, followed her to school like Mary's little lamb. Dogs pushed their hard heads into cupped hand, cats arched against her legs (her knee socks were always plaid for some reason, to be envied a little but rather common). Edna believed in happiness for mice as one might believe in Divine Powers. Her parents had not shared her faith, and her baby brother was too young to be allowed to maul anything but his pink fur rabbit, so that little Edna was not allowed pets of her own, at least for the time being.

Florence and Edna had played with dolls and with stuffed animals. Sometimes Edna would sit endlessly, stroking the head of Florence's teddy bear, making it seem like her own bear, which it was not. She had thought once of giving the bear to Edna but she had reconsidered, because her mother never approved of giving things away without permission. Of course, she could have asked and her mother might have said yes, only thinking about her child's generosity, but she was not that sure about giving the bear away. She had, however, given Edna several paper dolls and even a small plastic doll with jointed arms and legs and a change of dresses. It had not been the doll or the teddy bear that had made the difficulty between them, if you could call it a difficulty....

I *itch*, said the bag lady.

Then go to sleep and forget about Edna. There was a time when two little girls played together and then there was a time when they did not, and it had nothing to do with the teddy bear or the paper dolls or the plastic doll.

It had to do with a kitten, a black and white kitten with a clown face. Someone had been giving away kittens, a batch of them having arrived unwanted under someone's porch, and Edna had been so unexpectedly independent as to ask for one. She had known, of course, that she would not be allowed to keep it and she had brought it around trustfully to her little friend Florence. Florence had known at once that she herself would not be allowed to keep it but that she would not even ask and so risk a rejection. (She did not want the kitten, for all its softness; she was doubtful of cats. It was dogs she liked, and it was not necessary now, sitting here with the bag lady in a subway train going wherever it was going to remember that dog in the street not so long ago. In her mind now, she had extended a welcoming hand to that dog, and it had slunk away. She had, and she remembered it, tried to help the poor thing.)

"Poor kitty," Edna said, near to crying because she had been sure that her friend who shared the teddy bear would take the kitten. "I'd help you to take care of it," Edna kept saying earnestly, and her little sharing friend kept saying no, being obliged to say no in fear of that rejection, until finally it was clear that the kitten again had no home. It was not as pretty as most kittens, the black and white on its face made it look somehow smeared, instead of sweet. "You'll have to take it back," Florence had said firmly, and then, because of course she really did love Edna and because she really did want the best for the kitten, she had created a reassuring fiction. The kitten would find someone else, there would be some other little girl in a big lonely house who was wanting a kitten so badly.... By the time Edna turned away with the kitten held against her cheek, the story had become completely true to its creator.

There had been no little girl in a big lonely house. Things had gone even more oddly. Edna had marched straight home and announced that she had been given the kitten, and her mother apparently, unbelievably, had looked at the object and said, "Well, we can manage, I suppose." With the kitten clutched to her small chest, Edna had run to her dearest friend and told her the triumphant news. And then, instead of staying with Florence and both of them playing with the kitten, Edna had turned around and gone home.

The games with the paper dolls and the stuffed animals had become less and less frequent, and finally they had stopped entirely. It was as if the kitten had alienated the two friends, and if that was what something as small as a kitten could do, it was perhaps as well it had happened early. I did my best for her, she thought now, I always did my best. She didn't need my teddy bear or the doll either. Not after she had the kitten.

Whatever the mistake was (if there had been a mistake), she would not make it twice.

I still itch, the bag lady said.

The train was no longer a worm. It was slowing down again and there were many shoes moving toward the door. It was one way to shut the bag lady up, and Florence hauled her to her feet, too fast so that she jolted with the train and hit against a leather briefcase. Whoever was holding the briefcase hissed indrawn air, angry, and a man's hand, a clean hand, a soap-and-water superior hand, clutched the handle of the case until the knuckles turned white. He was cleaner than the bag lady, the knuckles stated that, and for a moment she wanted to thrust her knee hard against his leg. But then she, both of her, were caught up in the push toward the sighing door, like a great suction, and she stumbled getting out and walked into a pillar, ugly, gray, concrete. A shoulder hit hers, and she would have been spun around completely but for holding on to the pillar. She began to be very angry because she was, all at the same moment, back in time with Edna and the kitten and forward in time with the bag lady's itch and in the middle of time with the man with the too-clean hands and the leather briefcase.

She leaned against the pillar, the pillow, and then she parted the folds of her cape, reached down with her right hand and began to scratch—with exquisite satisfaction—the bag lady's knee. It was a deep itch, and the scratching fingers were so strong that for a moment they seemed to belong to the man, and then all at once the bag lady was seated, and the man with the briefcase had gone, and Edna was back.

Carrying Edna's kitten, she turned away from the pillar and prepared herself to wait for another train. When she heard it, it came as a high wind with more thunder than one would have foreseen, and the platform shook and the train she had meant to get on had gone before she could move, and she had not even seen it go past.

That was because of the hat, but it was not because of the hat. The train had never been there at all. She was hearing trains in her head, carrying Edna's kitten. (Perhaps, after all,

Edna's mother had said No, the kitten would be too much trouble; no, she had not said that.) *I would like to go to sleep again*, said the bag lady noisily.

She realized now what had happened. It must have been the Express train, on the middle track. If she lifted her chin up, only a little, she would be able to see the Express track. There was the sound of another train coming up in her ears, not as noisy, and this would be the one that would stop and she would take it and put herself down into a corner to sleep, herself and this woman who was traveling with her....

The eyes were closing already, anticipating the corner cradle. The chin would drop, settling deep into the collar of the cape, the muffler of sleep—like being home in her own bed, although the bag lady had never known a bed, only that corner seat where there was shelter.

Someone behind her pushed her through the door as it closed, almost closed on her cape. But that would not happen. Some kind of device kept subway doors from shutting their jaws completely, or was that on elevators? She moved toward the corner seat, and someone was already in it, she could see knees like bony coat hangers. There was another corner seat across the aisle, she knew that, and she stumbled toward it or someone pushed her. This train had a huge pushing hand, but at least it was pushing her in the right direction—into the seat across the way, closed in on two sides, where she could sleep.

But the seat across the way also had someone in it. Bony knees again. The skeleton across the aisle must have shuffled over to defend its second cradle. Where would she sleep now, no walls to encompass her, no windowshades to come down against the light, the bag lady silenced, the world whirling? If the skeleton had not been in both seats at once—

She must leave the train, which was already lurching

through the tunnel's space, denying her the rest she needed. Any doctor would tell her that she needed rest, Janet would tell her. Not Janet—Edna.

She *must* get off. The train shook, unraveled, the worm of her dreams was back again but she could not sleep because her cradle had rocked itself away with two skeletons in it.

"F'Chrissake," said a voice. "You coming or going?"

She put her head down, like a bull, so far down that she could see nothing but her own shoes like barges, and she drove ahead. She would go through the closed door and it would be no more difficult to do that than for the skeleton to slide from seat to seat.

The train stopped. The door opened. "F'Chrissake," said the voice. She got out ahead of it, and it pursued her, crying on Christ as if they were both in a church. She went up the nave, to the transept, to the High Altar, the hound of heaven pursuing her. I fled Him down the nights and down the days. The poet's name was James Elroy Flecker, and she felt a shout of glee at remembering the difficult name of the difficult poet, all three of his names. She had graduated, remember, magna cum laude, very nearly Phi Beta Kappa. Daddy, before he died, had not been disappointed. She could remember fitting the black mortarboard over her hair, short and thick with a natural wave, and she remembered the tassel and her anxiety about its position—forward, back, to the side? It had been a kind of game, because they were all so happy.

She distinctly remembered being happy. There had been several young men, any one of whom she believed she could have had, in that time before the choices narrowed, and there had been one young man ideally suitable. Florence, how lucky you are!

Her mind veered off this obstacle and ran into another. Her memory had cheated her again. The name of the poet

97

was not James Elroy Flecker, it was Francis Thompson. Flecker was not to be compared to Thompson, and now, in front of the whole class, she had stood up and named the wrong person. She felt the shame rise in her cheeks, but at that moment the transept and the altar melted and the bag lady rose from the bowels of the earth, surmounted all the subway stairs as one flight, and burst out into space.

You are not to go back into the subway, Florence told her.

The bag lady said that she had only wanted to sleep.

We'll find a place, Florence told her quite kindly. Kindness was the only way to shut her up, and, since there was no question about who was the superior, it was easy to do. Walk away from subways and subway stairs, walk somewhere else. The worm was the pursuer, the Worm of Heaven.

Just to sleep for a little while, said the bag lady pleading. You used to let me sleep. On your bed. Can I go back to your bed?

No. You never slept on my bed.

She did not know what direction to walk in, only that she would not go back into the subway, which had seemed so sheltering at first and which was now full of skeletons. She stood on whatever corner she was on and turned slowly around, listening for someone to speak, to give instructions.

It was quite warm, a warm September this year, mild, season of mists and mellow fruitfulness. The college student whose major was Literature was elbowing in on the two inside the cape. Next thing, she would be trying to get under the cape for shelter, sheltering Keats. One could not get Keats' name wrong, his first name was John and he was lucky and died young.

I don't mean that. I mean he died young, but not that he was lucky. But he *was* lucky, said the bag lady very peaceably. One night he laid down and went to sleep, John Keats did. No one, said the bag lady resentfully, kept John Keats from going to bed. If we were home now...

The telephone would ring, Florence reminded her. You would have to get up and answer it. Telephones live by being answered. Sometime, she thought vaguely, I must telephone Millicent, and the thought was so immediately distasteful to her that she stopped herself turning around in half circles and began to walk in the first direction that presented itself.

There was a breeze, coming from the water perhaps on this September-humid night. Sluggish, not humid. Oppressive, not sluggish. Strive for the right word, Mrs. Lane had told her as early as fourth grade. Mrs. Lane had heavy glasses and a way of being autocratic about anything connected with the English language, and one student at least had loved her passionately—back in those days of passion being possible.

Perhaps *I* should have been a teacher, she thought, and then: Keep on walking, you're headed into the wind. The breeze. That barest zephyr. Now both of us want to sleep, and now the breeze gets fresher as we walk into it. Easterly? Westerly? If she was still in New York City, which she must be because of the Worm, she must be near water, rivers, estuaries, canals, underground streams undermining construction plans, filling excavations with still waters, making lakes that had to be pumped out.

Her feet were pumping, one in front of the other. She must be arriving somewhere, and there would be a place in it for the bag lady's head and shoulders, her cape and black gloves and everything that made her insist that she was real. Under the hat (the realest thing of all), the bag lady was searching for her cradle, and there was only a line of feet, all pointing in one direction, pointed into the wind, the breeze, the zephyr. The feet were not walking, only shuffling a little,

99

forward. She looked higher, still safe under the hat brim, and saw knees and thighs and hips, all properly clad, of course, one did not bring the actual knees, thighs, hips out into the city streets. There was a bus-stop sign, and at her left the fat side of the bus, blue and white. People were getting onto the bus. There would be seats.

Hush, she said to the bag lady. She walked her to the end of the line of feet, knees, thighs, hips, and moved her into it, and stood waiting until the whole line began to shuffle again and to move forward.

She realized suddenly that she would have to have money for the bus fare, and she clutched her shopping bag in a moment of panic. Her purse would be at the bottom of the bag, and there was going to be no time to get it out. She was already moving up to the front, up to the steps, inside the bus. Someone behind her pushed, not roughly but very firmly.

So she was in the bus. From under her hat, she could see the driver's body and legs. His thighs were fat. It was not like her to be thinking so much of thighs, and it made her uncomfortable, but the coin box was now directly under her hat brim, and the person behind her was saying Excuse-me-excuse-me-excuse-me like a talking doll. A woman. Men did not talk like dolls.

She muttered and moved forward a little, and the doll behind her said Well-thank-you and went on past after there had been the sound of tumbling coins. The bus driver's voice said, "I'm waiting, lady."

She stood there, in front of the whole class, trying to find the page in the grammar book. But she could recite it from memory. When the coin purse at the bottom of her bag delivered itself into her hand, she could feel the warmth of Mrs. Lane's approval. Wordlessly, by instinct, trusting in God and His Holy Worm and Mrs. Lane, she opened the purse and let some coins slide into her black-glove hand. She held them out.

"These," said the bus driver, the fingers of his hand appearing in the palm of hers. His fingers were flesh but as black as the glove; she had not expected that and was immobilized. The black fingers chose the coins and held them out to her. "You put them in, right?" said the voice now known to be black.

She put them in, closed her purse with a snap that could surely be heard through the entire classroom, turned and moved up the aisle. The bus was not moving but it was unsteady, and she had to hold onto the backs of seats until she came at last to one that was blessedly empty—two seats, side by side, a double cradle. She slid with a sign into the space, which was like the space she had moved into under the lion. She remembered the lion, just before the bag lady closed her eyes and, in doing so, took them all away together. This time, without any dreams at all.

IV
THE TOWN

1

A dreamless rag doll, she woke several times. Once, her forehead was hard against the window, safe enough behind the hat brim but causing a mild discomfort. She escaped it by closing her eyes, and whatever landscape there may have been was annihilated by eyelids. They were drawbridges, cutting her off from the enemy, but drawbridges were meant to be pulled up and eyelids were meant to be pulled down. The thought slid through her mind with perfect mindlessness.

The second time she woke, she was lying across the double seat, although she had paid for only one. Her moral nature balked at the knowledge, (one must pay for what one gets in life, she knew that) but no one was looking. Or—more important—if someone was looking, she did not know about him, her, them. What one did not know about did not hurt one. One pays for what one gets or one gets hurt. It all ran together in her mind, and she felt a kind of muddy despair. But then the bag lady settled her head more firmly on the plastic cushion, which was hard but not terribly hard, and made a grumble, a snort that sounded like that head on a pillow that had once been next to hers, legally....

The drawbridge went up instantly and the moat defended the castle, and the bag lady, who only wanted to sleep and who was so good at it, was sequestered again. Sequestered? Like a jury. She had served on a jury once and she had not liked it, except that the telephone had at last understood that she was not to be bothered. Millicent saying, Hush, Mother's not to be bothered. Janet saying, Mustn't call Florence, she's on jury duty. Duty was something Florence understood, thought Florence now. Something to be proud of. Something to *do*.

The bag lady turned her head and pushed her face into the plastic cushion, pulled all the eyelids down and the drawbridges up, and went peacefully back to sleep, taking Florence with her. Again, there were no dreams.

2

She was wakened by her husband James shaking her shoulder. It was humiliating because she had gone to bed without undressing, laid herself down on the counterpane and gone to sleep, and in the early days he had waked her sometimes to nuzzle.

What a distasteful word! But she did have a sense of duty, and it wasn't as if she hadn't known what to expect. She braced herself under the insistent hand on her shoulder, but the bag lady resisted and burrowed deeper into the plastic cushion on the bed. It was not a suitable place for plastic, and she had always disliked the kind of women who covered upholstered chairs with plastic headrests and plastic arms. It was—well, it was common. She had known a woman once who.

"Miss, wake up. You okay, ma'am? Ma'am, you want a doctor?"

She put her hand next to his (and whoever he was, he was not James) on the bag lady's shoulder, and together they were able to wake her. She sat up, mumbling like an animal. The hat, which was always so blessedly low on her forehead, had been pushed even lower by the plastic cushion.

"Lady," said the voice, whoever's voice it was, "we're at the end of the line, we're here. Is here where you want to be?"

Yes, said Florence, answering. Here is exactly where I want to be. If I must get out, I will get out.

She put the bag lady's hand over Florence's mouth, and for a moment the confusion she felt was terrifying. Things inside her head tore at each other, and she raised her hands to the hat and held onto it tightly, until everything came together and the animal-mumble said "Yes" out loud.

The hand moved off her shoulder, and she pulled away from it at the same moment and put her feet down on the floor. She knew she was inside a bus, and she accepted the fact that she was at the end of the line somewhere. She would not think about being at the end of the line because that was where telephones were. She had promised to phone Millicent.

You don't have to push me around, she told the hand voicelessly, and the bag lady, who had some kind of dignity under the mud-gray cape and the hat's horizon, got to her feet quite nimbly.

The owner of the hand, who could now be perceived to be belt buckle, dark pants (she remembered them—the fat thighs) and brown shoes with real scuff marks, was standing in the aisle. The owner of that hand and those packed trousers and scuffed shoes backed off, also nimble. "Well, you're okay," he said, having become *he* and not *hand*. That was what clothes did for you. "You live around here maybe?"

The bag lady said "Yah" like a Swedish cook. Her mother had once had a Swedish cook, a Swedish housekeeper, who had always been looking for lingonberries in the grocery shops.

Finnish, perhaps? not Swedish at all? Large and bony and raising her voice to thunder at the little girl of the household, named Florence certainly, who had only endured it once and, the second time, had gone to report to Mother and Daddy. The cook had left within the week, and she had been so teary that the little girl of the household had forgiven her with dignity. That was why it was surprising about the bag lady being dignified, one expected it of the upper classes although they no longer existed. We are all middle-class now, as Janet so often pointed out quite merrily. Janet *was* merry.

"Yah!" said the bag lady merrily, trying it out.

"Talk English," the man said. "You live up the road maybe? You work up the road somewhere?"

"Yah." She did. Leave her alone, thought Florence, watching the bag lady get up, watching the black-gloved hand holding the shopping bag and the back of the seat at the same time, watching the clumsy shoes poke out from under the heavy cape-skirt, one shoe in front of the other, until all of her had arrived at the open door, folded back and with a handrail to hold. She stepped out onto a curb, onto a wide sidewalk with grass at the edge, grass turning a little brown. Not a city sidewalk.

Behind her, she heard the bus pull away, having a place to go. She herself need only follow the clumsy shoes of the Yah-sayer. They would go to the next place, get something to eat, somewhere to sleep. It was a very narrow world and sleep always lay at the end of it when the sky came down to meet the horizon and could never be seen because of the brim of the hat.

Interiorly, the bag lady declared hunger. Lunch, dinner? Breakfast, maybe? The sun was warm enough to be at any time of day, and none of it mattered. She looked ahead, not up, never up, up would only be the blessing of the hat brim.

Ahead was a lawn, on the lawn three red-coated green-hatted plaster elves with idiot grins on their idiot faces; beyond, a porch. The elves said a great deal, they and the bag lady made a fine quartet. If it wasn't elves, it would be a brace of white ducklings on a lawn, iron ducklings, like the bag lady's iron shoes. Never mind. The bag lady could go find the food she was demanding, she was good at that kind of thing. Trust her, give her her head. Mumbling and quacking, she would have her own way, rightly knowing that a house with a porch in a town with a wide sidewalk would have food, and a house with elves (Elves! Imagine! My dear!) —Such a house would provide.

"Do what you want," said Florence, out loud before the bag lady could say anything at all. The sound of her own voice startled her. It was as if the telephone had rung and she had answered it. She had meant to let the telephone ring, everyone knew she was out, visiting friends in this town called Last Stop.

She had a city person's feeling about towns: they would offer food, shelter, perhaps a bed in someone's attic behind a dormer window. Towns had rooms with attics; where there were elves, there would be attics.

Meanwhile, while she thought of attics, the feet were taking her up from the sidewalk, up a path, to the steps of what appeared to be a real verandah. Porches were for anything; verandahs were for small-town Fourth of Julys...or Fourths of July. It was a grammatical crux. She remembered, in high school, encountering a literary crux in Hamlet, the play was assigned reading, but the crux was her own discovery. She had read all around Hamlet, even a text called a— Called a Variorum, she thought triumphantly. It was not fair to have been accused of showing off when she stood in front of the class and quoted from the Variorum, mentioning the crux.

She had looked up *crux* in the dictionary, and—good Latin student—found that her guess had been right; it came from crux, a cross. *Abi in malum ... cruciatum*—go and be hanged.

No, it had not been fair. The class had thought she was showing off her knowledge, when all she had been doing was hunting down words as if they had been the foxes running ahead of the hounds. In college, there had been Linguistics, and an old fierce teacher, a man, who had been marvelous at first but had given her a B grade when she was an A student. However, no one in her family had been disappointed because no one in her family knew what Linguistics was. Were?

She was obliged to take note of the bag lady, who at this point had mounted the verandah steps and was hammering on the door. It was the verandah that had thrown her back in time, to college. Except for the Linguistics professor and a few other barriers and traps, she had been quite happy in college, rooming with Janet. She and Janet had been arm-in-arm friends since the day as high-school freshmen they had met in the cafeteria line. The cafeteria smelled of damp sandwiches and milk, a baby smell. Millicent in babyhood had smelled very like a damp sandwich. She wished the bag lady would stop beating on the strange door in the strange town called by the bus driver the Last Stop.

"There's nobody home," she said. Out loud again. She felt a rush of anger because she had left the city so she would not have to respond to anybody, and here she was in this town responding to this idiot fool who was hammering on a brown door with elves and toadstools and for all one knew white ducks marching up from the lawn behind. There were no chairs on the verandah. If there had been chairs, she could have dropped into one and slept, safely distant from the school cafeteria. The bag lady could go and eat at the cafeteria while she herself slept, and it was she who needed the sleep now, because the bag lady had slept herself out on the bus.

If they both beat on the door, perhaps someone would come and answer the questions.

When the door opened, the first question was answered. There were feet in the doorway, firmly planted in bone-colored sandals, women's feet, not large, not small. For a moment, she felt an intolerable pull—the desire to look up from under the brim of the important hat and to see, only for a moment, the face itself.

But she knew, supernaturally perhaps, that if she once looked up and beyond, the bag lady would be lost forever, and she would be left alone swinging in wild space, too frightening to conceive of. She could see, anyway, as high as the waistline—a print dress, mid-calf, an ugly print with blue and red and yellow flowers, all very small but bright to hurt the eyes. A print so ugly that it could only be stared at.

There was a voice, very loud. It said "Go away!" not nicely at all, not in the friendly way she had said *Go away* to the dog on the New York street—she had been friendly, she was certain of that—but *Go away* the way one would say it, angrily, to a tramp. Or (she grasped for the revenge) the way one would say it to anything as ugly as the blue and red and yellow print dress.

It was a triumph really, because even the bag lady understood and wheeled herself proudly around and went down the verandah steps she had just come up. Hate would have boiled over if there had been anything to hate, but, when the door slammed powerfully, the whole house fell down behind it. She heard it fall, beam by beam, brick by brick, until it lay in rubble, and the print dress covered nothing but a heap of bones under the chimneypiece.

And to think, said Florence, walking primly down the path which had led to the verandah and which now led nowhere, *to think that all we wanted to do was to borrow the telephone.*

Perhaps the print dress would call the Police; perhaps it

was calling the Police now, and an arrest would follow. For vagrancy. In jail, they would feed the bag lady, but they would expect endless responses in return, and they would hold her overnight and find out who she was and call Millicent, or worst of all they would call Gerry who would be angry for Millicent's sake, my God! she's having a baby and you get yourself thrown into jail.... She sought another scenario. The policeman (she could see his shoes, like the shoes of the policeman so long ago in the subway) would track her down and, by the time he found her, she would have taken off the gray cape and the clumsy black gloves and she would be wearing the navy blue dress that was under it, the dress that Janet told her had such nice lines. The policeman would ask her if she had seen an old tramp, a bag lady, a female bum, and she would say no, indeed, no one like that, but perhaps he could suggest a nice little place to eat, she had accidentally gotten off at the wrong bus stop and she thought she should get a bite of breakfast. Lunch? Or would it be supper? Better say a bite to eat. She would like a bite to eat, and she would look up at him very candidly, very ladylike....

Oh, no, no, no, no! She would take off the cape and the gloves but she would not take off the hat. It was the only thing, the *only* thing. Her heart started to pound as if she had been running, and she realized suddenly that was exactly what she was doing: running. Past the elves and across the street and onto the opposite sidewalk, leaving behind her that household which was smashed to bits and it was all her fault. She was the one who had done it.

She stopped running. She had done it, but she would not say she was sorry. *You never say you're sorry,* James had told her once. But it was James who had never.

We're sick, said the bag lady. We want to eat.

We'll eat. Anything but James. James is back there in that

house which is all rubble now. We'll eat, and then we'll sleep. You'll like that. She had no idea how far it would be to the next house, but she was in a town, not a city, and houses could be very far apart and doors could close and she could not go on forever destroying houses as she had destroyed the one now safely behind her.

But there was another house already, just at the limit of her running. Again, she could see front steps. The town was full of neighbors, then, and here was a neighbor to the ugly print dress, but if the policeman was already following her ("She came to the door, right to the door, and she threatened me," said the print dress. "She's got a gun," it said)—if he was following her, she must not be caught knocking on other neighbors' doors. It would not be safe until she was forgotten by the print dress.

But the print dress was dead, it was crushed under the heavy stone of that mantelpiece. She could see the mantelpiece quite distinctly, straw flowers in ugly vases on either side of it, hideous things, all rubble now. We wouldn't go back if we could, she assured herself, and we wouldn't like any of her neighbors. A woman like that. We'll walk.

We're sick, said the bag lady. We want to eat.

Obedient at last, suddenly remembering, Florence stopped, put down her bag on the sidewalk, and reached into it. Down the sides, along the bottom, creeping in the bag's dark, her gloved hands felt and groped and felt again. Four granola bars, granola knights in armor, Excalibur. She put three back and held one in her hand. The bag lady started to yammer, but she would not open the paper wrapping until they were safely somewhere else, until they had walked far enough.

Do you know, said her eyes under the hat brim, that it's getting dark?

So, it was dinner time then, which would be followed by darkness and sleep. She would have to resort to bribing the bag lady, there, there, you will be fed when there is a place to lie down, which will be more difficult in a town than it was in the city. In the city, any angle had formed a crib, walls and lions cradling the hat with the head inside it, indifferent as God Himself.

She had not used to think that kind of adjective about God, having been brought up in churchgoing ways and having enjoyed at one time the soaring arches, the solemn pews, the kneeling-stools covered with plush.... Ahh, she thought. If she could find a church, that would be a place for eating granola bars and leaning back in a luxury pew and being surrounded, not by lions but by saints. But we were Methodists, she thought. Mother was extremely Methodist, she would not have liked me sleeping with saints.

The person with whom she had slept, with Church approval, had not been a saint. She turned that corner in her mind unintentionally and bumped into him when he was the last person in the world she wanted to think about. And she had no need to think about him. *That* was all over. *His* fault. All over. The bag lady did not even know his name.

What she needed to do now was simply to find a church, somewhere in the middle of this town, all towns had churches. The policeman would not be able to follow her into a church, she would have sanctuary *and* the granola bars. It was a fair bargain. No place to sleep; no food. That was that.

That's that, Florence. Don't tease.

She had given up the idea of a house, and, as she walked and reached only nowhere, she began to give up the idea of a church, unless she stumbled on one in what was beginning to be a grayness of twilight. It was difficult. She had credentials for entering churches, but there were none to enter; she was barred from houses (even though the print dress was safely dead under the mantelpiece). Front doors and back doors were locked tight, but might she not find a shed somewhere, outside, separate? She thought suddenly, marvelously, of garages. A garage would be neither church nor house. A garage would be like a lion. There would be a sheltering animal, an automobile, inside, and she would open the door of it and the seat of the automobile would be real. You could eat the granola bar and then leave crumbs on the seat that no one would notice.

That is what one wants, not to be noticed. She could almost feel the bag lady quivering, like a dog waiting to be fed. I'll not be quiet until I get my bone.... Don't tease me. ...Don't tease *me*, the bag lady retorted, I only want to be fed.

She moved her feet with energy now, since they were going somewhere, and, when the sidewalk was interrupted by a narrow gravel roadway, she followed the roadway and, as true as a church nave, it led straight to the altar. One side of the double door was open to let the worshippers in, and she walked through it into an empty stall. The next stall had the shiny body of a shiny automobile, just as she had pictured it all—fenders, chrome, gleaming door handles, whitewalled tires. Its people must own two cars, which meant this was a wealthy house. Perhaps the whole town was wealthy, perhaps the ugly print dress had wrapped a servant. She was offended by the idea of having been dismissed by a servant, but the print dress was no more now than a rag in the rubble and need not offend her further.

She began to reason, doing it very well. There was one car inside, space for another to come. If car two came back, surely nobody would look into car one to find if there were people inside it. It would not be in this rich comfortable town the way it was in New York—two locks to a door, peering peepholes, savage chains. That was why one really didn't want visitors; the effort of peering, unchaining, unlocking was all too much. She had Janet's apartment key, Janet had hers. She forgot just why, it had seemed the right thing to do.

Now she put her hand on the shiny handle of the shiny car, and for a moment the black-wool glove looked very elegant, a kid glove going out for an evening, even the long skirt of her cape was operatic. The handle, however, did not give to the elegant hand, and she had to grasp it with both, which an opera-goer would not do. How long was it since she had gone to an opera, or even listened to one on the radio? She could answer that, she had lost the radio's support when it had begun to hurt her ears. Everything hurt her ears nowadays, noises too sharp, sounds too high, hummings and vibrations. She looked down at the two black-gloved hands folded over each other, folded over the door handle that would not give way to them, and they had a peaceful look. She bowed her head on them and stayed so, thinking perhaps that if she stayed long enough her spine would crumble slowly, her skin would shrivel, her nerves go silent. That was what she really wanted, and she closed her eyes which were looking at blackness already because of the blackness of the gloves.

In the very silent garage, only the bag lady shouted, waking all the nerves, turning the skin to plastic, the spin to a rod of living pain pointing up into the head. The head, as always, was safe, because the hat was there. She lifted the hat and the head came with it, and the bag lady took advantage of the resurrection and pushed heavily on the shining handle of the shining car. This time it gave way, and the door opened. Shoe over shoe, glove over glove, wrapped in the cape, dragging the shopping bag, the two of them clambered into the darkness of the back seat.

The back seat—that was truly clever of them. No steering wheel to be bruised against, no horn to shriek out, no gears, no dials, no wires, no radio, nothing connected and harmful. Only this fine dark spaciousness, a car seat upholstered and yielding, a place for the head, a place for the body and its feet, and a granola bar for the wolf.

No crumbs, please, she told the wolf, this is my house. She broke the bar in two and doled out the pieces. The wolf snatched both and gulped them down, asking for more, asking for a real meal. Crumbs are the sign of a slovenly mind; this is a very creditable thesis you are writing, you show discipline. Crumbs were not disciplined, and now the wolfing bag lady was spilling them on the upholstery on the back seat of the strange car in the strange backyard of the strange town. I wish I had not brought her with me, Florence thought, but someone had to, and she would come. Be still, animal. Be still, wolf. Be still, whatever your name is! You can have your bag for a pillow, and your cape for warmth, and you can go to sleep and leave me here to manage somehow.

People were always expecting her to manage somehow. Manage the things that had gone wrong, manage the lost plans and the sourness, manage the Millicents, the Jameses....

No! said the bag lady, saving her from going on with the thought, and then went to sleep. The light turned off in their heads, it was warm, quiet, dark and dark and dark. She ran to meet the darkness in her head, and it lapped around her like waves. She remembered a seashore with long sand and crisp foam and her mother calling her to come back, come back, and of course it was the mother who was responsible, always the mother. Millicent, come back at once. Millicent!

Dark met dark in collision. The curtain came down absolutely. There were crumbs on the back seat and perhaps on the floor of the car too, but nobody would know. That was

117

what was so important, that nobody should ever know. There was this secret. She sighed, fell, and began at once to dream.

She was wakened by a flashbolt of light and by voices. She thought they were part of the dream, and she lay dazed with no idea where she was or why. Finally, when the light, which was so strangely placed, went out suddenly and the voices went on, she recognized the where and why of her being there. It's the other car, she thought, and I expected it. The words were so clear in her head that she knew she was not only wide-awake but extremely wise. They were not police at all, they were householders, a strong solid word. If she stayed as she was, very calm and very wise, they would go away and leave her alone. They were householders who owned the garage and the house, and now they had driven their car into their garage and they would return to their house. They were rich people; they had two cars, and, perhaps, two houses. It was not important. They would leave her, and she could go back to sleep between the saint's paws. The bag lady was behaving beautifully, not a sound out of her, tranquil, unfussed.

One of the voices said something—a woman's voice, misty and light like a blue violet—and then a door slammed that must have been the car door, and there was a man's voice, solid and dark.

Why a blue violet? Violets are purple. Something of Shakespeare's, perhaps. She had pretended once that she had read all of Shakespeare's plays, and her professor had believed her because she had dredged up such appropriate quotations. I did read them, of course I read them! She so nearly said the words aloud that her glove crammed into her mouth to stop them, and she tasted wool instead of a professor's approval.

The professor was not really important. The color of the

violets was not important. None of it mattered. She could now
listen to the voices again, which were still going on.

What were they doing out there, standing in the dark,
talking to each other in those voices that curved together, very
accustomed, terribly contented? They were voices that would
go through the door into the house, would go up the stairs
hand in hand, would go into the big room with the wide bed.
...She was shaken by a fever of jealousy; her body jerked,
and it woke the bag lady, who whimpered. Shh, ssshhhh, it's
all right, we're dreaming the whole thing, go back to sleep.
Listen, the voices are going away. Listen, the other door of
the car has slammed shut, the footsteps are making echoes,
there is a sound of an overhead door coming down like a
waterfall, there is the sound of a lock.

Oh God! they've locked me in, I shall never get out!

Thank God! they've locked me in, I don't have to get
out.

There, she said, I told you I would manage, people expect
me to. We can both go back to sleep. In fact, we never woke
up, there were no blue violets, no upstairs room with a wide
bed, no lock clenching its teeth. In the morning it will all be
as it was, we will be here on our own good upholstered bed.
There will be no other car next to our car, the jaws of the
lock will have been pried open, the door will be standing wide.
Shakespeare will have gone, and the professor too.

And, hours later, it was so. In her dream—or perhaps
she had wakened—the lock gave way, the waterfall of the door
flowed upward, the car engine stuttered and roared. Tires
skittered on gravel, sound expanded, diminished, leaving
everything behind.

We must get up at once, she thought. *She*— the one with
the blue-violet voice—might come back. She might get into
this car, the one where we live, and drive it and us away.

Nowhere was safe, everything had scandals. I never had scandals, it was James who made them, not I.

Her mind felt quite proud, being so scandal-free. Her body felt nothing. Although all night it had been wrapped up in the cape, colliding with the bag lady every time one of them turned, still it was a nothing-feeling. And there had been no woman. *No* man. The truth was that those two had had a very unhappy marriage, they had divorced. Poor Florence, they had said, and they had put blue violets on her grave.

She woke fully and sat up, just before the bag lady could announce her inevitable natural needs. Together, they climbed out of the back seat of the car. The space next to it was empty, as she had known it would be. The other car was gone, if it had ever been there. The door was open. I can take her out on her leash, to a bush, she thought. A dog is better company than a wolf. I am becoming as clever as my professor. She thought this softly because she had had such a good night. She had seen a dream of two people, and then she had been able to kill it.

3

Overhead, in a tree, there was a bird. In this town, there were trees along the streets, and she walked in their shadows, never thinking of the leaves or branches or the sky over her head. She had stopped under this tree to rest because of the long distance she had come, not because of the bird which sang oddly as if it were clearing its throat. A September bird, left over from someone's summer.

She leaned down to rub the calf of her right leg, which

was aching a little. Was it a large town, or was she walking in circles? So far, there had been only the sounds of a few cars passing, unpleasant, aggressive. A postman's canvas mailcart stood on the sidewalk; a child's red tricycle was upended in the gutter. She hoped the child would not reappear, because she could not avoid seeing children, even under the hat. They would enter under the brim, because they were small and fitted there, and they were visible in whole, not in part—real humans, however tiny. They were unpleasant and aggressive, too. She must put her attention on important things, like the breakfast the bag lady was already urging, one need satisfied, another imminent.

After that car left its garage, she thought, I should have gone in at the back door of the house, gone into the kitchen, and straight to the refrigerator. He would not have locked the back door after his going, would he? He had not even locked the garage door until both cars were inside it. Of course, there was always the danger that the blue-violets person might be in the kitchen, standing in front of the refrigerator where there would be milk and, perhaps, cold chicken. She disliked intensely the way she could taste the milk and the cold chicken now, on her tongue and in the roof of her mouth, but she was able to blame this on the bag lady, who was Greed, as Athena was Wisdom.

I have quite a lot of money, she remembered, and then she straightened up with the cramp in her leg quite gone. I am very healthy and I have quite a lot of money and there is no reason why we cannot eat whenever we choose to. She could see white bread, as well as milk and chicken. She could see them right before her eyes, but when she put out her hand to take them, there was nothing there, just a black wool glove in front of her face. If she fainted from hunger, they would find her on the sidewalk and take her to a hospital and feed

121

her. But she would not go to a hospital to be fed, she would stay where she was and die on the sidewalk, as good a place as any. It was the fault of the blue-violet woman, whom she now hated, wrapped in her blue-violet life, upstairs, so happy— so *meanly* happy.

The bird had stopped or flown or died. She looked beyond the tree shadow and saw the bottom of a telephone booth, a sentry box without a sentry, and she thought at once of Millicent who would have to be called, telephoned from that mythical place on the Island, from the happy home where Millicent's happy mother was staying with all her happy friends.

If you don't call her, said the bag lady, they'll set the dogs on us.

I don't remember the telephone number.

Yes, you do.

I don't.

Yes, you do.

I won't.

Won't is different. Call, and then I'll have my breakfast, my lunch, my supper-dinner-tea. My *meal!* If you don't, I'll set the dog on you, the dog you didn't help when it came up to you in the street.

She went into the telephone booth, and it was impersonal like a box. She put her large shopping bag down in the small square space and bent over to feel for the small square coin purse. Would she need only twenty-five cents, or would she need more to reach the Operator? She did not know where she was—perhaps in another State of the Union by now, she had walked so far—and, even if she knew, how would she know how much money it would take to talk to Millicent? There was no way of stuffing a dollar bill, a five-dollar bill into the coin slot. She looked up to see the place where the coin would go, and the hat brim cut it off. If she looked higher, she would be looking out from under the hat brim, and the idea frightened her.

She would not call Millicent. She would simply stay here within these thin walls, until they came and took her away. She leaned against one of the walls and it was more firm and reasonable than she had expected. The question was, Which of them would die first, her self or the bag lady? The other question was, Did it matter?

If I called Millicent collect, she thought suddenly, it would serve her right for going away and leaving me alone when I needed her most. She went away to college, just after James— No, we sent her away to college, we did the right thing, *I* sent her away. No, she left me; it would be perfectly fair to call her collect.

This was so clear that her hand reached into her shopping bag without her will, no longer groping, and it found the coin purse, which was tan with a brass clasp. It belonged in another bag, but the other bag had worn out, it had been used too much by someone— With a little care, one could move everything into the passive tense. Grammar she understood, and, while she stood there, understanding it, her wooled fingers opened the purse and found a quarter. She lifted the receiver off its hook. Now all she had to do was to look up a little way and find the place to drop her money, and she could hear the dial tone like a seashell....

When she was a junior in high school, she had spent a week at the seashore with a classmate who had been almost her best friend but not quite because of Janet. Janet was best-friend and Janet had not been invited to go to the seashore with them, though there was plenty of room, and, although she would have liked Janet to be there, she had not missed her because of the satisfaction of being asked when Janet was not. Come now! she thought briskly. Of course she had missed

Janet, and there had been no satisfaction at all. She had been sorry her best friend was not invited, and she had brought her home a conch shell, an intricate palace of a shell—Build-thee more stately mansions, O my soul, Janet had said reverently. Later on, they had both learned that The Chambered Nautilis was a bad poem—no, one did not say a *bad* poem. It was a mediocre poem. *Bad* meant you made judgments; *mediocre* meant you had sensibilities. The classmate at the shore had made judgments, which meant that Janet was really the better of the two, which was as it should be. And the conch shell had been so really beautiful that she had wanted to keep it for herself but had, instead, generously, given it to Janet. Pressed to the ear, it held the whole of that summer week with salt air and wide white winds and screaming gulls.

The phone booth was a cabin. There was rage at the porthole, and she looked out and saw the bag lady screaming like a gull, and she remembered that she had promised the bag lady to phone Millicent and then take her (the bag lady, that is; a dangling pronoun, a dangling bag lady) to where there was food, milk, and cold chicken....

All this time, she had been holding the quarter in her hand. Now, she reached up without looking and located with her fingers the hole that fitted it. The dial tone sprang into her ear, the conch shell. In a moment, there would be the ocean.

Nothing. Just the dial tone, not the ocean. There was something else that had to be done, some very strict action that called for memory. The fingers remembered. The O/Operator place for the finger was visible from under her hat. She poked her finger into it, and then, slowly, with luxury, she pulled the dial around, let it go, and heard it purr back. She wanted to do it again, for the quiet spinning, but then a new sound came in between, and she dropped her hand as guiltily as a child. Why was the hand guilty? Who was there, watching?

The phone was ringing in her ear, which she had not expected. Bells rang, not conches, but before she could hang up a calm voice, like a good nurse, said, "This is Miss Ryan. May I help you?" It frightened her so much that she almost dropped the receiver. The fear was like a cold second hand on a clock, but then it went away swiftly because it was obvious that the nurse was going to be kind.

"May I help you?" said the voice insistently.

Someone had closed the porthole. She searched first for the words and then for the voice to say them. The voice was rusty, and she had to clear her throat several times. "I am sorry," said the other voice, very precise, it would not use any contractions, "I cannot hear you."

Well, it was a long time since she had talked to anyone, and she had forgotten what the tongue was supposed to do. It was hard even to remember the words. She said with extreme difficulty, "I want to call collect," which was a triumph, because the word *collect* had come back just when she needed it.

The other voice asked patiently for the area code and the number, and the thing in the brain which was now working so well gave it all with great precision. "I'll speak to anybody," she said, triumphant again with the right words, able to talk quite like other people even in the company of a bag lady. I will not call person-to-person, she thought in the inner voice that was as precise as the Operator's and without contractions, remembering the proper phrase. She was doing marvelously well, remembering also that person-to-person was expensive, thinking of Millicent's expenses. Millicent would be home, sitting lazily in an armchair with the baby inside her, worrying about Mother perhaps, waiting for Mother to call.

125

The operator-voice said, "Your name?" and Florence said, "What?" "May I have your name, please?" said the voice, still patient.

She looked at the hole where she had put her finger to invoke this voice. It had all been a mistake. She was being asked for her name and she did not have one. The name she used to have was left behind in the apartment, and this person who was making the phone call had no name, except Millicent. If she said to tell them that Millicent was calling, there would be nothing but misunderstandings, matters to clear up. It would be better to put the telephone back on its hook, the Operator would not be able to reprove her, the Operator would have lost her completely....

"Tell her it's her mother," she said, and found that she was shouting.

There was a pause. The Operator said, "Their mother," as if she had been studying the words, then she said "Yes" and "Thank you," and then her voice disappeared altogether and turned into a steady ringing.

The ringing went on and on, and after a while it became a bore. Millicent must be doing the laundry or saying good-bye to guests or putting the baby to bed—No, there was no baby yet. I don't know what *time* it is, she said into the telephone, and the Operator said nothing but *ring*.

Except for the ringing in her ear, the cabin of the phone booth was rather pleasant. Safe from the elements of wind and wave, she leaned her back against the glass wall and waited for the ringing to become something else. The classmate whose seashore she had visited had not invited her back in their senior year, but that was because the classmate had gone to Europe with her family and hadn't invited anyone. "That's what you told Janet," said the bag lady with sudden anger, "and it wasn't true. Nobody went to Europe, and you know it. She didn't invite you again, she invited someone else."

The attack had no effect at all. She was becalmed, and all she said was Hussshhhh, like the shell at her ear which had been ringing but was now as still as the sea outside and which now said, as sudden and as angry as the bag lady, "Hello! Hello?"

"Millicent!" said Millicent's mother, although the hello-voice was a man's. It must be the wrong number. Millicent was too young to have a man in her house.

The operator-voice cut in between them crisply with a message from mid-ocean, Will you accept a collect call from your mother, will you ... Florence heard her own voice rush into the space between the waves. "It's me, Millicent," she said, "it's Mother." The other voice said, "Oh, yes, sure, I'll accept the call," and the Operator gave a kind of sigh as if she had lost a wager and then, once more, she disappeared altogether.

"Mother! Where are you? Millicent's not home! Where are you calling from?"

It was her son-in-law, and he had a name and she could not remember it. She could not remember the name of her own son-in-law. Joseph, John, James ... No, no, no, not James! Not—James—not—James—ever.

She dropped the telephone, and it fell down on its long cord and barked like the dog. She buried her face in her hands, terrified because she could not remember the name of her son-in-law. The receiver barked again.

Jerry, that was it! Only he spelled it Gerry, the J was there only in the voice. She needn't have been terrified after all, it was silly of her. The silliness of it grasped her fleeing mind and pulled her back. She reached for the cord and, like a sailor with a rope, hauled it in. Up the mast, up the spinnaker, up the mainsail—that was the damn bag lady howling sea-chanteys, she should never have let her inside the cabin.

She said, "Gerry dear," in a perfectly placid voice, an example to the howling wretch at her side. "It's Mother."

His voice came down. She remembered Millicent saying, quite often, that Gerry was hopeless on the telephone, which was true. He depended on his wife or his secretary or his nanny, which was perhaps why Millicent had married him.

"Gerry dear," said his mother-in-law, utterly calm. "I'm so sorry to have to call you collect." She gave a little formal laugh, which pleased her, just amused enough. "It's too absurd, of course, but I don't want to charge my calls to—" She got frightened again. Who was she staying with? who had she said she was staying with? Whom, not who!

"—charge my calls to my host," she said cleverly, and then it all came back and she was in command again. The Endicotts, Liz and Douglas Endicott, beautiful people living in a beautiful house on the Island. She gave the amused laugh again, it soothed her vocal chords like honey. "Liz and Doug won't let me do a thing for myself. I just wanted you to know that everything is fine...."

"You sound fine," Gerry said, breathing out. "Look, Mother, Millicent said to be sure to get your address if you called."

"How is Millicent?"

"She's fine. Your address. She said I was to get your address and your phone number."

"The doctor's satisfied, isn't he?"

"She's fine, the doctor says everything's great. Mother, I promised Millicent that if you called..."

"And here I am, calling" said Gerry's mother-in-law brightly. "I can't give you a phone number, darling, because we're leaving for a quick trip to the Cape tomorrow so I won't have one. We're flying, of course. But, anyway, I'll be back home before long and everything's been perfectly wonderful.

Tell Millicent I'm getting a lot of rest, give her a kiss from
me, love to you both—Darling," she added considerately, "I'm
sure this call is costing you a thousand dollars. Just give my
love, love...love..."

Her voice trailed off. He said something, she could not
hear it, he was suddenly miles and miles away from her. Where
was he? where was she? The telephone fell from her hand
and dangled again on its cord. She turned around and started
to go away and leave it dangling, but all at once Gerry's voice
came out of it, loud and clear, shouting Hello, hello! She knew
that he would stay at his post forever, like the boy on the
burning deck, shouting hello, hello, until the line went dead.
She would have to kill it herself; nothing would satisfy Gerry
except the click of an instrument being hung up, relieving
him of responsibility. She's having a great time, he would tell
Millicent, they're flying to the Cape so she couldn't give me
her phone number. The Cape, he would say, we should have
it so good!

She turned back and lifted the instrument firmly, and it
was still saying hello, hello, a puppet in a voice-box. She put
her mouth close to it and said very distinctly, "I have to run
now, dear, Liz is calling me." She searched for a final word,
found it. "Bless you, dear. Bye-bye." Bye-bye like a taxi driver,
a doorman, a friend, a stranger, a mother-in-law.

When she stepped out of the telephone booth, the cabin,
she still had her coin purse in her hand. There was money
in it for food, but for the moment the bag lady was keeping
quiet, intimidated perhaps by the fine-lady voice of Gerry's
mother-in-law, Millicent's mother. She smiled to herself and
felt it as a small cold smile just at the corners of her mouth.
It was some kind of victory.

There were no birds in the trees any longer, and the sun
was warm through her heavy cape, reaching between her

shoulder blades, making her feel both heavy and light. She walked, watching her feet move ahead of her and counting the steps she took, limiting her view to the circle of the hat, not even looking ahead. There was the road to the left of her with cars going by, not many but enough, and she began to count them in with her steps. 101—102—103, one car, one car, two cars. 104, but it was really 106, because she had not remembered to count the steps while she was counting the cars. Her head began to ache slightly. That's from being hungry, she thought, admitting for the first time that she shared the bag lady's wants. She stopped counting and looked sideways, furtively, under the hat, sub rosa, under the rose, hunting for a sign from a store window. It was not long in coming. In fact, it leaped at her and screamed. CEREAL BOXES SOAP LETTUCE CANNED TOMATOES CHILI, hugger-mugger, hocus-pocus through the plate glass. A door was open, and she went through it like a stalking hunter.

Empty, echoing, large. A pile of wire baskets, a stand of shopping carts. It must be a supermarket, and so she could lounge along the shelves, take her time, scavenge, spend money or not spend it as she chose, being careful not to buy more than the shopping bag could carry, not to look up toward the top shelves beyond the hat brim. They would only hold things like salad oil, maple syrup, canned beets, nothing she would want anyway.... She knew this place like a map, because it was a mirror image of her own supermarket. They recognized her there, but just sometimes, not always. Sometimes there would be a snip of a girl-clerk who had to be watched when she rang things up or gave change.

Eye contact, she remembered, was the thing to be avoided, Watch the hand giving the change, the dollars, the quarters, the nickels, but never look into the eyes belonging to the hand. It was important.

She had come to the cookie shelves, and the bag lady cried out like a squeak-toy. Not macaroons, Florence warned her. Macaroons would perish like white mushrooms. Not sugar cookies either! they would crumble into fine sand. Ginger cookies would make one thirsty. There was a plastic bag full of raisin cookies, fat with raisins, though the raisins were probably only at the top where they would show....

The bag lady was making rude tongue-sounds like an animal snapping for a bone. Take the cookies, take the cookies, if the raisins are only on top, what's the difference? Everybody cheats anyway. That's the one thing you learn: Never trust anybody, said the bag lady.

I learned that before you did, she answered. *Never trust anybody.* Not ever again. It won't matter about the raisins, it won't matter if there aren't any raisins inside them, I never expected there would be. It's when you believe that there will be some, and then there aren't any...

Oh, get on with it, said the bag lady.

She got on with it, and was rewarded by a whole shelf of raisins, seeded, seedless, golden, sultanas, all kinds. If the cookies cheated her, their cheating would not matter. She found nuts, too, almonds in a bag, and, best of all, she found a package of dates. They were wrapped in gold foil, king-like, suggesting opulent banquets, and she took them down eagerly, but only one package because their elegance was unique.

Rejecting canned soups (how would she heat them? she asked herself, pleased with her foresight), she found a row of vegetable juices, even little cans of tomato juice in packages of six. Too many. She pulled a package apart, very neatly, and abstracted two cans, pushed the torn box well back on the shelf. No one would know what she had done.

Should she get milk? If so, in a carton or a bottle? A carton, she decided, but she would have to drink it all at once or it would slop about in her shopping bag, go bad in the September sun (if it was still September), turn into a nasty cheese, curds and whey like Little Miss Muffet's lunch. A nasty child, Miss Muffet, deserving of a nasty spider.

Stop it, she told herself but not unkindly. Really, she was being very patient, and patience was rewarded by a row of objects called Breakfast Bars, which were—as one read in the small print on the box—a meal in themselves. My eyes are still sharp, she thought proudly, and then she remembered that, after all, she was only fifty-two. Unless she had been a bag lady for longer than she now remembered. It was possible.

One box, chocolate. She took it into her already filled hands, wishing she had picked up a shopping basket. A basket lady. A basket case. That was a nasty idea, like the spider.

She turned another corner, and fruit rushed at her in noisy colors. The oranges hurt and so did a sliced-open cantaloupe and bite-red apples. She narrowed her eyes against the shock and selected, very carefully, an apple that was pale green like the underside of a wave. Somebody's wave, glassy, cool, translucent, she could not remember the somebody because all that kind of memory had been beaten out of her long ago. Passive again. Somebody had beaten it out of her. No bruises, no scars, nothing so respectable. What was the Court's phrase, the phrase wrapped in judicial robes as she was now wrapped in the cape of a bag lady—

Mental cruelty! that was it. And the name behind the translucent wave was Sabrina, and the name of the author of the poem behind Sabrina was John Milton. Giddy with self-esteem, she took another apple and, without thinking, put it to her mouth and let her teeth sink in.

It was all tartness and juice, as sappy as Spring, and she could taste the pale green against the enamel of her teeth. She had not brushed her teeth since she left home, if you could call that home. Home is where your toothbrush is. Pleased by the fancy and by the sap, she bit into the apple again, deeply, chewing with her mouth open. ("Millicent darling, don't do that." But hadn't it been, first, "Florence darling, don't do that"?) Etiquette demanded. Society frowned. She chewed and bit and then she chewed again, and, when she came to the core, she spit out a seed onto the floor of the supermarket and then she threw the core after it. Because this was her home, and in it she could do anything she pleased.

Marvelously soothed, she picked up two more apples, and this time they were red, as red as Adam and Eve's. Eve's apple. An Adam's apple was something quite different and decidedly unattractive, so that she shied away from it in her mind. After all, she had enough to do with all this difficult balancing, cookies, apples, milk in a carton.... She must get some bread, but no jam or jelly. Jams and jellies lived on high shelves. She would get brown sugar and spread brown sugar on the bread. But that would need butter too, and butter would spoil like cheese, and now she was back at the spider.

The gods intervened. Peanut butter was at eye level, and she snatched too large a jar, put it back, took a small one— Oh, she was sensible. She found the bread, chose a small loaf. After a while, she found sugar—not brown, but white lumps that would be nice to suck. Lump sugar in a yellow box, and now her hands were much too full and everything was going to fall on the floor, and she was turned around from her walkings and no longer even knew where the door was.

But she found it, as she had found the groceries, and arrived at the checkout counter. The clerk was blue jeans from the waist down, which was all she could see, and the blue jeans had a bulge at the middle. A fat girl, a fat woman, a fat man, a fat boy.

"This it?" said the clerk, and his voice said he was a fat

man. She jerked back, as if for a moment she was afraid of anything inside blue jeans, but then she rediscovered herself and nodded. Or, rather, she lowered her hat and raised it again, so that her eyes went only from counter to bulge and then back to counter again. The problem now was to find money, but it turned out not to be such a problem after all. Money was instant-found, like treasure, down there at the bottom of the bag, a careful infinity of green bills folded each inside the other.

How clever she had been. She would have congratulated herself further, but the clerk was holding out a fat hand and saying a sum, and she thought automatically that it was too much, the cost of living going up so terribly, everything going up terribly, everything terrible. Millicent had said once, "I suppose you could come and live with us, Mother, if the worst came to the worst." Dear Millicent, always so tactful. But, of course, she had not meant it the way it sounded, not at all. It was simply a phrase, like don't-chew-with-your-mouth-open. The worst coming to the worst was more the kind of thing Gerry would have said, really, though he was such a *good* son-in-law. She remembered telling Janet what a good son-in-law Gerry was. Janet, thank goodness, had troubles with her own son-in-law, who drank.

What does *thank goodness* mean there?

Whatever the amount of change due her was, it was being put into her black-glove hand, and she spilled it down into the bottom of her bag. Later, she would count it, perhaps in piles. She took the bag of groceries that the clerk, the fat clerk, the fat *man* clerk, was pushing across the counter at her, and she thought she would put all of it into the shopping bag, the real bag, before she left the store. But then she decided not, and she went out, away from the counter, through the door, out onto the sidewalk, her own shopping bag and her handbag on one arm, the grocery's bag held in both arms against her caped front, her chin clamped down on its edge so it could not tip. Walking so, she continued along the sidewalk until she found the front steps of somewhere, of someplace—stone steps, formal and wide, the lion's Library perhaps?

She sat down anyway, spread her cape out around her, pulled her hat down hard over her eyes, put the grocery bag next to her, carefully, and settled herself. The bag lady was being quiet, expectant, watchful, slavering but silenced, waiting for the moment of the red, red apple, not a green one, a juicy red...

It was only then that she realized the green apple had been stolen.

No. Not passive. She had stolen the apple and eaten it, she who had never stolen anything in her life. Once you stole something (she had read this somewhere, or someone had told her), you became a thief, and once you became a thief you could not go back ever to the purity of not being a thief. Not even if you never stole again. It was like being a virgin.

The bag lady interrupted, just in time. The bag lady said calmly that, once you were a thief, then you were a thief. It would make it easier to get food later on if the money ran out.

Somebody's feet were going past her, up the stone steps. She marked their passage, holding in suspense the bag lady, who, having delivered her moral judgments, was now stretching itchy fingers toward the grocery bag. The feet, nicely shod in high heels, went up, and then other feet came down— man's feet, blue-striped socks just visible below gray trousers, respectable socks, respectable trousers. Perhaps the stone steps belonged to a church and this was Sunday. Perhaps she should not be preparing to eat on the steps of a church, but surely a church was sanctuary and one could always appeal to the

Bishop. If it was a synagogue, it might be more difficult, but towns seldom had synagogues, Jews were city people. Not that she had anything against Jews. Jews were really no different from anyone else, except in some of their ways from which, indeed, some of them had been able to escape. The Jews she had known who had not escaped had always seemed to her a little too ornate. Baroque.

The word pleased her. If this was a Christian church, its steps would assure sanctuary, and she would be very careful not to leave scraps about. If it was a synagogue, they would have to forbear her presence. Minorities had to practice forbearance, although she was not certain that, in New York City, the Jews really were a minority. Or the Negroes, either; the blacks.

Contemplating all this, so vividly, grateful that she was educated and tolerant, she was at the same time spreading the contents of the grocery bag around her. The bag lady was instantly at her elbow, inside the bag, nudging, reaching. She pushed her aside and pulled the wrapper off the bread, tearing its waxed protection. *Rye* bread. A disappointment. She had meant to get white to go with the peanut butter, but rye was healthy. Anything coarse was healthy—seeds, roughage. It was difficult to get the top off the peanut-butter jar, and then there was no knife for spreading. She used her fingers, only two of them, dainty black-wool teacup-fingers which she wiped on the skirt of her cape.

Wait! she said, using her elbow to nudge back and to push the other body away from her, nuzzling as it was like a horse for a sugar lump. When she was twelve, she had wanted to have a pony, she had been such a nice average little girl wanting ponies at just the right age to want them. Now there were all sorts of psychiatric theories about little girls and horses, nasty ones, like cheese and spiders. Everything was spoiled nowadays. She had thought so for a long time, though Janet said not. Perhaps that was the trouble between her and Janet, Janet was not a realist.

What trouble? There was no trouble at all between her and Janet. Janet was her dearest friend.

She took out the carton of milk, opened it, and put it down beside her on the stone steps in the warm sun. The question now was whether to bite into the bread-and-peanut-butter first, or whether, first, to drink the milk. These were the same urgent questions that had persistently followed her about in her own kitchen back at the apartment. The kitchen walls were painted yellow, sunshine yellow, everybody said the kitchen walls were lovely.

Bread first, or milk?

She put the carton to her mouth and drank, gasping, like an upturned fish-mouth, one of those drinking fountains in Italy. I never went to Italy. I thought I would go to Italy someday and see where Byron lived, and the Brownings, but no one ever let me go. You can have a bite of the bread now, she said to the bag lady. It's better to drink first and then bite.

Gulp, swallow, gulp, swallow, gulp, swallow. She kept her head down, her eyes on her nourishment. Feet went past her, one pair stopped, pausing for a moment as if the shoes wanted to say something, male shoes ascending. If it was a church behind her, the shoes would go inside, select a pew, genuflect toward the altar, sit down and reach for the hymnbook, perhaps confess or take communion, sit listening to the sermon, or just sit in contemplation, believing in Buddha or the Devil, but raised Christian. Mea culpa, mea maxima culpa. One was culpable, not wicked.

Gulp; there was no more milk. Swallow; there was no more bread. The bag lady belched with reasonable restraint (poor thing, eating much too fast, the lower classes) and now inevitably she wished to sleep, as if black gloves were for nothing but to fold in the lap. It was necessary to shake her into wakefulness because of gathering all the things together into the shopping bag, and besides, this was not a good place for sleeping, more feet going by all the time. What was needed was a quiet private place like the sunny yellow kitchen everybody admired so much.

Of course, one did not sleep in the kitchen. One slept in the bedroom, properly, on the bed. On the single bed, meant for one sleeper only. If the bag lady was in the kitchen, she might be allowed to sleep there, but now she would have to get to her feet and move on whether she wished or not. Everything was stowed away; she had been functioning very well, even while she thought about a place for the bag lady to sleep. Stowed away, safely stowed, like Polonius. Once, in high school, she had been given a B minus on a Shakespeare essay—"You know more than the teacher," Janet had said loyally. Janet had got an A. The B minus was meanness. It wasn't me who said I knew more than the teacher; Janet said it.

She had the shopping bag full now and on her arm, and around her feet there was a rubbish heap: milk carton, some of the waxed paper, bread crumbs, a blob of peanut butter dropped on the stone steps. She was sorry about the peanut butter, but since she no longer had an apartment, a doorman, a mailbox, she was not a householder and the problem was not hers. The neat shoes that had stopped to examine her (to examine her? had she been examined from above when she was helpless to defend herself from eyes? how mean!)—the neat shoes would come back down the church's stone steps....Synagogue steps. Was it a Jew who had stared down at her? She remembered now that the teacher's name had been Levine. Or Levinson?

Does it matter? said the bag lady wonderingly, and yawned like a cave.

She would have to find a bench for them to sit on or a tree to sit under or a corner of a wall to sit within, and she would have to find it before those neat shoes came down the synagogue steps and discovered the milk carton, the waxed paper, the peanut-butter blob. The shoes might come at any moment.

Hastily, she took the bag lady's rough hand into her own smooth one, and she led her carefully down the steps, careful because of the judgment that would be held over the milk carton and the paper, the crumbs and the peanut butter— I'm very tired of going over that list, she said under her breath, stop making me do it. I need sleep. We both need sleep.

She took her away then without argument, down the stone steps and out onto the sidewalk—cars going by at the edge of the sidewalk, a few tree trunks, bicycle wheels. Hurry, hurry, before they all come at you.

She began to stumble. When a brick wall presented itself, she found its corner and fell into it, brick at her back and on one side. She put the shopping bag and the bag lady between herself and the wall, and then she put her cheek against the wall although the bag lady was, confusingly, between her and it. She pulled her cape up around her shoulders and down around her ankles, then she reached up out of it and pulled her hat as low as it would go, blocking out what appeared to be sunlight but might, of course, be a street lamp or a full moon as white as milk or the white bread she had not been allowed to have.

She closed her eyes against them all. Her body flowed beautifully into the space that held it. The other body, the one between her and the brick wall, sagged, then slumped into utter weight and unconsciousness. Someone ought to stay awake and look after the baby, thought Millicent's mother resentfully.

Whether the light was sun or moon or street lamp no

longer mattered. It flickered out, went black. Her last waking thought was, how often this had happened before, how often the light had turned itself out, and left her to fall through the space that it left behind. She might as well be home, but, of course, this *was* home. Space between brick and air, space between bag and bag lady, space between lost and...Lost. Space between lost and lost, that was it.

4

When she finally woke, at the end of a long tunnel of sleep, the light was mild and so was the air. If this was still the same month she had started out in, it was a mild month. She woke without angles or edges; she was a ball of body with a tiny pain between its shoulder blades. That came from hunching, Mother had been right to tell her to stand up straight. In her teens, her full height had come upon her suddenly, making her alarmingly taller than the boys, aggravating her muscles and nerves, but later on the boys had all grown past her, although too late for dancing. Of course she had stooped, putting the boys at their ease. Millicent had grown gradually, like a tree, but now Millicent was much taller than her mother, taller than her husband, in fact, or at least as tall. Gerry (she remembered his name without difficulty)—Gerry was exactly the same height as Millicent, and the baby would be huge. She could see the baby clearly, gigantic in a football helmet. Harvard, or Yale?

Yale, or Harvard? She closed her eyes against the mild light and mumbled the colleges between her lips. Nowadays, even girls went to Harvard and Yale, to Princeton and Dartmouth, to Oxford and Cambridge. They were pampered nowadays, given every kind of chance. She should have been born into this pampered time and been allowed to go to Oxford or Cambridge.

Cambridge or Oxford? Her mouth mumbled the new choice. She was always being asked to make choices, she who had found all choices disappointing. If she kept her head down very low under the hat, she would not have to acknowledge the mild sun and could stay here forever, making no choices at all, wherever this place was. She remembered only a brick wall, a carton of milk, and the bag lady's sloppy greed.

A horn blared, something as heavy as a tank shook the ground around her, a voice called from a cloud or a second-story window. She lifted her head slightly under the hat and pulled the bag lady toward her. The bag lady was not awake yet—good! one less person to think about. Under her feet was a sidewalk, a sidewalk bed with a brick counterpane. She drew her feet in, but there was no escaping the sidewalk. Someone else's feet had stopped beside hers, someone's voice was saying "Are you all right?" Without her will, her hat bobbed up and down, enthusiastically. I am certainly all right, I know just what I am doing, I am here because I wish to be here, the bag lady wishes to sleep, she will wake up later. *Go away.*

The hat was so powerful that the voice went away, taking the feet with it, and the bag lady woke up and said, This town is too big. Before the point could even be argued, a tan spaniel went by on the end of a leash, towing a pair of sandals and a bright green skirt, and after it a tricycle pedalling its wheels furiously. She could not lower her head quite fast enough to escape seeing the firm bare legs in blue socks and stubby brown shoes, the blue shorts, the little white shirt, the fair shining head like a duck in sunlight.... The hat was cheating her safety. She must be more careful, the hat must be more careful. The bag lady was right, this town was too big.

We'll get out of it! and her noiseless scream woke the bag

lady up. Oh God, now she would want to be fed, want the bathroom, demand her bottle of milk, make a mess of the shopping bag, wallowing around in it, looking for money and a way back to sleep through its dark bottom. But, unexpectedly, she did nothing at all. She was not hungry, she was not anything. She was still the round ball of a body that she had been all night. It was not Florence who had been a ball, it was the bag lady. No one should have nagged Florence to stand up straight; it was the bag lady who had curled and hunched and turned herself into the round shape of the world. If she got up quietly, she could pick the bag lady up, round and balled, and put her into the shopping bag and take her away before anything happened. Before she started to demand things.

We'll get away from this town which is too big, she thought, and she got to her feet and began to walk. Her limbs responded, oiled, fluid, she had no feeling in them at all one way or another, they did what she wanted. She had power over them and over the bag lady and over this too-big town which she was leaving at once.

The bus was waiting for her at the next corner—or perhaps the fiftieth corner, she could not tell which. But she could tell that the bus was there, its heavy wheels, its long shiny side, its steps leading up. The bus being there showed that she had power over her own life too.

She went up its steps agilely. When the driver (of whom she could see more than she wanted to, but not his head so it was not frightening)—when the driver said, "Lady, I can't wait all day," her power continued and she dived her hands into the bottom of the bag, bringing up a dollar bill which she thrust at him. He said, "Je-sus! Put it in the—I can't take paper—now don't give me a hard time." He thrust the money back at her, and she stood there, swaying a little because the bus was starting up. She held the folding money in her hand

and thought that the driver wanted coins and she was not sure where the coins were or that the power she had felt was going to stay with her.

A voice, a woman's voice, from behind her or to the side, said, "Here, driver," and an arm stretched across the space under her eyes. Coins clinked in the coinbox. The arm was covered with a tan linen sleeve, rather nice. There was a flash of gold-link bracelet, very fine, narrow.

Inside her head, she knew that a transaction had taken place, redeeming her poverty of small change. Inside her head, she remembered thank-you and how-kind and oh-but-you-shouldn't. Inside her head, she heard the driver's grumble, rising a little at the end like a pig's tail, mollified. Inside her head, she heard the charity voice saying "Not at all," a very cultured voice.

She went up the narrow aisle, away from charity's voice, holding on to the backs of seats. Some heads jerked themselves away from her. She found a double seat, empty, as she had found it before on another bus, and she wedged herself and the bag and the limp bag-lady body all into it, and she closed her eyes under the hat.

Under the hat, she told herself a story. She had boarded this bus, and there had been an old lady in trouble, no money at all and very confused. She had seen what the difficulty was, at once. The bus driver had not been polite, there was a time when bus drivers had shown respect for passengers but not any more. The labor unions, it was a pity. She had reached across in front of the old lady and had deposited just the right amount. "Not at all," she had said gracefully, and then she had withdrawn her pale hand in the tan suit of nice quality linen, with the tasteful gold-link bracelet. "Not at all."

"Not at all," Florence murmured under the hat, pleased with her graceful performance.

She was paid for. She had paid her own fare. She could

go to the end of the line, and, when the bus driver told her "This is the end of the line," she would get off the bus without speaking to him. He would know then who was really powerful. The gold-link bracelet flashed at the edge of her black wool gloves, she noted it with disapproval before it disappeared forever. Then she settled down, quiet, satisfied, with the bag lady rolled up inside her bag. She let the bus take over. She was not responsible.

V
THE VILLAGE

1

Dark, light, dark. Move, stop, move.

She dreamed meaninglessly and steadily. The shopping bag cushioned her, and inside it the bag lady jounced and tumbled like tennis balls. She was fat and light and soft, and she went in and out of the steady meaningless dreams, a marshmallow of a woman, mutely obedient.

When the bus driver woke her, shaking her shoulder, she hushed him by putting her fingers to her lips so he would not wake the marshmallow-woman. He muttered something about "You hafta get off," and she suddenly, very cleverly, pretended to be mute and deaf and pointed at her lips again and then at her ears. He said Ohhhh like air escaping from a tube.

She got out of her seat, not arguing, bringing bag and companion, dragging them after her. It was still sunlight, the sun was somewhere, and she went down the steps and off the bus with the driver yelling "Be careful!" at her deafness. Out of a sudden notion, she yelled back—she, the secure deaf-mute, yelled, "I will! I will be careful!" Then she began to run, clumsy as a cow, bag hitting her knees, cape wrapping around them, bag lady lumbering behind (or was she ahead?), escaping the bus driver, the Hound of Heaven. She was not frightened, but she must have run a long time before she began to stumble, then slow down, and finally come to a dead halt. It was because of the fire hydrant that she stopped running. The hydrant was brownish-red, and it had made a puddle of water around itself. In the puddle was sky, clouds, but that was only on the surface. When she looked down, the sky fell into a well that had no bottom.

For no reason she began to tremble. She leaned over, not bending her knees, like a young girl, and started to dip a black wool finger into the well, but she withdrew it instantly before it could get wet. There was something she had to do first. The water would tell her.

She looked into it again, and the sky was gone, cancelled by the wide brim of her leaning hat. Very carefully, she pulled the black wool glove off her right hand. The trembling continued, but it was the bag lady's, not hers. It came from anxiety, or perhaps from terror. With the gloves off, might she too not be cancelled?

No. Be calm, she told herself. Only one glove.

She smoothed the one glove and put it into her bag before she leaned again toward the black well. Her hand was white, as she had known it would be, and the fingers, extended, looked like a mandrake root. Go and catch a falling star.... But there was no danger of stars because of the surrounding hat, unless they rose from the sidewalk and shot upwards. I'm afraid! cried the bag lady, and watched with fierce fascination the descending fingers of the mandrake.

When the tips of the white fingers touched the water, all trembling stopped. She hesitated a moment, holding them— four fingers and one thumb—just skimming the surface, then she plunged her whole hand in up to the wrist and gave a cry.

"Poor crazy old thing," said a voice that might have been at her shoulder or at a milestone distance. She looked sideways and saw shoes, walking away. She did not like shoes.

She felt the ocean lapping at her wrist, cold where the

wide blue vein ran up into her arm. She leaned closer, trying to see deep into the dark water, and from this new angle she saw her own shoes as black as the wool gloves.

She did not like shoes. She hated shoes.

The bag lady began to tremble again. Be calm, she told her softly, only one shoe.

It was quite difficult to bend over and undo the laces on the right shoe, which belonged to the right glove, the left one could keep as it was. *The others shall keep as they are.* She had been given an A in Shakespeare. Had she not?

The shoelace gave way in her hands—one wet to the wrist, the other in its black glove. She pulled the shoe off by putting the toe of the left one against the heel of the right, and it came to rest beside the ocean like a black scow. This pleased her. She had forgotten that she was wearing socks as well as stockings. Men's socks. Not James's socks, however. The bag lady had begun to whimper again, and, still hushing her, still bending over, she pulled off the sock, then the stocking.

Her foot was far cleaner than she had expected it to be, and far less familiar. It was white and narrow, like a sailboat. She plunged her right hand into the water once more, and then, shuffling, she brought her white right foot up next to it. The foot found the water colder than the hand had found it. Her mouth opened in protest, and her tongue dropped into its cavern. If she had not been a deaf-mute, as the driver had once known her to be, she would have cried out.

The water was delicious. A thousand miles away, but delicious. Some message reached up from it to her head, and tongue slid back into place, mouth closed. The word *cool* spelled itself in front of her as clearly as if a finger had traced it. She took her own fingers out of the water, and then she stood up. The white right foot was distorted and wavering under her eyes, cool under the brim of the hat which was salvation.

She stayed so until all the sensations left her, and then

she pulled the foot out of the water and studied it, flat on the sidewalk, alongside the fire hydrant. She studied the toes, which were long. When her head under the hat instructed the big toe to move, it moved, and for a while this amused the bag lady. But they would have to put the stocking on again—the stocking and the sock and the shoe. They would have to sit down by the water, at the ocean's edge, away from the wetness that might threaten the bag or the cape or the other shoe or the other glove.

Painstaking, that was it. She took pains.

She had the stocking on and was reaching for the sock when someone on top of the hydrant, or at any rate standing near it, said "Are you all right?" She was being plagued by voices making such remarks or asking such questions. For all she knew, this voice—coming out of a cloud or the hydrant—was the same one that had said poor-crazy-old-thing, a voice that had gone away and then come back, determined to be kind and responsible, a good-citizen voice. The voice was like Janet, Janet who would take you by the hand and see you tenderly through the cemetery gates—Oh, that was horribly unfair! It was Millicent she was thinking of, but that must be a mistake too because she had just talked to Millicent's husband on the telephone. She had talked to the baby too, hadn't she? There was a happy marriage!—a threesome, blessed by God, made in Heaven, like all marriages surely.

The voice (it was overhead, from a cloud, not a hydrant) said again, "*Are* you all right?" and, by way of answering, she pulled on the sock that had been dangling from her hand. When she was twelve-going-on-thirteen, she used to sit forever on the edge of her bed, dangling a sock or stocking or shoe, while she dreamed of being a new age entirely, of being thirteen. But when it came, her thirteenth birthday was no different from her twelfth. Her body had kept rearranging its habits, its genes and chromosomes shifting about in embarrassing ways, but the person who wore the body was no different on the new birthday than she had been on the old one.

She began to pull on the sock, breathing hard to show how intense the effort was so that the voice from the cloud would have to go away. As she pulled, she reflected with some satisfaction that she had always been very sensible about disappointments. Disappointments such as finding thirteen no different from twelve. Disappointments such as finding that marriages were not made in Heaven.

Well, of course, said the bag lady, no one ever believed...

"Come on!" said the cloud voice above her, a double-gender cloud, speaking now with a man's deepness. "She's perfectly happy, Kathy, you can see she's perfectly happy. Leave her alone, darling. She's all right."

She knew a great deal about the cloud already. It was male and female, full of responsibility and of detachment; it believed in happiness even for bag ladies, but it also believed in leaving well enough alone. Worst of all, it called itself *darling*.

She could not look up, because of the hat. Would not look up. She dragged her shoe on over the sock. The big toe, which had moved so effortlessly on instruction, was now imprisoned, but the whole foot felt cool. It had drunk at the fountain and was fresh and, possibly, immortal. She thought she could hear things moving away behind her. The man-voice that said darling, the woman-voice that said are you all right, the bag-lady voice that said, impiously, that she hoped to God they were through paddling in the fire hydrant. I thought you liked it....I did, but you always go on too long. ...You never called me darling, not in all your life, you called me Florence.

You called *me* James, said the bag lady sharply.

151

Anger masquerading as energy brought her to her feet, and she began to walk away very fast. The bag lady panted after her, wanting to be fed; as punishment, she would not be fed. She would have to learn how to behave herself, stop talking of things that were in the far past, unbecoming to gentlefolk to talk so, nobody's business, never anybody's business.

I'll die if I don't eat, said the bag lady, we'll both die and then we won't be gentlefolk anyway. It will spoil everything.

Beg for your meal, said Florence, taking long strides, not getting anywhere.

I shall.

You shan't. You would disgrace me.

You're disgraced already. Don't you remember?

Nobody remembers. Beg for your meal, and then we'll see who's disgraced.

They turned, together, like horses in tandem, and left the sidewalk for a green lane that had bushes on either side. It was a village lane; in a moment, church bells would ring down its narrow center. There was a tangle of weeds under the bushes, with a few stiff yellow flowers, past-summer-going-into-autumn flowers, well within the compass of her hat. She leaned over and pulled a stalk out of the ground, roots and all. It was not a mandrake and it did not scream, but something about the dry caked dirt and the stiff fingers which, until she wrenched them free, had been gripped deep underground alarmed her, and she threw it away with a clumsy jerking motion.

Village people, she thought, live in village houses. They are friendly, not like city people. If *she* wants to beg, *she's* welcome to do it. She kept on walking but her mind walked backwards, scraping at the memory of the yellow flowers and the roots in the dry earth, wilting in the sun and then rotting.

She was angry again, angry with the stupid things because they were still clinging in her mind, now when she wished to be free of them. She strode in anger, the cape flapping. She was careful not to look to right or left or straight ahead, only down to the circumference that belonged to her, the circle she had chosen so thriftily in a thrift shop.

When a house thrust itself upon her, it was a small house, planted in her path. The moment she came to its neat, Noah's Ark steps, she also came to the dog, and she drew back from it as if she had trod on a serpent. It was a shabby dog, brownish in color, of no great size, a booby that wagged its tail when it saw a stranger, then put its nose between its paws and went back to sleep. But a non-barking dog was a good sign, and that was important because she was as hungry now as the bag lady, the two of them unfed, in the heart of this village in the heart of this—this State? Connecticut? New Jersey? Still New York State? She was in a State—you're in a state, said the bag lady and heehawed so noisily that the dog looked up. She went up the steps heavily to find the door, the bell, the knocker, the thing whatever it was that would tell whoever it was that she wanted to be fed. A pair of feet would answer if she rang, not a face, because of that blessed facelessness of people provided by the hat.

My car has broken down, she said, rehearsing her speech. May I use your telephone? Oh, of course, come right in. Would you like a cup of coffee, a bite of something, while you're waiting for the tow truck? Well, just a little something, she would say, how kind of you, the way she would say it to Janet or to some other dear friend. *What* other dear friend? Never mind what other dear friend! Her heart was pumping uncomfortably. She did not really want to ring the doorbell which she had now found. There was a door knocker too, brass and well polished, a very bourgeois door knocker of no imagination. For the same money, she found herself thinking fussily, they could have gone to an antique shop and bought something really nice. For the same money.

I have money, she said placatingly to the door. If you don't believe me about my car breaking down—and you might not, because of the cape and the shoes and the gloves and the hat—you would believe the money. People always believe money.

The dog got to its feet, stretched fore and aft, and came walking over slowly to sniff her shoes. In a moment, it would certainly bark, and then people would come and see—not the well-bred woman whose car had broken down, but a broken-down bag lady, a freak.

Who are you calling a freak? said the bag lady ungrammatically.

Shut up. Please shut up.

Perhaps it would be better to go to the back door. In villages, people lived in their kitchens, close to the coffee pot, the bread box, the refrigerator. They would not be suspicious at back doors the way people were suspicious at front doors. That was the trouble with city dwellers—they huddled into apartments where there were no back doors and where everyone was frightened of what might come through even a front door. Although, of course, there would be a doorman.... Her mind leaped to the last doorman she had seen, the one whose name she had not known and who had helped her into the taxi. She would never see him again. She would never know his name.

Under her breath she told the dog to be quiet, but it had already gone back to the same place and the same position, nose between paws. Watchdogs were better than doormen, doormen took your elbow and put you into cabs. Feeling suddenly confident, she turned and went down the steps, walking briskly around to the back of the house, to the friendly kitchen that was waiting for her.

Once she had lived in such a house herself—a village house, with a bright kitchen she had copied from a picture in House and Garden. There were copper saucepans on the wall and her friends came in for coffee cake fresh from the oven and there were smiling children—No, she had never had that kitchen and there had been no coffee cake. Somewhere she must still have the page torn out of the magazine with its picture of the kitchen she was never going to have, out of which she had been cheated. Live in the *suburbs?* James had said, making her sound as bourgeois as the door knocker.

James was bourgeois. Only a bourgeois person could believe that it mattered what a door knocker or a kitchen looked like. Incompatability, the judge had said. Not said; decreed. Decree awarded. In absentia. Uncontested.

She ripped her mind away as one would rip sticking plaster from a wound. It was not a wound, of course. James, and James's incompatability—nothing could matter less. She had made all her adjustments, and now here she was at the back door of a village house with copper pans on the kitchen walls and coffee cake coming hot and fresh and cinnamony out of the oven. She could taste it. The bag lady could taste it too and was licking her lips in that bourgeois way she had—gross. That was it. She was gross.

When the back door opened to let her in, she would leave the bag lady outside.

The door did not open, although she had been standing there for hours while, out front, the dog slept. Very carefully, she reached to turn the doorknob, pretending this was her own back door, she had just come back from the market, she had just come back from taking her little daughter, no, her little son, to school. She had just come back from taking her

155

husband to the railway station, he worked in New York. His name was Malcolm, and her son's name was Danny. Malcolm read story books to Danny when he got home from the office. But now Danny had grown up and married the wrong girl and they were going to have a baby.

I've decided to have a baby, she said to the bag lady aggressively.

Good. Push on the door.

It gave under her hand, and she walked through it into a kitchen that was all white and red. Janet's kitchen in Janet's apartment was avocado and gold; I warned her she would get tired of those colors, and I was right. My kitchen is (was?) yellow and white, sunny as a child's morning face, sunny as a daisy in a meadow, sunny as butter in an earthenware crock. Sunny as hell, but that was the bag lady talking and it was the bag lady's big black shoes that now trod on the linoleum floor which had a pattern that zigzagged and made her dizzy.

Ignoring the linoleum, she headed straight for the refrigerator, a solid white mausoleum, unblinking. Its door when she opened it revealed a well-stocked heaven. The black-glove hands snatched selectively, rejecting chopped meat ruddy under a plastic cover, rejecting some kind of pudding in a china bowl, not portable, not to be snatched and run away with. She tore Christmas-silver wrappings off a chunky package and revealed half a chicken, cooked, a feast for the Magi. Stuffed it into her bag. Lunged at raisin bread, raisin bread was expensive, they did themselves well, her host and hostess. Cheese, *good* cheese? She sniffed it. Very good cheese. I know quality, she thought, and stuffed that into her bag too.

There was a noise over her head, shaking her with sudden fear. Then she righted herself like a shivering boat in a squall, stood and listened quite calmly. The noise stopped. Someone lived here then. Someone had brought everything home and put it into the refrigerator. Someone might come down the stairs any moment now and stand, transfixed and staring. She would be pretty, blonde, a housewife in a pink housecoat with a zipper up the front. Her husband had gone to work. He was tall and lean. They had a dog and two children, where were the children?—Oh God, she had lost the children! She must rush away at once, find them, make them safe. She was bringing food to them—chicken, raisin bread, cheese. That would do very well for them until they were found.

Overhead, the sound came again and turned into steps, firm calm woman steps. Perhaps this was a kind woman, coming down her staircase? But she had been careless, had lost the children, and one must put the children ahead of everything. She had always put Millicent ahead of everything, and now Millicent didn't even answer the telephone when her mother called, leaving it all to James.

Not *James*. Gerry. She stared down into her bag, at the things she had stowed away in it, and then suddenly she turned and ran, a crab scuttling, shoes too heavy and too large. She ran through the back door she had left open behind her, down the steps, past the dog out front. It still lay there, nose between paws, not getting up, not caring at all.

She thought she heard the woman scream, but perhaps that was inside her own head. Anyway, it was only a little bit of chicken, a little bit of bread, a little bit of cheese. No need for anyone to fuss. What she must do at once was to find the children. By now, the children must be famished.

Nonsense, said the bag lady happily. There are no children. The food's for us.

It was the first time that the bag lady had used the plural pronoun.

They ran, clumsily, hand in hand, until they were both out of breath. They ran into the roadway and off the roadway, and into a yard and out of a yard, and into an alleyway and past a grinning wall and a mailbox, until they came to a vacant lot that was all weeds and flowers going to seed. Near a corner by a fence there was a tree, and, when she stumbled in sudden weariness, catching one foot in the cape which had become too long, she fell under the tree against its broad trunk. The bag lady, stumbling too, fell on top of her, and the shopping bag was underneath them both. They lay under the tree together, breathing hard at first, then evenly, then lightly. It was all quite pleasant, and after a while the bag lady got off her back, and she sat up and got off the shopping bag, and the smell of good ripe cheese rose out of all the warmth and the crushing and ascended into the branches overhead where it sang like nightingales.

This was a good place. Under the circle of her hat, if she turned, she would see the fence at her side and the tree at her back. When she leaned against the trunk, rough bark dug into her spine, counting each knob, 1-2-3-O'Leary, 1-2-3-O'-Leary. Was it a skipping game or a game of childhood jacks? That was it! She had come to find the children, and here they were ahead of her, skipping rope, playing jacks, in an eternal sunshine of being young and safe, having known she would come and would bring them their food. She would never let them starve.

Her knobby spine against the tree, she stretched her legs out in front of her, pulled the cape across her knees to make a picnic table, and opened the bag. She thought she had put a red-checked tablecloth inside (for picnics, for her husband named Malcolm and the little boy named Danny), but she must have forgotten it, because there was not even a red-checked napkin. No matter, she could wipe her hands neatly on the skirt of her cape. "That's the advantage of these good sturdy woolens," she said to Janet who was sitting beside her.

"They wear well. They're an investment."

She opened the Christmas-silver package first and revealed the chicken. Its half-breast was plump, its single drumstick curved like an image of desire. She tore the drumstick off and passed it to Janet, but the bag lady's hand snatched it first. Janet was a lady, she said it was quite all right, she had just had a large dinner, and they all nodded, all three of them.

The chicken breast was tender and sweet and moist. The raisins in the bread were tender and sweet and moist. The cheese was not tender, but alive and assertive, the singing nightingale. She ate all the chicken and a quarter of the loaf of bread, and then she ate quite a bit of the cheese, sucking at it as if it were a baby's bottle. Millicent will never be able to manage a baby, she thought. She's exactly like her father. *He* had never wanted to have a baby either. He had never cuddled the pink baby she made for him, never chirruped at it.... She could see him cuddling and chirruping at it now, little Millie, his little Millie. No, that must be wrong, she could not remember that, it had never happened. He had not wanted the baby, it was *her* baby. She had not even wanted him to want the baby, but he cuddled the baby so much that it became bad and screamed.

He never cuddled his wife. He cuddled other women.

"You can't prove that," Janet said calmly.

I can't prove what? I never said anything. It's no business of yours. For a moment, she felt a wet glob of teary misery rising inside her throat, because Janet was turning against her and Janet was her only true friend. She stared at Janet, sitting there beyond the bag lady—stared very hard until Janet dropped her eyes and turned into a rag of mist. *I* am your only true friend, the bag lady said. Can't we just go to sleep together, here in the warm day, under the shelter fence, the nanny tree....

She pulled her hat down so far that it covered her eyes completely. Limply, luxuriously, she felt her body sag, roll to the left, fall forward onto side and shoulder, curl itself, become tranquil. It took her mind with it. The mist that was Janet breathed itself away to almost nothing. She could destroy Janet with one puff. Magnanimously, she chose to let her live. Closing her eyes against that tiny remaining vestige of Janet-life, she breathed deep enough to suck in everybody. She would sleep where she was loved. Loose in the naked palm of her own hand lay the bag lady's black-gloved paw. Their breaths mingled quietly. They slept.

2

When she woke, it was because the sun had circled behind the tree and reached the picnic place. The children had gone, having eaten their fill. Janet had gone too, although Janet had received absolution. She pushed her hat back off her forehead, just enough to see who had gone and who had stayed but not enough to see anything that might make her shiver. (What could make her shiver in the sunlight that had sought her out? Why did she expect to shiver?)

Sitting up straight, quietly because the bag lady was still asleep, she packed her bag, the chicken bones on top of what was left of the raisin bread. She could not throw the bones away because all bones were mysterious. The cheese seemed to be wilting, like a meadow flower.—Actually, it was more like a runny nose, that was the bag lady's simile, she had woken up. Waked up?

She rubbed her hand across her forehead, below the hat

brim which was contracting and causing a small ache in her
left temple. The temple had been raised up to the Lord to
keep the antique chicken bones in, she supposed, but she
would study that later. For now, she ought to get to her feet,
do some of those exercises she had done once, after Millicent
came, getting her middle section back into shape. They did
not call it a middle section nowadays, they called it a midriff.
She had found the exercises in a women's magazine and she
had done them quite faithfully for at least two weeks because
she had thought James had not liked her thickening midriff.
Thickening. Sickening with a lisp. James had not said that,
however, he had just looked. James's midriff was flat. James
was dead, wasn't he? She had divorced him, and he had died
of the divorce immediately.

Sighing with satisfaction, James so nicely dead in all this
sunshine, she leaned back once more against the tree she had
just bought. (She had stolen the food, but she had bought the
tree with her own money. That was important: *with her own
money.*) Pleasantly confused, she laid her hands across her
midriff, moved them up to feel the arch of the springing ribs,
moved them far down to feel the ... She changed the direction
of her hands swiftly, raising them high up until they were
under her chin, flat on her breastbone, on her chicken bone.
It was better for hands not to travel below the waist. It led to
impossibilities, and, anyway, James was nicely dead.

She sat up again, because the sun was too persistent and
she would have to move away from it. When she got to her
feet, the cape fell promptly around her legs and the bag leaped
to her gloved hand as if it were part of her. She shook herself
like a dog coming out of water, glanced at the circle of grass
on which she—they—had lain to be sure that it was tidy, and
then began to walk by putting one foot in front of the other.

Annoyingly, she was a little stiff. She should have kept

on with the exercises, she supposed, but now that Millicent was born, Millicent took up all her time. A real baby now, not a threat and a terror but a real live baby, a dear cuddly little thing with dark curls, so much curly hair for a baby, everyone had exclaimed, cooing their admiration, praising Mommy. Triumphant Mommy.

A car went by very fast, and then another not very fast, and then after a short waiting time another car that lingered. The third car was blue and white, and foolishly she looked too high and saw that it had one eye in the middle of its forehead like that giant in mythology. She could not remember the giant's name, but he had a single eye like this police car....

Police. Car.

On absolute instinct, as if her whole life had been spent running from the police, she turned and ducked and stumbled and fell behind the nearest bush. It had sharp cruel twigs and one of them scored her face, just below the right eye. She would be forever blind in that eye now, she would be one-eyed like the nameless giant, but at least the police car could not see her. She peered through the bush at it, and it was no longer lingering. It had stopped, and her heart stopped with it.

She knew exactly what must have happened. The woman upstairs in the house where she had stolen the food—I did not steal it, sir, it was there all spread out like a banquet. I did not steal it, officer, I was starving. I did not steal it, God, the lady came downstairs and shared it with me. We ate at a table with a red-checked tablecloth, and when I left she packed all the leftovers into a picnic basket and she said, "Oh, do take this, do take that." If you will escort me to the lady's house, she will be glad to explain everything to you.—No. They would escort her to the police station and the police officer at the desk would stare at her like cruel ice and they would shove her into a cell and the door would clang.

No, again. It was not done that way. First, they would arraign her, and, if words like *arraign* came so clearly to her mind, she was in no danger of losing it just because she had forgotten the name of the one-eyed giant.   ·

Cyclops.

There. Her good memory was with her. She was all right, she was not losing her good clear mind at all. And she was not—although she appeared to be—lying full-length now under a cruel bush, whimpering into the ground. It was the bag lady who sprawled. It was the bag lady who would be arraigned.

Encouraged, she looked again, and the police car was gone. "There!" she said, loud enough for the bag lady to hear. "There! I told you!" and the whimpering stopped.

She got to her feet, suddenly confident, came out of the bush, went to the edge of the road. Nothing was coming from either direction now, perhaps the parade of cars had been a dream. Her cheek stung a little under her eye, the eye had not gone blind. She was not sorry for Cyclops, not sorry at all.

In contempt for the giant and the police and the whole panoply of authority, she turned and went back to the bush, behind it, hiking her skirt up briskly. Nature, as a Convenience. Her mind began to giggle, but this was not disturbing. She had not only produced *arraign* and *Cyclops,* but *panoply* as well. She was in no danger whatever.

Rested, fed, relieved, and triumphant as a Juno, she felt as if she could walk all day long, from sundown to sundown, or sunrise to sunrise, whichever end of the Zodiac was approaching her. She had been born in late May under the sign of Gemini. She did not believe in the Zodiac, which was merely nonsense, but newspapers and magazines carried horoscopes and one could not avoid seeing them from time to time.... The Sun is your powerhouse all month.... This is an ideal period for self-improvement.... Stay on guard against treachery and deceit.... There will be a romance in your life....

James had believed in horoscopes or said that he did. To annoy her?

James was a fool, she thought, and her mind sliced him in two. An instant later, her brain made the correction: James *is* a fool. James was born under Virgo, most unsuitably.

It doesn't mean anything, she told the bag lady who had never been born at all. Oh yes I was, the bag lady said unrepentantly, I was born under Gemini, and you are my twin.

She was striding now, they were both striding. One would have supposed that being the twin of a bag lady might be demeaning, but it had an opposite effect—four feet to walk on, four hands to hold bags, two heads to reason. Striding, she turned a corner and saw the police car from under her hat brim, recognizing it by color. It must have gone around in a circle and was coming back to trap her.

The bag lady spit at it. Florence said, Don't! They'll see you.

The police car went on past, but it left a trace of ice behind it. Perhaps, she thought, it was another police car altogether and knew nothing about her, or perhaps it was the same car, cat-and-mouseholing. It might not be a good time to be a Gemini? they were not in their ascendancy under the Cusp? The Cusp was like the Holy Grail, to be sought malely anc purely in the Crusades. It could be fearful in its seekings.

I think we will leave this village, said Gemini to Gemini. We would be safe in the country, the trees and animals and birds would not move against us. If we stay here too long, in this village, they will all join the Crusaders, wear gold crosses over chain mail, branches and thorns, beaks and talons, fangs and claws. But not in the country, the country would be safe.

She put up her hand and pulled her hat down very low, and instantly she felt strong and secure. Her mistake had been in allowing herself a view wide enough to include a police car. Under this lowering brim there were no cars, no feet but her own, no road but beneath her own feet. The feet began to move without her, and she watched them carefully. They were clever, moving so steadily. She had only to follow them.

One and two and two and one and, when her Gemini twin insisted, two and four and four and two. The feet moved, and the road moved with them.

She paid no attention to the sun, which was sometimes under the brim of her hat and sometimes, like the breeze, on her shoulder blades. She was satisfied with a treadmill on which no one asked questions or demanded answers or, worse, left undreamed dreams about where one could fall over them, meanly, selfishly. Little stunted knobs of people who clambered through her head, silly candle-ends, harmless. She need not remember anything. The sun pushing under her hat could reach no higher than her eyebrows, the breeze had died away. The day stood still, and through it the Gemini moved. The country would be unpeopled, roadless, houseless, *hers*.

The road—sometimes concrete, sometimes asphalt, dirt, even grass—refused to stop. All her walking had no effect on it, she was not reaching the country, she would walk forever and get to no place. Her head felt dizzy, then it began to ache, and she felt a sudden longing for a room she had left long ago, in the city, where Venetian blinds would be closed, there would be bed to lie on, aspirin in medicine cabinet, water in faucet, telephone summoning help. She would call a number, any number, and she would say that they were back again and lying on the bed—two of them now because Gemini had brought her sister.... I will *not* be Gemini's sister, Janet is my sister, and she will bring me the bed to lie on, the blinds to close, the aspirin to swallow. I must telephone her.

I must telephone Millicent, too. It would be terrible if the baby came and I had not called and everyone would hold me responsible. It was all so unfair, and there was no place to telephone. She must somehow get into the country, then it would not matter whether she telephoned or not because in the country no one would expect anything of her, or of her sister. She is *not* my sister, I just told you that. Janet is not my sister either, not really, but perhaps Millicent will have twin girls and there will be two new sisters in the world, and then, *then*, they will leave me alone. I suppose I could call collect, the way I did the other time.

A pair of shoes went past her, and she watched them closely from under the hat brim. Shoes with sensible heels, wide, a little run-down. They might belong to a schoolteacher, to a librarian, to a Mrs. Florence Butler who was wearing a secure hat, an enveloping cape, and carrying a bag that still had chicken bones in it.

It did? It had chicken bones?

She was offended. Chicken bones were wholly inappropriate for anyone traveling to the country, and in any case there was no nourishment on them. She stopped short and set her shopping bag in front of her, between her legs so it would stay upright, spreading the handles wide to give a clear view of the contents.

It was true about the chicken bones, they were on the very top. She scooped them out and, holding them, gnawed and useless, she leaned over to see what was below them. It was very reassuring; the bag was stocked with her excellent choices. She could travel to the country, where they were expecting her, of course. She could travel appropriately.

166

With a large gesture, she tossed all the bones out onto the road. They jumped a little, made a brittle tinkling sound, scattered themselves. She stepped into the road to scatter them further with her foot. In front of her, appearing suddenly like an archangel, a bus pulled up. She had grown so accustomed to buses by now that this one seemed no more important than the bones, perhaps it was a bone grown large and useful.

She nodded to herself as the door of the bus opened, and she put her foot on the step, the well-stocked shopping bag on her arm.

She could see the driver just as high as his chin from under her hat. She limped heavily, she trembled, she pointed to her mouth, to her ears. The driver shrugged, and she went on past him and up the aisle, accepting the archangel's benevolence. It was all so simple and so clever, as simple and clever as the good food she had got together inside her bag. I am entitled to it, she said to the bag lady who was either behind her or at her side. . . . It was tiresome, the way she moved about, thoughtless, really.

It was too late to reprove her. She was already asleep in the back seat. I'm the one who needs sleep, Florence thought. I'm the one who has to do all the thinking. She was very tired from being so wise and clever and thoughtful. . . . She was very tired. Soon she would be in the country, which would be restful, the rest to which she was entitled, just as she was entitled to the food in her bag and to the bus that was carrying her free. The country would be free too.

Reassured, she leaned her head back and closed her eyes. The country would be free.

VI
THE COUNTRY

1

Now, she moved through passages of time and place and sleep. Sometimes one Gemini woke, and sometimes the other. Sometimes, a bus driver moved her out. Then she stood, swaying under her hat, waiting for another bus to come and take her somewhere else. There was an infinity of buses that came and went and she came and went with them and everything ran together, but not unpleasantly.

Somewhere, finally, she would be put down in the country. There would be almost no people there, only Nature and Gemini, and stars she could not see because of the hat but which she did not wish to see.

A very female voice said acidly, "If you would be so kind as to move your bag, I could sit down."

The bag was supposed to be on her right side, nearest the window. She was always very careful about that, all her life she had kept the bag there, she had been raised to remember this important point. Now she snatched it away, feeling the groceries solid inside the bag. "*Thank* you," said the voice, elaborately, sardonically.

You don't think that I know words like *sardonic*, Florence snapped inside her head. You think I'm a frusty old monster, a hag, a bundle of clothes. You wouldn't sit next to me unless your feet hurt, I hope they hurt forever.

Resentment prompted a simple and logical revenge. She

171

would get out of this bus at the next stop, no matter where. She would climb over the knees next to her, over the fat lap, over the hands clasped on a black handbag. She would push hard against the knees and make them know what they had done. She would, if she could, hurt.

Her exit was a success; the knees shrieked. With the greatest care and dignity, she managed even to knock against a shin, becoming a moving bulk of contact. I am a battering ram, she thought confidently, breaching the walls, terrifying the citizens. The bus lurched as she started down the aisle, and she seized a shoulder for support, another shoulder, another. It was like being drunk, although she had never been drunk or wished to be, but as a battering ram she was able to accomplish the same result.

She knew very well that the hands pushing her on, making her behave so unnaturally, were Gemini's. The shopping bag that swung at her side was now propelled into an arc of small destructions. The Arc de Triomphe. How civilized we all are, are we not? She thought she had said that aloud to the bus driver, having reached him at last in his safe bucket of a seat, but, in answer to her civilized comment on civilization, he only muttered loudly, "Doesn't stop here, wait, lady!" She mumbled at him then, letting her mumble rise very loud, but he would not let her out of his bus. Behind him marched demons more terrible than the Gemini, authority even out here in the deep country. She knew she was in deep country now, she could smell it.

Her impatience became unbearable, her body bounced with it, she could not wait for the next stop. She would explode or faint or die. Through her mumbling lips there escaped another sound, almost a squeal.

Either they had reached the stopping place or the driver could not stand the sound of her. His mutter had matched her mumble, but he had nothing to match the squeal. The door folded back like an accordion, she clutched the rail and her shopping bag tangled with it, but she pulled it free with a savage triumphant jerk and stepped down.

There was concrete under her feet that could not be sidewalk since the countryside would not have sidewalks. Road then, end of road, an ancient mysterious parkway constructed by the Romans. She let her vision of it blank it out, kept her head so low under the hat that all she could see was her own feet, and stormed ahead like a Roman legion. Latin had always come easily to her. Oh God, just let her get into the country where no one was!

Under her feet, the road persisted, asphalt, concrete, something man-made and hostile. She went up, sideways, down, on the unforgiving way until at last, her eyes darting under the hat, she saw bushes, grass, tangle. Such things had betrayed her before, leading only to more sidewalk, more people, more cars. She thought she could hear voices behind her and the sounds of tires and horns, but she was not sure if they were real. If they were, this was not country and she was lost again.

A tiny cry, not hers, came from her closed lips, and she knew she would have to risk everything—risk that there would be tall buildings on the far side of the bushes, civilian people, neon lights, and police cars. This time, inevitably, the police car would take her away. She was resigned to that, and resignation gave her enough will to make the plunge.

The bush was level at her throat. It could strangle her, or it could throw her back into that blind civil service she called existence, or it could swallow her whole in its comfortable country arms, impersonal and welcoming.

A crowd of thorns. No, that was a crown of thorns. She could feel them now lash across her face. That had happened somewhere else, hadn't it? She would be scarred forever.

Get on with it, said the bag lady. It's a bush, not a crusade.

She plunged deeper, arms straight out, bag swinging from her wrist like a spent scimitar. Instantly, she was swallowed up.

And here, at last, was the country. Here was where she could be calm and safe, away from everyone and everything. Here was the forest, the jungle, the prairie, the canyon. Voices were left behind, eyes and ears could not see or hear her, no network of flesh was even within reach.

She pushed strongly. From under the hat, she could see her black-gloved hands, formed into a steeple, like a diver's, slitting leaves and branches and thickets. She lowered her head between her raised arms, a diver plunging to the utter depth. The waters of the countryside for which she had been longing closed around her, gave way, opened into a path, then closed again. She had a feeling of marvelous power, swinging herself blindly, a sledgehammer.

It went on, it seemed, forever, and she went on within it, but then the sledgehammer became a metronome and the force dulled. She stumbled, her cape caught, her hat hurt her behind her eyebrows, and the bag lady began to whimper with fear that they were getting deeper and deeper and there would be no end. You got me into this, Florence accused her fiercely, but the whimpering only denied any responsibility, the whimperer now only wished to lie down and rest. It was so nice when we were lying side by side under the tree ... remember the chicken bones?

It was true. It had been nice. If they slid to the ground together now, here in this tight cage of bushes, if they stopped crashing through undergrowth, if they lay down, lay down, lay down ...

Just as she thought she had the answer, just as she was trying to estimate exactly how to fall full-length in this jungled forest where the earth itself was knit into a conspiracy of branches and vines and thorns—just at that exact moment, she blundered head down into some kind of wall, so solid that it nearly felled her.

She would have staggered back, but the forest held her upright and she could not fall. A long-ago memory struck her of a hot New York subway so dense with bodies that, no matter how the train lurched and thundered, no one would even sway. I cannot sway now, she thought, and raised her hand to explore the wall. It curved away on both sides, she could feel its roughness through the wool of her gloves. It was something more human than a wall, but less dangerously human than a subway car.

Her mind, which had first been a sledgehammer and then a metronome, now became an instrument of impressive clarity. She was pleased with her mind, the sharpness of its edge, its keenness. It gave her back her dominion over the silly whimpering bag lady. Contemptible, she said not quite aloud, contemptible of you, it's only a tree.

I was just pretending, said the bag lady. I knew all along that it was a tree.

Brushing such defensive nonsense aside, she considered the situation calmly. She would have to move to the left or to the right, and this might be the portentous decision on which everything else hung. She stood and waited for a sign, and it came. The fingers of her right hand began to crawl of their own volition around the resistant bark, her wrist followed them, her arm, her shoulder, she moved to the right, stealthy but firm. Whatever awaited her, she was in control for the moment at least. Her fingers left the bark of the tree and groped in space. Directly overhead, a bird let out a sudden shout of music, and the sound frightened her. Her hand in space tried to come back to the tree but it had lost it already and there was nothing for it but that black shoes should follow

175

black gloves. I cannot strike the bird, she thought, I cannot reach that high. They will understand, she thought, I tried to reach and everything was too far away.

Her mind, which she had believed to be cooling, suffered fire. She said hush to the black shoes and the black gloves and the bird, and from that moment none of them dared to answer her. The gloves moved, the shoes moved, under her orders. The trunk of the tree was circular. She had known it would be circular, of course. Her mind was not heated, it was cool like the glade, or she could not have known that the trunk would be circular. You're repeating yourself, someone said, but it could not be the bird which had fallen silent. Had been ordered to fall silent.

She held her arms out straight ahead of her, the black hands at angles, as if she were in a lightless room groping for an electric-light switch. She had done this often in her own apartment, going from bedroom to bathroom in a night need, instead of turning on the bedside lamp. I had a bedroom and a bathroom? she thought incredulously.

And a lamp. That was the bag lady, nodding, but she could not have known about the lamp, could she? They had not lived together in the apartment, had they? They had met on the street. They had met next to a lion, not under a bedside lamp.

She began to realize that, for some time, she had been moving forward, her hands out at right angles, and that nothing now was stopping her. Her feet were moving too, there was space under them, grass. The bushes that she could see from under her hat were low and green, no longer giants with scimitars. The glade, she thought. The glade in the forest where the sleeping princess lay on a golden bed to be awakened by a husband.

Her mind jerked. Not a husband, a prince.

What about him? said the bag lady promptly.

Nothing.

What about him?

Nothing.

What is it that you don't want to talk about?

Florence said, you're a crazy old fool, I don't have to listen to you, I don't have to answer you. This is a *glade*, fool. We can sit in it, we can eat, we can sleep.

The bag lady could almost be heard to pant at the sound of those gilded, silvery, delicious words. There was no more talk of husbands; the dialogue slipped to the floor of the forest glade. Tiny sounds came out of Florence's mouth for which she had no responsibility; they came from quivers of excitement, of lust for food and peace, and for the aloneness that was now complete.

She sat down, upright on her floor, her cape-covered legs straight out in front of her, the shopping bag at her side, the table about to be spread. Very slowly, she began to empty the bag of its booty, standing each separate piece of grocery upright next to her. She had altogether forgotten about the almonds and the dates, and an instant craving for them seized her. The dates, especially, seemed a desert triumph, to be ingested slowly, delicately. To be absorbed. I am absorbed in finding the dates in the bag, she reflected; the dates will be absorbed in me. The dates were so beautiful in their gold-foil wrapping that she was almost unwilling to open the package, but after a moment she began to pry at the edge of it, so careful. The gold foil must not be torn. When it had all been taken off, she could spread it on her knee to make a cloth-of-gold napkin. For the prince.

For the husband, said the bag lady.

If you are not silent, said Florence who was in control of everything in the glade, you shall not have anything to eat at all. Millicent used to be naughty too, and she had to learn to sit in her chair at the table and not have the cake, only look at it. That way it punished *him,* too.

What on earth are you talking about? she thought, astounded. There was no *him.* There was James, but he had been erased long since. Millicent would be allowed to eat the cake now, of course, because she is eating for two, for herself and for that little baby she insists on having....

She had freed the package at last, and now she spread the gold damask across her knees and selected one date to place upon it. The brown slim perfection, slightly glossy, of the fruit blotted out everything else. She knew precisely how it would taste on her tongue, very sweet and a little dry, with the pale brown slim seed lying inside it. She would plant the seed of this first date, and from it would grow a giant tree under which she could shelter forever. And ever, and ever.

She bit into the date, and it was everything she had hoped for it. Better than a daughter, better than a husband, better than a home, sweet and safe.

She selected a second date and put it down on the grass for the bag lady. A black-glove talon reached out and took it, a beak nipped it, a craw received it. Florence nodded slowly and licked her own lips. When they had finished the dates (and she would share them, scrupulously), they would have the almonds, but when she and they came at last to the almonds, they were a disappointment. Dry, unsalted. One could taste only the hard wrinkled skins. She could substitute a slice of raisin bread for them, of course, the raisins would taste fresh, but she had no butter. She wondered if there was something in the bag that she could drink and, vaguely, she remembered the two little cans of tomato juice. Digging into the bag like a terrier, she found them both. They had neat silvery-pasted openings to be pulled off, and the brief worry about a can opener that had flickered in her mind subsided.

The silvered opening resisted her wool-thick fingers. She could not get a grip, and when she shook the little can in anger it made a gulping sound, aggravating her thirst. She would have to take off her right-hand glove.

Reluctantly, she pulled at the index finger of wool, then the middle finger, the second, the thumb, the little finger, loosening each in its wool case, one by one, not off but coming off. She tugged, and the wool at the wrist moved up to the palm of her hand and she saw a glimpse of white skin. It was the bag lady who screamed, of course. In deference to the bag lady's fears, she did the only thing she could do—she hastily pulled the whole glove back into place. The skin vanished in blackness, and she patted the wool wrist.

The little tomato can, however, was still in her hand. She extended one finger determinedly, began to scratch the opening, scratched and scratched, risking the wool. She triumphed. The paper dam began to rise, could be lifted up, finally gave way. She raised the can to her mouth, put her lips to the tiny opening, tilted her head far back....

She saw the tree overhead, saw the branches, the leaves. Saw, most terrifyingly of all, the sky. The bag lady screamed again. The little tomato-juice can almost slipped from all their hands. Four black-wool gloves snatched it to safety, held it tight. Close your eyes, you fool, someone hissed.

The eyes closed, the tree and sky vanished, the head could be tilted chin-up and there was no danger. There were other things than the hat to make everything safe. Eyelids.

The thick clotted juice trickled down the two throats. Gulps at first, then grateful swallowings, then lady sips. Between the taste and the coolness, she inserted pieces of raisin bread, relishing them. As her interest in food and drink slackened, she began to roll tiny balls of bread between her fingers.

179

Gloves seemed excellent for this, hygienic like a well-kept bakery. She lined up several bread-pellets on her lap and leaned sideways to poke small holes in the ground beside her, difficult but worthwhile. She planted five pellets, one by one, seeds to grow into what kind of tree? Was it the mad King George of England who had planted bits of meat in his garden? She felt sorry for him now because no one had understood what he was trying to do. Not mad at all, but very sane, trying to make things grow.

It had made King George comfortable to plant the little bits of meat, as she was comfortable now, having planted her bread-seeds. She lifted the tomato-juice can, closed her eyes so she could turn the blank eyelids toward the sky, and drained the last drop. Leaning backward so, she leaned further backward. There was the tree trunk behind her, as once before there had been another tree trunk. It was reassurance itself. She was not sleepy, but placid. Here, in deep country, where she had always known she belonged, she did not need to sleep, only to be. She could leave her mind alone, she could let it think about anything it wanted to, anything.

Even James? said the bag lady, settling down like a child to hear the story.

Yes, said Florence, even James.

Once upon a time.

2

I remember meeting James. Begin there.

I was just out of college, she told the bag lady, on the threshold of life where you've never been. He was attractive, not good-looking but attractive, different from the college boys I went out with, you know everybody goes out with college boys. I had to plan things sometimes to be sure I would have someone to go out with but, in those days, it was important to have a date. By the time Millicent was my age, it didn't matter so much, women were finding their place in the world, most women don't have a place in the world even now, you know, although *we* have this place (she explained to Gemini) under this tree where we can talk and no one will hear us.

I didn't have many dates. I wasn't what you call popular, but popular usually means being a little cheap and I knew too much for that. I was well liked, I had friends. Girls were my friends, and there was the boy who took me to movies, he was nice, a little awkward in his manners so I never brought him home. Mother thought young men should have nice manners. James had them, of course, or I would never have married him. A little smooth, perhaps. You can see that I'm being very truthful, this is a true story that I'm telling you.

It's quiet here, isn't it? I've found you a good place to be quiet in. I've found you food and a home and a bed and someone to look after you. You would have liked James, I suppose. I don't think Janet ever liked him much, but I suppose *you* would have liked him.

I think Janet was a little jealous. We had been first-friends
for a long time, she was such a good schoolmate for me, and
Mother and Father liked her. She was always nice and not
pushing, and then James came along.... Well, naturally, she
didn't like that, but she never showed it, and then, of course,
she got married herself. Just two years later. She married
Richard Johnston and he was only an accountant at the time
but he got to be a banker. Janet cared about things like that,
status. James was more of a—a—there's a word for it, entre-
preneur, that's the word I want. He moved from position to
position, he was lucky to have me for a wife because I was
very understanding and tolerant, except that time when he
didn't bring any money home at all for months and I had my
child to consider. My daughter Millicent, the one who's going
to have a baby.

I know, said the bag lady. Why didn't he bring any money
home for months?

That's a vulgar question. You're far too interested in
money and food.

I knew you wouldn't tell me, the bag lady said. She had
found the box of raisins and opened it, and now she was
licking them, one by one, and putting them into her mouth,
and chewing. She seemed to be able to chew on one raisin
forever. It was gross.

You're gross, Florence said.

Go on about James and the money.

You should share your raisins.

You have some already. In our lap.

It's not our lap. It's mine.

Suit yourself, said the bag lady, and reached over to take
the raisins which—it was true—were in her lap. They looked
like bugs of some kind, flies or cockroaches. Cockroaches were
something that James had been very common about, he told

guests that everyone had them and he talked about bug sprays. She had told him later that it was offensive, and he had not done it again or at least not in her presence. Having roaches was bad enough without talking about them. They were dirty. But the raisins were not roaches, and they were not dirty. She picked one up and licked it, merely to see why the bag lady ate them that way, and the taste on her tongue was quite pleasant. She pushed the raisin into her mouth, it was small for a roach, but if one chewed slowly...

She spat it out.

Wasteful, said the bag lady with hideous calm.

Florence said furiously, You tricked me into that. You tricked me into eating a roach. She felt spasms all through her body, not nausea but anger, shaking her like a dog shaking a rat, like herself shaking Millicent.... I never did that, mothers don't shake their children, I never. It was James who shook her, I remember it distinctly, I am not the kind of woman who, I have never been the kind of woman who.

She picked up the box of raisins and tipped it, pouring a handful into the palm of her black-gloved hand, lifting the hand flat to her mouth, pouring the raisins in, grinding them with her teeth. There, I told you, they're not roaches.

Who said they were? said the bag lady and grinned at her hideously. It was the first time she had seen the bag lady full face, and for a moment she was terribly frightened and then she was reassured, knowing that someone was *there,* someone listening, it was all such a comfort. I believe I'm beginning to miss Janet, she told the bag lady, but you will do though you're not educated. That was one of the troubles with James, common, not educated, I thought it was attractive at first, even if he didn't have a station in life. Mother didn't like him.

What about Father?

You're talking about God, Florence said accusingly.

Your father.

There were no raisins left in the box, she must have been eating them at a great rate, very selfishly. My father was gone by then, you know that. He was always terribly thin, my father was, and one day he just vanished.

There was a silence. The tree trunk against her back filled up with silence, stuffed with the hard plaster of it, waiting for someone to say something more. He's in his grave, Florence said sullenly. He ran out on me and died, Mother was very gallant, she kept a brave face. I learned it from her, never let anybody know when you're dying.

It was your father who died, not you, the bag lady said quite nicely.

Yes, but that meant he was out of it all, he escaped, he didn't say *Ask your mother* or *Wait a little, Florence, you're too impatient* or *They're laying off people at the plant*—Not the plant, he didn't work in a factory, he was a custodian, very high up. Not very high up, perhaps, but responsible for a great many things. Mother said he could have been anything he wanted to be, but she said he was...

Was what?

Well, flabby. She didn't mean it, I suppose. Thin people are never flabby. Father was very thin. Mother is quite stout.

You mean your mother's living? Is there any cheese left?

Yes, yes, there's cheese, we'll have cheese. It's in the bag, I'll find it for you.

She must be very old, the bag lady persisted, old like good cheese. I had no idea about your mother, Millicent's grandmother, the little unborn one's great-grandmother.

Florence thought angrily, I never told her about Millicent, I never told her about the baby. How did she find out? Why did I tell her about Mother now? She's going to use it against me, everybody uses everything against me. She could feel the dog shaking the rat again, inside her head. There was a mist around the dog. "I telephone my mother quite often," she said out loud, and the sound of her own voice which she had not been using startled her, and she went on, but inside her head now. I telephone my mother the way Millicent telephones me. She's only eighty, you know, it's not such a great achievement to be eighty. The reason I never see her is that she lives so far away. I'm a very good daughter to her, she says so quite often—Florence, you're a very good daughter. She's in a very good nursing home, one of the best, it's better for her to be in a warm climate and I write to her too, I telephone her and I write to her.

The dog had stopped. She selected two slices of bread and wedged cheese inside them and took an enormous bite, leaving a crescent of space where her teeth had been. The cheese warmed her, she could feel its zest all the way down her gullet. Mother had never liked James, except at the very first when he had taken her beloved daughter (beloved-daughter-beloved-daughter) to the movies. Their first date. James had picked her up in his car because in those days young men had called for their dates politely. The dates she had just eaten had not been as good, that was a different kind of date, all this talking was making her sharp brain very tired. The bag lady's brain was on a much lower level, there was no communication between them, all she could say was *Go on.*

Go on, she said, and Florence felt a brief satisfaction at her own prediction. I don't have to go on, she thought, I don't have to talk to you.

She had worn a very pretty dress, she went on. In those days, dresses were very pretty. Now it was nothing but jeans, pants, sit-on-the-floor, be-common, people always talking about—

185

Sex! the bag lady said, speaking through cheese.

Be quiet, you talk too much. He was wearing light pants and a dark jacket. He was older than I was, you know, eight years older and he always came around and opened the car door to let me out. Later, when I didn't like being out in the car with him so much, I sometimes had to open the door myself, but that was later. Not important. Not important! Don't keep asking questions. I don't know why we're doing all this talking anyway. I just wanted to sit here and eat a little, take a little nourishment, lean against a tree, be quiet. I had a successful marriage for a long time. He changed, I didn't. I had a very successful marriage.

Suit yourself, said a shrugging voice which frightened her because it was not the bag lady's but had come from somewhere else. I had a very good marriage, she said firmly. James was the one who spoiled it. I had to tell him to get out.

3

Into her head, there fell a silence. Behind her back, the tree leaned toward her, waiting on her next words, The bag lady said nothing. In her own hand, the cheese sandwich was more silent than the grave, more silent than the pits of the dates she had let drop. There were pits in hell, Miltonic pits, great yawning abysses. She felt melodramatic and a little dizzy. Why was she thinking about pits in hell when they were only date pits and of no consequence?

Everyone knew that she had been obliged to end her marriage. As she had told dear Janet, all sympathy, friendship, and calm blue eyes over calm cups of tea, "I had no choice, dear Janet, I know you understand," and Janet's murmurs had been tender and compassionate and rightly deserved. "It has not been easy for a long time," she had told Janet. "I never talked about it because of the child."

The Child. Millicent. There was something about Millicent that she was supposed to remember, wasn't there? to telephone her somewhere, for some good reason. It became clearly remembered through the dizziness. The child Millicent was going to have a child of her own, was carrying around within her (even now when her mother sat under a tree and ate and felt dizzy) another body that no body wanted as Millicent herself had not been wanted. Millicent's body had been assaulted by (she could not remember his name, Millicent's husband, it would come to her in a moment)—and now there was going to be a living reminder of the assault. She burst out, "It is cruel, it is all cruel," and then the silence fell onto her again.

When someone finally spoke, it was the bag lady, sounding mean and meanly indifferent. You're probably jealous, the bag lady said. She's quite happy, isn't she?

I won't talk to you, said Florence. I wish you would die.

She put her cheese sandwich down on the ground beside her and folded the black wool of her hands together on her lap. The black wool trembled slightly, as if wind was passing over a black field of wheat. I never saw wind over a wheatfield, she thought, how do I know about it? She remembered books with wheatfields, Nebraska, Willa Cather. Once she had read all the time, piling books up against her heart and around it, fortresses where she could be alone and happy. Now she was just alone. James had not liked books, he had read a few paperback mysteries, cheap things, comic strips, the sports page, and he had watched television. He called it TV. Why can't you say television instead of TV? she had asked him.

Once there had been a wind blowing Willa Cather and she had felt it in her own chest, bosom, breasts. She withdrew the last word and substituted *lungs,* which was more accurate. She had felt that Nebraska air in her lungs. "You're always reading," James had said, wanting her to go out but never to places she wanted to go to. He liked late-hour places, places with bars and women who glittered, a little cheap.... Poor James. She had married beneath her.

You married beneath you, the bag lady said dutifully which showed that she was listening.

I wouldn't say it to anyone else, Florence answered. It's because one has to keep one's dignity. He stopped asking me to go out, after a while, because I was pregnant. I was having Millicent, and my health was fragile.

I thought you were the one who didn't even have morning sickness, the bag lady said. She had found some more dates somewhere and was spitting the pits into the palm of her hand. It was disgusting.

My health was fragile, Florence repeated. From the first. And Millicent was a large baby, you have to remember that. James sat home evenings and watched television until I wanted to scream, you know very well that mothers-to-be have a special strain on their nervous systems. One night he said he was going out by himself, and I was nice about it. I said Of course, dear.

You said Thank God, the bag lady said.

I said nothing of the kind. I never say things like that. I only tried to make it easy for him, that was all. I tried to make the marriage work. It was never my fault that I finally had to tell him I wanted a divorce. Millicent was old enough by then to share her mother's burdens, James was a burden, but that was years ago. You know Millicent has really married too young, she's too young to have a baby. I was twenty-three when I had Millicent. Too young to have a baby, my mother said so at the time, it will tie you down. Well, it didn't tie *him* down, he started going out two or three nights a week. But, when he came in late, all I had to do was close my eyes and be asleep, and when he got into bed he would know I was asleep and an expectant mother needs sleep. So when he got into bed he would not push against me and start—well, start reaching. He would lie there restless for a while, and I would breathe deep, which was good for the babe....

The *baby*. You sound like your mother.

You don't know how my mother sounds. It was good for the babe, and James would be restless for a while and then I could hear him listening and sometimes he would—he would reach anyway, and I would get up and go to the bathroom for a while making sounds, as if I was sick, not sick really just a little nauseated, and when I came back he would be asleep, or quiet anyway. That's what I would like to be now, quiet, really quiet. Reading Willa Cather, or Tennyson perhaps. I know Tennyson is supposed to be old-fashioned, but he was so lovely. I can recite him if you want—willows whiten, aspens quiver, little breezes dusk and shiver, or Ulysses, or tenderest of Roman poets, nineteen hundred years ago. *I want to be quiet,* she shouted.

The bag lady, for once, did not retort, and everything became quiet, just as she wished it to be. It was a smother of quiet, smothered in all around her. Mother, smother, brother, lover, husband, wife. I was a good wife, he was a bad husband. I had to tell him to go, I had to tell him I wanted a divorce. It was for Millicent's sake more than my own, and for the sake of the unborn babe, although of course at the time of the divorce Millicent was not marr-ied she was in coll-ege no she was in high school and very hap-py like I was. *As* I was.

She raised her black-gloved hands up slowly in front of

her face, and then, as slowly, she put her face down into them, feeling the rough texture and the blackness and, of course, the quiet. She thought of letting herself weep, if only to ease the pain at the breastbone and between the shoulder blades, but she was unused to weeping and it would break the quiet. She felt fearful and, at the same time, secure. She knew these sorrows and this melancholy so well, knew she only had to wait and sleep would come on little cat feet (that was fog, the little cat feet, but sleep was fog and more comforting). Sleep would come, all the shutters would be pulled down, nobody would ask her any more questions.

What did he do that was so bad? said the bag lady. What did James do?

You know already, she whispered.

I want to hear about it.

I don't want to tell about it.

I'll wait.

Without raising her head, she began to draw the gloved hands away from her eyes, letting the fingers slowly trace her brows, temples, cheekbones, jaws. Someone had done that once, someone with bare hands, in the automobile, knee touching knee, someone pushing. She jerked her head up, and the automobile vanished and the hands with it, naked hands without gloves but, of course, it had been a warm night and nothing more had happened. She had expected more to come but nothing did, and perhaps that was why, later, she had been so trusting. Later.

Later?

Later. I'll tell you about it later. No, I'll never tell you. She leaned back against the tree once more, her face free of her hands, but the brim of the blessed hat censored all upward vision and the tree might be full of leaves, for all she knew or as barren as sin. Sin, of course, was not barren; sin was fruitful. I never sinned, not once. Not *that* way.

Not that way, the bag lady echoed. If not that way, how? Never. He wasn't a good man really, I suppose I knew that from the start. Maybe Mother knew it too, but nobody else because I was very proud. I *am* very proud. She looked up, saw the brim of her hat, looked down gratefully. Some kinds of pride were sins, but hers was not pride but self-respect. Her mother had taught her to be self-respecting, and she had taught herself not to be bourgeois, which was what self-respecting people were so apt to be. Reading had made the difference, education. Millicent had never been much of a reader, but Millicent had self-respect. I will say that for her, said her mother, she had self-respect. *Has* self-respect, if she's still alive.

She hesitated, uncomfortable. There was no reason to believe that Millicent was dead, healthy-as-a-horse Millicent, full of Baby. It was all rather vulgar. I suppose I ought to telephone my daughter, she thought reasonably. But I did telephone, didn't I? I got her husband whatever his name is— Gerry, that's it, Gerry with a G, and quite a superior type too. Perhaps the baby will be a reader. One missed, so much, culture....

Oh, but it wasn't *culture*, it was happiness. I used to read every kind of thing. The books understood me, the poems understood me, everything I read was kind to me. I could read Chaucer in Old English—no, Middle English—he sang in my head. Aprille with its shoures soote and long dreams of words and rose-red cities half as old as time. I planned to be so much happier, and there was that time in college when I was really happy. I didn't stay in college, you know, I got married. I left college to get married. Mother was so pleased, and so was Father, his little girl getting married. He pretended he didn't want me to get married, but he really did. He liked James so much.—No, of course he didn't like James. He didn't like him at all, he saw through him from the beginning. I was

191

the one who believed that James was a good man. If Daddy and I could only have had a Talk, if Mother and I could have had a Talk.

We could have a talk, the bag lady suggested greedily. Now.

Be quiet. Once upon a time there were three bears and a girl named Goldilocks. Once upon a time there was a girl in an automobile with a boy, a boy with fumbling hands that got surer every time they were in the automobile together, a girl who said No very clear at first but, after so many times, only whispered it, no, James, we mustn't, his head against her heart which was permitted but his hands somewhere else which was not. There came the time when No wasn't enough and she had tried to save herself. . . . No, no, she had tried to save him but he was so insistent, determined, frightening, she kept moving away on the seat cover, which was slippery and she remembered how slippery it was and how it stuck to the backs of her legs. He had been brutal, almost, she had been quite right to be afraid that he

that he

that he

I said, Don't, *don't,* James, and he said I don't know what he said, and I said *Later,* I think I said Later, and he said Promise, promise! and it was like the song they sang at Julia's wedding.

Julia?

My cousin Julia. I went to her wedding and it was beautiful, the kind I dreamed of, the kind I had, you know, I had a beautiful wedding. It was all I really wanted then, a beautiful wedding.

She sighed tiredly, put her hands down into her lap, looked up and saw nothing, under the security of her hat, looked down at her hands. There was still that gold band on the left one, but the bag lady's gloves hid it. She had no right to be hiding other people's belongings, the gold band had been a part of the wedding with Mendelssohn and the small, tiny-small, tiny-quiet minister. Do you, James Harold, (it was the first time she had heard his middle name) take this woman, Florence Ellen, to be your wedded wife? It was the first time she had heard herself called a woman, it had been sweeter than, sweeter than...oh, not honey. What was the French word for honeymoon? *lune de miel.* Sweeter than *lune de miel,* which had not been all that sweet, but in a bed not an automobile, and sanctioned, of course.

I am going to talk about something else, she warned the bag lady suddenly.

The bag lady whined. You didn't finish, about the night when the seat cover stuck to the backs of your legs.

You are very vulgar. I am not obliged to listen to you.

It was you who told me about it, said the whine. I never even asked. *You* told *me.* You'll get a reputation for being cheap unless you explain. What was the name of that girl in high school who was so popular?

She was a tramp, Florence said shortly.

What was her *name?*

I don't remember it.

You do, you do. What was her name?

Flo.

Oh. (Rhyming it.) Florence, like you.

No, just Flo.

I remember her, the bag lady said. She was very popular. Whatever happened to her?

How would I know?

Could James have told you?

(Icy now.) Stop asking questions, silly, you sound silly, you sound mean. That's what you are, isn't it, silly and mean.

I won't listen to you any more.

What happened to your cousin Julia?

She was Goldilocks, she lived happily ever after.

How mean of her, the bag lady said. Now you can finish telling me about that night, now that we've got Julia and Flo out of the way.

There isn't anything to tell. Nothing happened.

You mean, in the *car* nothing happened. Go on.

Why should I go on? Nothing happened. James saw me to the door, up the steps, he always did that, he had good manners on top, surface manners, very nice sometimes. That was all. He saw me to the door.

Your mother let you in. Go on.

If you know all about it, why do you keep asking? Yes, Mother let me in. Why shouldn't Mother let me in? She always waited up, we weren't late anyhow.

And James came in with you. You pulled him in, really.

Her mind disconnected abruptly, and she stopped responding, but her disconnected mind went on talking by itself. I pulled him in, what was wrong with that, my escort of the evening. I had others—no, I didn't have others. I had James and I pulled James in because, because. His face was still—I don't like the word but it's what it was—still flushed, and his eyes were shining. Not shining, shiny, that's a different thing altogether.... I have a feeling for words, you know. If there was someone here I could talk to, someone else who had a feeling for words, not a stupid bag woman with a black glove hiding a gold band, the only gold band she ever had. She may have stolen it, but if I ask her, she won't tell me the truth. As a matter of fact, she did steal it. I've lost my gold band, it's been stolen.

I have it here for you, said the bag lady coming back.

Here, under the black wool of my black glove. Why do you keep running away from me? Go on. *Tell.* About your mother and James.

I told you, there's nothing to tell. He came in with me.

You pulled him in.

If you insist. I pulled him in. His face was—

Flushed.

If you insist. His face was flushed.

And you said to your mother...

I did not I did not say it I never

You said to your mother.

I'll kill you, Florence said to the bag lady, I'll poison you. You're nothing but a common blackmailer.

You said to your mother.

I said to my mother, I said Mother, James and I are engaged.

That's the part I like, said the bag lady contentedly. The part where you trapped him.

Florence screamed.

There was silence in heaven for about the space of half an hour. Don't be alarmed, said a still small voice, that's only Milton. It's the Bible! Florence said in a small hysterical voice, I had the Bible as Literature in college, it was all lovely music except the bits that the professor left out because they weren't musical and I read them to see what they were. Do you know, she said, calming herself, that some of them were *nasty?* In the *Bible?* I'll be quiet now, I didn't mean to scream, we'll talk about something else.

You said to your mother that you and James were engaged. That's what you said you said. That's what I was waiting for.

Someone else said that, Florence said, talking again but

195

talking through her forehead, near the hat, because her lips were sealed and her throat was tight. You're trying to put words into my mouth.

Well. What did James say then?

Nothing.

What did your mother say?

You're trying to trick me! Florence shouted. You're trying to trick me into answering.

What did your mother say?

Nothing.

Well. What did your mother *do?*

There was silence in heaven again for a longer time. How did you tell heaven from hell in all that silence? How could you know? There was so much danger. She felt a long painful shuddering inside her bones, but nothing about her moved.

What did your mother do?

She kissed James.

Your future husband.

Yes.

She could see all of it now in her head, she could see her mother standing in the living room, facing her dear-daughter. She could see the dear-daughter's hand holding the dear-future-husband's. She had led James into the house with that hand—drawn him—pulled him—did the exact word matter so much? They were holding hands, that was it, as they had been holding hands in the car, only if they had been holding hands what had his hands been doing.... (James, no, don't, I promise.) He wanted to marry me, she said, suddenly severe and much surer. He *wanted* to marry me. He dropped my hand when Mother kissed him, no, I dropped his. I can't remember. You want me to remember too many things, she said fretfully, nobody remembers anything exactly. Mother kissed him, she was very happy, and then Daddy came in and Mother told him and they shook hands. James didn't say anything because of course he was a young man just engaged and very—not shy, really, very *reserved*.

Struck dumb, I would say. The bag lady's voice was singularly dry.

Please, Florence whispered. He wanted to marry me, everything went very well after our engagement was announced. It was in all the society pages, the New York Times, the London Times, the ... If the bag lady's voice got any drier, it would curl at the edges, brown faintly, blow away, be gone forever.

Be gone. Begone. No, she said, it was in the local paper. If you weren't so stupid, you wouldn't ask. You have to have influence to get into the New York Times, and what would the London Times have to do with it? I don't have to talk to you any more, you're stupid.

She had closed off the dialogue. It was over, behind her. James and she were now engaged to be married; no matter how it had come about, they were going to be married. He had wanted to marry her, and she had helped him through the difficult part, which was asking for her hand, such a nice old-fashioned thing to do. She had given her hand to him, and everyone had been very pleased, and they had a short engagement.

He never said anything about it? said the bag lady.

About what?

It. The trap you set.

She said *No* and went on pleasantly.

We set the date for the wedding, and he said anything that suited me was fine. Suit yourself, he said, it's your arrangement, he said we could get married in a registry office for all of him. You see! she exclaimed. He did want to marry me, he said that about the registry office. He didn't mean that I had *arranged* things, he only meant that the wedding is the *bride's* day.

He shrugged. I remember that.

You don't remember anything of the kind, you weren't even there. No, of course, he didn't shrug. She turned her head away from the blank air in front of her where there was no one except her enemy. She remembered James's shrug as if it were written on the air, saying to the air What's the difference, one's like another, why wait around in parked automobiles. She was imagining the shrug, of course, it had been fabricated by the bag lady. After the engagement was announced, she said formally, he never did anything wrong. I mean he didn't even try, except once, and that one time I said no, and he said OK (as if he was buying groceries, one day or another, what's the difference?). He shrugged. No, of course he didn't shrug. My classmates gave me a bridal shower, I still have the hand-embroidered guest towels that Janet gave me. Janet didn't think I should marry so young, she thought James was the wrong man perhaps, maybe she was jealous. She married quite a bit later, his name was Richard, he was a Richard kind of man, nice if you liked him, all I wanted was for her to be happy of course

of course

don't echo me, I don't like it. She had a very happy marriage for twenty years and then he widowed her. Richard widowed Janet and Florence divorced James, it was like that, only Janet didn't have to tell Richard to go and I had to tell James. I was sick for quite a while later. You remember that. I was sick. Millicent said I had done the right thing, she told me I had been very brave and wise and she told me that so sweetly. She put a wet cloth on my forehead one time, I remember, I was lying down.

Millicent didn't come.

Yes, she did. She came right away.

Millicent did not come.

I think she did.

Millicent did not come.

Florence put the back of her black-glove hand up to her forehead, holding in the headache. The headaches had started when she first made up her mind to divorce James. It was cruel to bedevil her now with silly statements, when that kind of thing brought on headaches. What she must do at once was to go and lie down on her comfortable bed in her comfortable apartment. She would take off her shoes in order not to hurt the blue bedspread, and she would lie quiet with her black-gloved hands folded like a knight's on his tomb, and she would not have to answer questions.

It wasn't a question, said the bag lady. It was a statement. Millicent did not come.

She shrugged what's-the-difference. Very well, Millicent did not come. Millicent telephoned as soon as she got my letter saying that I had had to tell her father I was leaving him, that I wanted a divorce. Not *leaving* him—putting him out of the house, showing him the door, as they say. I wouldn't leave him, why should I give up the house? I gave it up later because it was as big as a tomb but it belonged to me under the settlement, the Court gave me everything I asked for. She looked sideways, rapidly, to both sides, under the hat. You remember that? The Court gave me everything I asked for because I was in the right, the Judge was very kind and understanding because I was the, the, the, I've forgotten what they call it, I've forgotten what the Judge called it. It's nice what the Judge said, nice like chocolate candy and little cakes. I started eating too much after I got rid of James, you know, but I soon put a stop to that. If I had given James the satisfaction of getting fat and ugly—what was it that the Judge said?

He said that you were the wronged party, said the bag lady in a totally strange voice.

You sound like an actress, Florence said angrily. You

199

sound like an actress acting Portia. The quality of mercy is not strained, it droppeth as the gentle rain from heaven, but had there ever been a time when it was gentle and it came from heaven? The ungentle mercy and the hard cruel rain. Once, in high school, I recited Portia's speech in English class, required memory work was what it was, I always memorized very easily. The teacher said it was a moving—a moving—If you didn't keep interrupting, I wouldn't forget words.

A moving rendition, the bag lady said in the Portia voice. And you were the wrong party.

Wronged! Not wrong. How can you be so stupid, so mean, so ugly, I'd hate you if you were important enough to hate. I'm going away now and lie down on my bed with the blue bedspread and wait for the headache to—to—to—

Subside.

She felt like crying, not being allowed to finish a single sentence, interrupted so endlessly. Only, she never cried. She had not cried even when she told James that she was putting him out of the house, showing him the door, rejecting him, demanding a divorce. She repeated it carefully in her head: demanding a divorce.

The bag lady was completely silent, which was a relief.

No other woman would have tolerated it, Florence said. After a moment of waiting, she said Where are you? Have you gone somewhere?

No one answered.

She waited again, and then went on.

I knew every time, James. Every night you didn't come home, I knew. I even knew who they were, and I kept lists, so the Judge would know too. You knew that I knew. You knew why I was always asleep when you came in, why I slept at the far edge of the bed, even before I was sure about you. You never even bothered to lie.

The bag lady came back. Lie to you? she said. Or lie on top of you?

A pain went through the skull of her head and appeared before her eyes, violently colored, shrieking. I was a good wife, she shrieked back at the pain.

I was a good wife, the bag lady said obediently.

After I had made my lists, I knew I had no choice. I had to say it to him. He knew perfectly well why I said it, I didn't have to say anything more. All I said was, James, I want a divorce.

I was a good wife, the bag lady said again dreamily. I don't know why James divorced me. I don't know why James stood in the doorway and said, Florence, I'm leaving you. Florence, I want a divorce.

If she moved, the colors of the pain in front of her eyes would explode. You're lying, she said with her own voice hammering in her ears. You know that wasn't the way it happened, you know that *I* divorced *him*. You're trying to turn it all around....

If you insist, said the bag lady.

Of course, I insist. It's the truth. The first person I told afterwards, after I'd told James—the first person was Janet. She was so kind, and then I had to tell Millicent and Millicent was not kind, do you know that Millicent has never really been kind to me, not unkind really, but ungrateful. Millicent is the one who's going to have the baby. Wasn't I supposed to telephone her? I talked to her husband, Gerry his name is, he's my son-in-law. I talked to him and told him how concerned I was and to have her call me back...I don't know if she could reach me here, though, there's a tree behind me, I think, not a telephone booth. But if she really cared, if anybody really cared—

There was a wind coming up behind her, out of the

telephone both that Millicent could not reach. On the brown ground, in the space she could see from under her hat brim, there were à few dead leaves, and they were stirring as if a hand had reached into them. It's going to rain, her mother said sharply, help me get the clothes off the line, Florence, don't stand there like a little ninny. She never really talked like that, did she? She loved me and she loved Daddy, they had a happy marriage, and I knew what a marriage ought to be like, and that was why I had to say it to James. I had to say to James, I want a divorce.

You didn't say that to him. He said it to you.

She knew how to handle this, she had handled such things before, the silences and the accusations. She stared down at the brown ground and the leaves and the hand that was stirring them. The hand was not black-gloved, it was naked. She ought to close her eyes. He did not, she said. He did not say that.

Yes, he did. The bag lady's voice was measured out in little spoonfuls like a sweet poison. I remember exactly. He stood in the doorway and he said, *Florence, I'm leaving you. Florence, I want a divorce.*

No! I threw him out of the house.

No, you didn't. He said, I'm going. He said, I'm not coming back. Didn't he say that?

No, he did not. I was the one who told him to get out. I was the one who told him never to come back. (Oh God, the unsplit infinitive, the syntax, the safety.) You're not listening to me, you stupid thing. You don't care. Nobody cares any more. I could die, and nobody would care. I know, I know! I know what he said. I know how he stood in the doorway and how he said it. Florence, he said, I'm leaving you. He said, Florence, I want a divorce.

Exactly, said the bag lady. You see? I was right.

She heard herself scream, but this time her mouth did not open. She put her black-gloved hands to her head, but they still lay there on her lap in front of her. She saw the brown leaves on the brown ground turn to stone. I could die, she said, I will die. You won't be able to reach me any more, this is what I wanted all along, nobody will be able to reach me. I will die. I want to die! I want to!

Do so, said the bag lady.

4

She started to get to her feet, but she was not able to rise from the ground and she had to turn onto her knees, heavily, as if she was an old woman now, had to press flat black-wool hands against flat brown-leaf earth and push herself upright. When at last she was standing, she thought instantly of lying down again, lying on her bed, waiting quietly for sleep and blackness and silence.

But I don't want to sleep, she thought now, I want to die. It's what I've always wanted to do whenever I lay down. Now I lay me, to lay oneself, to be—She sheered away from the vulgar past participle, still clear about past participles, clear about everything that was orderly, but what had been orderly since she had learned to play everything out in endless lies? She examined the word *lie,* which had turned on her in a vicious pun, pouncing like an animal on its prey. Prey, pray. No, she said, I must get out of this, I know the way out now, it will be as simple as lying on...No, as simple as resting on my bed, with my eyelids closed, music that softlier lies than tired eyelids upon tired eyes. It's too late for all that now, too late for those soft, softlier words that were once so beautiful and so good. She had been good, hadn't she? There was nothing to spoil the good knowledge of her own goodness, was there? It was James who had told her that he was finished with her. No, no, *she* had told *him* that, it was she who had driven James out of the house. Good wife. Goodwife.

We've been through all that, the bag lady said wearily.

I know. I'm sorry. I don't mean to bore people. I'm timid sometimes. *Do so,* you said just now. Go out and die, you said. Well. Do so.

It's not that simple, she answered. If I could lie on my bed and not get up again, I could do it. That would be simple. I've wished about it a lot of times. I've pretended, not opening my eyes until they came open of themselves and everything was gray.

Gray?

Tired. Dirty. Gray.

Hunt for it, said the bag lady.

Hunt for it? Hunt for death? Stalk it like an animal?... Hunt for death. When she repeated it without the question mark (she could be rid of question marks forever, could she not?), she began to believe it. Hunt for death, find out death. Find out moonshine. But that was a happy play, a midsummer night's dream. I used to enjoy things like that but I stopped somewhere when everything stopped. I could start now, I could hunt. Queen and huntress, chaste and fair. I'm losing my mind, you know, she said to the bag lady, I used to be very fond of poetry. It's true that I tried to impress people with it but one has to impress people, doesn't one? else how does one live? How do *you* live?

This time she did not wait for an answer but answered herself, terribly. You feed on me, she said, that's how you live. Do you know that I can kill both of us at once?

Do so, said the bag lady before she could be stopped.

She was standing up perfectly straight now, alongside the perfectly straight trunk of the tree. She pictured it towering over her, up and into branches and leaves and sky, but she was safe under the brim of her hat, and what the tree did, beyond this rough gray bark, was not her concern.

She bent over and picked up the bag, or she lifted it out of the bag lady's hands, or it jumped to her and hung itself upon her wrist. They could now begin the new journey together, but this time it would be shorter, with the way out and the open door and the not waking up after the quiet sleep. She thought, for a moment of dismay, But I have no idea how to go about the hunt! and then she started merely to walk, the bag striking against her knee like the pendulum of a clock.

Gemini, twin. Double, single. Everything began to move together, to move apart. It would all go, softly or noisily, but it would all go. There would be no more lying on beds waiting for waking. There would be no more lying at all. There was nothing left for her but Diana's hunt, her leashed dogs, her victim stag.

She moved one foot in front of the other, the bag lady at her elbow and under her hat which moved with both of them. What she could see from beneath its faithful shelter was darker than it should be, but then it might be that the day had gone and it was time for the night. When night closed in, the Telephone Company would reduce its rates. She ought to call Millicent as she had once promised to do and tell her what a happy time she was having on this visit to these friends— on the Island, was it? on Long Island, the cloud Long Island, the cloud-long island—it was not her fault that the Operator would not answer, would not say, Number, please? There had been days when she had dialed O for Operator just to hear someone's voice. The radio was a monologue, the television was a monologue, when you said Where am I? no one answered You are here. She could call Janet, of course, and all the other people she knew and who knew her. She had so many friends....

No, I don't, she said. I used to have friends, but James didn't like them. We never talked much, you know, though we must have talked sometimes because I remember very well that he shouted at me. Why don't you answer? he shouted, and I said, You don't have to shout.

Where are we going?

Not far.

Let's get on with it, the bag lady shouted above James's shout.

It was not James. It was another sudden noise, much louder, a crash come all at once and gone all at once. Around her, the ground lit up, and then the light went as quickly as it had come, the snap of a whip. When she looked down, she saw earth as brown as coffee grounds and wet. When had the wetness come into it? She put her hand down along the side of her skirt to feel if that was wet too, but there was no feeling through the black gloves. She thought about her arms, and there was certainly a coolness about them, and when she thought about her shoulders, she could feel the water dance.

It was raining, she realized cleverly. The noise was not James shouting at her, it was thunder shouting at her. The whip light was lightning, the coffee grounds were earth and leaves, gulping rain.

Very soon, she would be as sodden as the land itself. She should find at once a place to dry. A place to die. She was very confident that she need only find the dry place, the silent place, the dead place where the lightning and the thunder were not alive and playing with her—the dead place like her bed where she could lie down and close her eyes. When she had found it, the rest would come naturally. She would give up, and then she would die. She had lain down so many times, wishing never to get up again, and now it was going to happen at last. Here, in her own apartment, she could lie down forever.

In her apartment, the wind rose. The owl, for all his feathers, was a-cold. The telephone rang, and she started to get up from her bed (although she was standing already) and go to answer it, but then it rang inside her head and she put her hands to her temples and it stopped ringing. It had not rung, really, it was the wind that whistled for her to come.

He left me, she said aloud tonelessly. I tried to make him stay, and that was worse than his leaving me. I would have gone down on my knees and begged, but he left too quickly— Why would I have gone down on my knees and begged when I hated him so and wanted him to go? No! I wanted to send him away, I want to send him away, I wanted to *send* . . . I was right from the first, you know, wasn't I! It was always understood that he was the one who wanted to marry me, that I was the one who—obliged him. Would *obliged* be the right word? she asked, suddenly anxious.

Tricked him, said the bag lady.

I thought you had gone. I thought you left me when the noise started. It doesn't matter what you say to me any longer, you can't hurt me now because I've arranged to die. There will be a lace tablecloth, and those crystal glasses for the party, and the best silver. And no guests . . . James never loved me at all, did he? Did Janet love me?

I remember Janet, the bag lady said. She was a nice lady.

You mean that she was only being nice to me? You mean no one ever really loved me? Not Mother or Daddy or Millicent or my grandchild, when he, she, it comes. (Or when *they* come. Millicent could have twins, I suppose, twins would keep her busy, wouldn't they, really busy, not busy-busy-pregnant-pretend the way she is now, happy-home, happy-husband, no time for anything, no time even for her mother.—I've telephoned her regularly, you know, I telephoned just a little while ago. She said, Oh, *Mother,* the way she always does, she'd be just as happy if I never called. I'd be just as happy too.) Is it true that no one ever loved me?

Who did you love? said the bag lady.

Whom, not who, said Florence automatically.

Whom did you love?

Nobody. That's why I'm so free now, perfectly free to die. It won't take long, she added quite kindly. Are you afraid of it?

It?

Dying.

I don't know, said the bag lady, I've never tried it before.

5

They walked together, looking for it. Under the brim of her hat, her home, her sanctuary, she could see the lightning flash around her feet in a fury of light on leaves and earth. There was a whipping wind now, and thunder like a bombardment from the gods on Olympus, the place where Jupiter lived, or was it Zeus? Jupiter was Roman, Zeus was Greek, or was it the other way around? Oh God, she thought, oh gods, they'll be angry with me, he'll be angry with me, not remembering his name. James, was it? or Gerald? She had married one of them, her daughter had married the other, they say the owl was a baker's daughter. Too much of water hast thou, poor Ophelia, oh, that's a very apposite quotation. My college professor said that once about something I wrote, my college professor loved me, he gave me an A, though everyone said it was very hard to get an A from him. The question is apposite because ... because ...

Because, she knew with sudden relief, because I am drowning. The heavens, appositely, have opened on me, Olympus is on fire. Really, she thought quite calmly, I am going to drown. Here, in the middle of some kind of forest in some part of the world, I am going to drown.

Water and wind were everywhere. She was drenched in deluge, and there was no way of escape. Where water and wind did not find her out, thunder and lightning would. She knew now what the storm intended. It intended to kill.

But that's what I want, she thought. I will lie down here in the midst of chaos and old night, and I will go to sleep on this new bed.

The world ripped and tore apart in a strike of lightning. The blaze was terrible and swift, a burning stallion, and she fell to her knees, her flesh becoming swamp, her bones flood, her blood tidal. A waterfall roared at her ears, and a sheet of hammered silver closed off the closing-in of dark. Now I lay me down to sleep, she thought and felt a stir of excitement. She fell further forward and onto her knees and elbows, like some kind of animal, something bovine. She said good-bye but there was really nothing to say good-bye to. She let her elbows slide forward into mud, up to her elbows in mud like a child—See, Mummy, I'm getting dirty, dirty, dirty—Everything dirty, gleefully. In a moment she would be full-face down, the bones of her forehead would be pushing their way into this grave. Her flesh would melt, her blood would run blessedly cold. She had meant to die laid out, on her back, hands crossed like the knight on his tomb, but this was better. This was sweet because her eyes were blinder than ever, not just blindfolded under the shelter of the hat but blindfolded by earth and leaves and wild wet.

She leaned into the earth. Her elbows gave way. Her forearms rested long and narrow on the ground. Her hands were flat at last, at long last flat and black and dying quietly.

This was to be it then—this moment of luxury and letting go. Let go, let go, soft, cradle, dark. Her gloved hands began to creep forward, slide, bringing her down into this home of earth. In a measurable space of time, quickly now, she would be free. She would never again have to answer any questions. She would be dead. On the ground, before her eyes, she saw her hands turn over slowly, palms up. There was silence.

Into that silence, the scream came like a distant riptide of the storm. She heard it first, senseless and wordless, and then, when she heard it again, she heard the words and she knew the voice.

The bag lady was screaming wildly. I don't want to die! I don't want to! I won't!

She heard the scream quite plainly, but it was safely distant, out on the edge of a world that was fading. Nothing in her responded to it except the gloved tips of the gloved hands, which had been lying so quietly and about to die. The tips curved inward, just slightly, responding perhaps to a faint anger, a blurring resentment at being interrupted.

I don't want to die! the bag lady cried out again, but this time it was not a distant scream but nearly a shout, loud enough to stir the leaves and stride the thunder which was breaking in roar and thud, striped with lightning. It was all overhead, she need not look at it. Let the bag lady shout, she was now beyond all shoutings.

I don't want to die, di-ie, di-i-i-i-ie. The scream had gone, the shout had gone, there was nothing left but a baby's frightened whimper, a baby or a little hurt dog, something out there, something small between the high beating of wings in the sky and the cold of the cemetery on the ground. I don't want to die, the small, small voice said. Please, please, listen. I don't want to die.

She forced the tips of the gloved fingers to uncurl, because if once she let herself be angry she would never be able to escape. If she was very quiet and careful, this need be no more than a delay. Of course you want to die, she told the bag lady, her mouth pressed now against the earth, her lips moving gently because of the baby, the puppy. Of course you do. I'll tell you exactly how it will be, she said. E-zackly, the way children tell things to each other. First, we'll close our eyes very softly, very softly, then we'll open our fingers—See, I've done it already. Then we'll rest against this earth which is waiting for us....

I don't want to die.

Hush, hush, hush.

I won't hush. You're killing me. The whimper became shout again. You're killing me!

Hush became shout, matching it. I am not! You're perfectly free! Her fingers which she had undone so carefully were turning back into fists, muscles, nerves, veins, blood, everything that was meant to die. No fists. No *fists*. Do you hear me, you fool? she demanded of the bag lady through clenched teeth, shut mouth (the mouth that had been drinking sweet earth). Do you hear me? You're perfectly free. See? I'm not even holding you.

You must hold me, said the bag lady. I'm afraid.

It was you who told me to die, Florence said angrily. You said *Do so*.

I didn't mean it, the bag lady whimpered. Put your arms around me. I'll be good. I'll help you walk, we'll help each other. Please, said the voice tinily, and then it started to say

211

something else and there was a crash of Jupiter and of lightning to split the world twice over and a rush of killing rain, and all words but one were lost. Please, said the tiny voice at the tail of the slashing dragon.

You *told* me to die, Florence repeated. You agreed.

Please.

They were in water as in ocean. Tiny gold and silver and black flecks floated in front of their eyes and were snatched back, leaf-things, broken-off bits of lightning, little hooked claws.

Please. Please hold me.

Ahead of them was the tunnel of dark and endings. There's nothing to be afraid of, she said trying to make her voice very steady. Just lie with me here, just wait. It will come. You'll never be afraid again.

I'm afraid now. Please, please.

There was a jerking all through the bag lady's body, and it fed into Florence's body, at war with the promised peace. I will have to be at war with my own body, she thought in a kind of terror, or the other body will kill the peace that is waiting for me. If I could kill *her*, she thought, but I don't know how. Nothing will ever quiet her but being rescued. Nothing will ever quiet me but being still.

Being dead, I mean. I can't kill her. I don't know how. I said that before, didn't I? I didn't used to repeat myself all the time, I forget things, you know, because they need to be forgotten. I told James he would have to go, it's not true that James left me. He married again, he had planned that all along, I expect, someone got hold of him, he would never have left me otherwise, did he marry again or am I forgetting what he did? He must have, or he would never have left me. No - he - did - not - leave - me. I ordered him to go.

Don't leave me like he left you, said the small voice hopelessly.

He didn't leave me. I just told you that. I ordered him to go.

Don't order me to go, said the small voice. Please, it said.

The waves were rising around them, the tide was rising, the gold and silver and black fishes would swim into their mouths. She knew what she had to do—at once, or she would never escape. She must save this—this woman, this thing, this incubus, this bag lady who hung on her arm as if she was a bag herself and not a person. Somehow, she would have to drag Incubus (you never had a name till now, she thought for one moment of triumph), Fiend, Demon, Devil, poor devil, poor demon, poor fiend, poor *poor* incubus)—She would have to drag this monstrous It with the tiny voice to where It would be safe, dry, warm, surviving.

And then *I* can die, she said to Fiend.

Anything you want, said the devil-voice. I'm dying, said the demon. Save me, said the incubus. Please, said the bag lady, oh please.

She stooped, bending double (though she had not even known she was standing), and she pulled the bag lady's body up into her arms. It weighed the exact tonnage of the world itself. Lightning illuminated it, thunder rolled over it, wind extinguished it, but it still lay there as helpless as a baby, a puppy, a lamb, arms dangling, legs dangling, as merciless as it was massive, only the voice whimpering Please.

Hold on to me, Florence said grimly and shifted her own shoulders, braced her own back and thighs and hips, and began to stumble forward, not knowing where to go, only to keep moving. The wind at her back helped for a moment, and then it veered viciously and thrust the torch of lightning into her face, the shock of pouring rain.

I will carry her to a dry place, she told herself. I will put her down, all safe. She will have to let go of me then, and I will be free of her forever. Then I will be able to die, and I will be free of myself. Her thoughts were running like pebbles in an avalanche. To the rattle and the thud and the rising roar of the pebble thoughts, she began to walk steadily, not to stumble, body as mechanical as a marionette, thoughts as formless as the storm.

6

The path, if it was a path and not a channel of water, a tunnel of wind, climbed upward. She could feel it through the soles of her thick shoes, the heels dragging her down. Roots tried to trip her, and bushes snatched her cape. The bag lady lay against her as inert as clay, her arms twisted around the shoulders of her bearer, or was she lying against a reluctant breast, or was she being dragged with black-glove hands under hollow armpits? Flesh or skeleton, she had to be delivered to safety as Millicent's baby would have to be delivered, as Millicent had been delivered once. I didn't want Millicent, of course. Why *of course?* Mothers are supposed to want their babies, good mothers always want their babies. I was a good mother. I *am* a good mother. Stop talking, stop listening, she reminded herself. It doesn't matter now, I don't have to think any more. Just get up this growing hill and find some place to lie down before I drown, before we both drown. Maybe *she* has drowned already, she thought suddenly, maybe the waters have already risen so high that she has gone and taken her life with her, and I am left here alone and not dead yet, not even dying. I'm moving too strongly. I can't die until I can lie down.

She shook her burden, and it was still limp. If it was dead, surely it would be cold and stiff, having died all by itself and so frightened. A branch whipped across her face, but the hat defended her. She had forgotten the hat. So long as she was under its brim, she was safe, and the baby lady was safe too. The bag lady, not the baby lady. Poor soul, poor soul, you'll have to fend for yourself after I've laid you down safe and laid myself down dead. Fend, what an old word, old magic. Magic was once real magic. It got lost and then I got lost, and once a thing is lost, it can never be found. Can it be found?

She shook the bag lady, who was still warm. Can it be found? she asked and answered for herself that, no, it could not. There was a way out, but never a way back. Well, she would be there soon. Her moving body was resolute and tireless. She could, she thought fearfully, walk up this clutching wooded hill forever, never come to the top, never lie down. The brim of her hat had blown flat against her eyes, like a dark bandage wound around them by the wind and the rain. Her cape was as heavy as chain armor, link on link of solid water that would soon soak through her whole body. What was she wearing underneath the cape? She no longer remembered, she had not seen or touched her own body or what it wore underneath the cape for days, weeks, months, perhaps years. It was not important. The rhythm of the unviewed body had taken everything over. Her legs moved like pistons. Her shoulders, arms, back accepted their duty, bowed to the enduring weight at each step, lifted after each step effortlessly.

She walked, and the hill climbed, and the black sky, laced with torrent and wind, the sky she could not see, came down to meet her. She was in deep woods now, she could tell it by the ramparts and fortresses. There was a chattering in her ears, as if tiny vicious animals were pressing around her. There were streaks of blazing lights, edged in black, behind her eyes. She was dying at the top perhaps, an aging dandelion gone to seed, the stem still remorselessly alive and full of green

215

juice. If the top dies, she promised herself, the rest will have to follow. It will all go soon in the storm, after the storm. Once I have laid down this heavy woman, this woman that I carry in my arms, once I have laid her down in shelter, in calm, then I can escape. I can escape everything forever.

I am strong enough to carry her because, once I lay her down... Lie her down. There it was again, the evil punning. She should not think, it was better not to think. Her strong arms were carrying. Her strong legs were moving through this river of night, the dandelion stem was full of juice, green juice, bitter juice.

Very well. She moved, with terrible effort and with no effort at all. It came back to her that, somewhere, she had done all this before—single, double, Gemini, twin, tick, tock, tock, tick, left foot, right foot, hay foot, straw foot, where did that come from, some Army tag, where had she ever learned an Army tag? Army from armor, chain mail, chain male. Single, double, Gemini, twin. She knew now that, wherever it was she was going, she would soon be there. Stumbling but not from weariness, hurrying but not from haste, she would make her own way on some kind of an unknown path, toward some kind of an unknown place.

It's very near here, she said out loud, but the wind took her words and threw them behind her. She was deaf and blind and dumb from the violence of the storm, but it was no longer important. The woman, the thing, the *twin*, hung on her arm, across her shoulder, against her breast. Wherever she lay, she was still limp and silent and warm. She would lie wherever she was put down, when that place of putting down came into existence, into light. She would waken safe, but without her Saviour who would, finally, have escaped.

I will have gone, said Florence. It will all be out of my hands.

Her way of walking was no longer human. She walked now as if she was swampland, a marsh, gathering into itself its weeds, its muds, its gropings and suckings of tiny hands and mouths. Water poured from below her, rain above. Left foot, right foot, bones of feet and ankles and legs, thighs, hips, the thigh bone fastened to the hip bone, the hip bone fastened to the backbone, the backbone fastened to the jaw bone, the jaw bone... It was coming too close, too close now to the final bone, the bone that cradled the brain. When that bone cracked at last, she would be dead. She yearned for the last bone to break, but, first of all, the bundle of bones she was carrying, the old rags, the thing spilled across her arms, must be put down. A place, a place. She pushed forward against the wall of storm, clenched her whole body against its onslaught, fought the wind and the water until, in a sudden wild surge of motion, like a wave breaking, she hurled her body against a wall that was not water, but rock.

It threw her backwards and she almost fell, staggered, put out her gloved hand to catch herself and found solidity.

She stretched out her other hand, the shopping bag dangling from her wrist—and how could the bag lady not fall now, with nothing to hold her, nothing to support her? But she did not fall, nothing fell. The blind hands, blind in the gloves, in the rain, in the dark that was night under the brimmed hat (like a candle snuffer, if there was light anywhere the candle did not know it), the blind gloves felt, touched, crawled like blind moles on the unknown surface that had struck her. Crawling, they met an open space, a moat, a gate? A door?

Pulling, dragging, pushing, breathing like an old drayhorse, frantic in haste now to reach this place where it would all end, she fell to her knees, holding her burden in her arms. With a terrible effort, she managed to raise it above her head, like a warrior lofting his shield toward the enemy and the arrows, then flung it from her. She heard distinctly the sound of nothing falling, heard somewhere a sigh of relief, and felt cold dry air touch her face. With her own body, on her knees, she followed the shield, the burden, into the space where it had fallen.

Instantly, the rain stopped, and she knew with a clear triumph that she was inside shelter. She was enclosed. The bag lady was safe and would live. She herself was safe and would die.

7

All quiet here. The storm snarled outside this place. The thunder had no ears for hearing it, the lightning lit nothing. Black was total, it was diameter and circumference, latitude and longitude. Geometry and geography whispered along the tight encircling walls, which could not be seen but which were certainly there. The bag lady was lying close against one wall, perhaps, safe and laughing. Why laughing?

Because she is safe, Florence thought. I could laugh too if I remembered how, because now I am safe too. Safely, she let her body slide beneath her. Pressed down, on her knees in prayer, long past praying, she raised her gloved hands to her temples, wanting perversely to feel the last beat of life in the hollows, the bone-hollows, that circled the eyes. The gloves muffled everything, and in a sudden burst of rage, rage at any interference now, when she was so close to ending everything by her own choice, she tore off the right glove. With her newly bare right hand, she tore off the left one. Even in the black of this place, the hands glimmered like white ghosts. She put the ghost-fingers quickly to her temples, exploring once more the ghost-life behind them. The naked fingertips could feel it all now, all the distant surf of blood beating against the distant stone beach. Three waves broke clearly, and she dropped her hands.

Her fingers touched cool dry earth, and she snatched them away as if the coolness had burned her. Now I lay me down to sleep, she thought precisely, and she let her whole body fall forward. The earth that had been cool to her fingertips rasped her face, and she did not like it. With difficulty, which was strange because her body was featherlight now that the burden had gone—with difficulty, she turned onto her back. Very carefully, she arranged her body, straight and narrow on the coffin lid. A knight's lady, her lily in her hand, her little dog at her feet. I remember that, I remember lying so when I was little, in my bed. I was Elaine of Astolat then, I am Elaine of Astolat now.

She could feel the whole line of her body from earth to sky, head to heels, left hand to right hand. She brought her hands together, and they felt strange without the gloves, naked and frightened. She placed the right one against the left one, fragilely, in prayer at the altar of her breasts. Fingers were spires. At last, she thought, and she closed her eyes. Behind the absolute silence of her eyelids, the world ebbed away.

As she felt it go, her whole body sighed deeply. Her wrists failed, her hands fell, her blood drowsed, her bones melted. Very slowly, curving and curling toward some lost center, she rolled onto her right side. Her hand came up gently to cushion her cheek in her palm. She slept.

VII
THE WORLD

1

When she woke, whatever days or centuries later, she supposed that she was dead. Her body was intact, but it was as empty as air. Her mind was empty too, empty and cool, a seashell thrown out by the ocean, still carrying the sound of waves in empty chambers.

The sensation was calm and vaguely pleasant. Nothing had moved since she died. She was lying on her side, so she must have died in that position, although she retained a dim memory of lying flat on a coffin, a memory of joined hands and sealed eyelids. Her eyes were open now. She had not expected to be able to see at this stage of her death, but she could see, faintly. There was a mist of light in front of her eyes, or not so much light as an absence of the dark she had expected, as if there might be a beyond. Death released one from a beyond, did it not?

But, of course, you're not dead, her body informed her callously, you're alive. All that lying down and the coffin and the praying hands were masquerade. There was nothing for you to die of. Your health has always been excellent; it is excellent now. Death was just another one of those promises you couldn't keep, another of those lies you told yourself.

She closed her eyes to shut out the informer. The palm of her hand was still a pillow, and, moving it away, she felt gritty stone against her cheek, mausoleum stone. I am dead after all? she thought. You are not dead, the stone told her. Move, it said.

Eyes still shut, she shifted the bones of her body and arranged them narrowly. Certainly, she was alive. Her health was, indeed, excellent. The joints connecting the bones did not ache, the spine was not wooden. She was neither stiff nor sore, not even shaken. Close to her, she could smell drying wool, and when she reached out her hand, she felt the material of her cape, heavily damp but not sodden. (Where were her gloves? She remembered black gloves.) *Where are my gloves?* she said out loud, and waited for someone to answer.

No one did, because there was no one there.

But I threw her into a corner, didn't I, into an empty space somewhere? She could remember the abrupt stopping of the downpour-pouring rain, the feeling of a sudden roof over her head, of harbor for the bag lady. The bag lady had pleaded not to die. She didn't want to die and I did, but I made her safe first. I secured her, like a boat at anchor, before I lay down to wait for the tide. If she doesn't answer now, it's not because she's dead. It's because she is asleep, or because she has gone away.

If I open my eyes, I will know.

Her eyes were demanding to be opened. They were as restless as sea-creatures, and she could feel the eyeballs dart like fish. I must open them, she told herself silently, I must open my eyes.

Do so.

For a moment she thought the bag lady had spoken, and for no reason her breath caught at her chest and struck at her throat, but then she knew that she had said *Do so* to herself and that she was quoting the bag lady as she might have quoted Wordsworth or Shakespeare. So, there was no way out. She opened her eyes, staring straight up.

Directly over her in the faint light hung what seemed to be a ceiling of stone, so close that, if she reached up only a little, she would be able to touch it. She turned her head to the left, and the wall was as close as the ceiling and it too was stone. Infinitely slow, she turned her head to the right, back toward the mist of light that had first wakened her.

There was an opening. Into daylight. This ceiling, this stone floor, these walls, and then an opening, a doorway? into light. Beyond was color, shape of brown and green and blue, forest, sky, ocean? Her eyes blinked shut automatically against the threats of color and light, opened again.

It seemed to be a small, low doorway. I am, she thought with painful logic, in a prison with an open door, or in a room with stone walls, or in a cave.... A cave. She was in a cave, God only knew where, and fear conjured up for a moment a primitive snarl from some thing lying in wait.

No danger. There was no room in this small cave for savagery cloaked in fur. She turned her head once more on her careful neck, assuring her careful brain that there was no room here for anyone or anything except her body, her self. There was certainly no room for the bag lady. As for the bag...

The bag lay near her on the stone floor. She could see it lying there like the little dog, the faithful little dog that lay at the feet of the lady of the manor, carved on her tomb, curled close to her feet.

She jerked her body around and sat up. There was no room in this place, this cave, to stand, but she pulled herself over, feeling dirt and grit under her crawling knees, her cape trailing after her, her hands grasping ahead. When her hands reached the bag, they grabbed it, and the world that had lurched became steady again. I'm hungry, she thought, but there's food in the bag, I'll be able to eat. Unless the bag lady has taken the food—Taken the food and left the bag? She had a sudden, heartlessly clear picture of the bag lady, prowling while she slept, finding the bag and opening it, eating everything inside that could be eaten, burrowing, greedy hands, greedy mouth, then throwing the bag away and running out of the cave, away from the cave and the woman inside it.

I saved her life, Florence thought dully, and she has stolen my food.

She opened the bag, looked down into it, dim in the dim light, and thrust in her hand. The bag was as full as it had been, its life-preserving harvest intact. When she dug deeply, there was the box of bars, and she tore it open, stripped the wrapping off one quickly and sank her teeth into chocolate flesh. It was exquisite on her tongue, but, when she tried to swallow, it stuck in her throat, and after a moment she put it back into the bag.

I'm hungry, she thought, but I can't eat. Sooner or later, I am going to have to turn my head again and see that doorway, that caveway, and go through it. I can't stay here until my flesh changes to bones and my bones change to dust and I join the grit on the cave floor and become the dust on the walls. It's not that simple.

She turned her head. The light through the opening had become stronger. The Outside was obeying rhythm of moon, sun, and stars, revolving just beyond the caveway, carrying light into the cave. It would find her sooner or later, going or staying, alive or dead.

Beneath the stone ceiling, she began to crawl again, head down in order not to see the light toward which she was moving. When she reached the opening, she moved her head from side to side, the way a cave animal might, cautious of risk. Nothing threatened, and she crawled forward, then stopped, suddenly aware of stone on either side of her, solid, crouching, just visible to her fish-darting eyes. The lions! she thought in quick alarm. The lions at the Library, back where I started, back where it—whatever *it* was—all began. She shut her eyes against them, and then, behind her lids, she remembered with relief that the huge-pawed Library lions had been marble-white. These lions were iron-gray, dark, altogether different.

When she opened her eyes again, very carefully, the new lions were revealed as rock guardians of the cave that was now behind her. There was no longer a stone ceiling over her head. She could stand up, and she did so. *Do so* echoed in her brain, but she knew now that it was her own voice and not the bag lady's.

Standing full height, outside this strange cave, she could see all around her. She could see the earth at her feet and the bushes beyond, the tree trunks and branches and leaves and, the instant she looked up, she could see the sky. It was arched and blue, not deeply blue but a clear washed blue, and she was astonished by its color, because until this moment it had been gray. Had it not? No, said her eyes, it had not been there at all. No color, because no sky.

Everything tightened, everything screamed. She felt herself flung spinning into terrible danger, and her hands reached up desperately to pull down, over her endangered eyes, the asylum of the hat, to shut out all the sky. *The hat!* The shapeless felt thing that protected her from seeing too much, the wide brim that kept out the world ... There was no hat to be pulled down. She had lost it, lost it, lost it, sky, sky, sky. Her mouth mouthed *Help.*

She managed not to scream. She managed to hold on to the rim of the world until it stopped its monstrous tilting. Perhaps the hat was still inside the cave—no, she would have found it with the bag. More likely it had fallen off her head, in the night of dark passage and drenching rain when she had carried the bag lady out of danger into safety. She could almost see the hat lying somewhere in the wild black world she had come through, a wet bruised dog huddled on wet bruised leaves. She stood quite still, and the image went away. It was only a hat, and she had lost it, and she could not stand here forever staring at the ground.

Above her, the sky beckoned. She could feel it, as she had seen it only a moment ago, high and very blue. She raised her head slightly, letting her eyes travel upward along the trunk of the tree, into its branches, into its arch of leaves. The tree assembled itself; there were other trees around it. They had been there all the time, she supposed. She must have run through and between them, in and out of her stumbling nightmaze, staggering under the burden of that bag lady, that Gemini, who had been saved and who had left her savior to stand here alone and afraid to look up.

The sky insisted. She raised her head, her eyes open.

The blue was clear and vivid and endlessly wide, a roof without walls. Her eyes drank it in, even while her body shrank from it, trembling in a convulsion of terror. She could feel the messages of terror shooting through her like racing stars and shaking her with chill and fever, but she did not close her eyes. Shaking and staring, she stood there, outside a strange cave on a strange hill. When at last the chill left her fingertips and the fever let go of her bones (rattling together, be quiet, bones), she looked along the edge of marvelous blue and saw the trees against it in green silhouette. First, the trees closest to her, and then, over and beyond, more trees diminished by distance, and then the hills holding their roots, until it all sloped away before her and, moving slowly, she reached a place where she could see an open field and green grass and trees walking.

Men, as trees walking. *And he looked up and said, I see men as trees, walking.*

They were not men, walking. They were only boys, playing. She could see three boy-figures on the open field, and a large ball. She lifted her hand to shade her eyes, but the hand could not shield as the hat had shielded. She brought it palm down, like a visor, until sun and sky and trees and field were shut away and there was only the earth at her feet.

But she could not walk for the rest of her days with a visor-hand, and it was now too late for shutting anything out. Undramatically, she took her hand away from her eyes, and there were the boys once more and the leaping ball and the green field. Not summer-green, a September-green. So it was September then? It was in September that she had left home.

So it was *home*, then? Not the cave behind her; that was not home. Not the places she had been journeying in, wherever they were; they were not home. Home remained the place she had started from, the place she would have to go back to, without the bag lady who had been found on the way out and lost on the way back.

All her journey would now have to be unwound. She would have to find the city of New York again, the streets of Manhattan, the lobby of the apartment building, the hallway outside the apartment. The key in the door, the room waiting for her, the bedroom, the bed where she would lie down.

Lie down. Lie, lying—Lying.

No. Stop.

She stopped.

The sun had an immediate warmth, even here in the shadows around the cave, and on the field below it was full. She looked down at the cape, hanging from her shoulders like a shroud, faintly damp and faintly unpleasant to her ungloved hands. It belonged with the hat, she thought. Without the hat, the cape had become distasteful, or at any rate unsuitable. It would be unsuitable to enter that broad green meadow, with that ball and those playing boys, when—without the hat and without her companion—she was not any longer what she had been. Would someone find the bag lady lying inside the cave, would someone take care of her?

No, there was no bag lady.

My name is Florence Butler, she thought. I am going back to my own apartment in New York City. I shall walk down this hill and, quite sensibly and reasonably, I shall ask those boys who I am.—No, again. I shall ask them *where* I am.

She unfastened the large button and the safety pins that held the cape together, and let the heavy cloth slide off her shoulders. It heaped itself around her on the ground and she let it stay there. She had almost forgotten the respectable dress she was wearing underneath, and she looked down at it briefly and then further down at the shoes. Their black clumsy shapes were grotesque, but there was nothing she could do to hide them. She put her hands up to her hair, and then took them away.

It will have to do, she thought, it's the best that I can manage. Janet would say, Dear, you look a mess, but she never says it very often because generally—*generally*, she thought—I manage to look neat. I am a neat person. Who is Janet?

You know who Janet is. Stop running away. You have only to walk down this hill in your respectable dress and your heavy shoes. You have only to get from here to there, it's not that hard—even if there's no one with you, even if She is back inside the cave.

There is no She. There is a Janet.

Bending over, she picked up the shopping bag from the ground and then she remembered the handbag inside it and pulled it out. Slipping its double leather strap over her wrist, she felt the instant relief of her respectability. No one who had spent the night in a cave would carry a black leather handbag on her wrist. Clothed and in her right mind, she started down the hill.

She walked carefully. The ground was treacherously uneven, and she did not choose to slip, fall, tumble, roll—roll to the feet of the playing boys, and, there, try to account for herself. There were rocks and trees and bushes in her way, but the idea of rolling persisted—another ball like the one they were playing with, an idiot woman floundering.

If she had put a mirror into her handbag, she could stop now and look at herself. She could assure herself that her hair was not matted and stuck full of straws, her mouth grinning, her eyes askew. If she had a mirror, she would be able to see her reflection, and it would be, she supposed, ordinary enough. She knew very well, however, that she had not put a mirror into her handbag and she knew why.

She reached level ground suddenly, and the boys were in front of her, Greek figures in a Greek frieze. She cast her eyes down because she was not used to seeing faces and eyes. They were staring at her—and might attack?

They were staring, but they would not attack. They were all quite young, softer than teen-age, children really, only waiting for her to go past them so they could get on with their game.

Her hands fled to each other for reassurance. The boys were standing quite still, everything about their motionless bodies saying Go away. She took a shallow breath and said, "I—" and then, encouraged by the syllable, she managed to produce the others. "I got lost," she said.

One of the boys, the one holding the ball, nodded. He had bright foreign eyes but he had heard her.

She said, "In a cave?" as if it was a question, so that if he yelped his laughter at her she could pretend she really knew there was no cave, could not be such a thing. But he only nodded again, and the other two nodded with him like toys. None of them seemed surprised. "You know about it," she said.

"Sure." He was twirling the ball between his fingers, and fingers and voice were impatient. "Everybody knows about the caves. They're *old.*"

There was more than one, then, and the idea was unsettling, as if during the long night of storm the caves had gathered around her, making their choice. She started to say, "How do I get out?" and then she realized that they would think she meant, How do I get out of the cave, and their bright eyes would stop looking bored and become judgmental. The ball in the boy's fingers, twirling faster, would shout Crazy, she's crazy!

"Never mind," she told him quickly, "It doesn't matter," and then she turned around and walked away through the Greek frieze, before they could laugh or jeer or whatever it was they were going to do. Behind her, almost instantly, she heard the soft thud of a flying ball caught on the edge of a shoe. She was forgotten, and she kept her eyes on the ground until she was well away.

When she did look up at last, she saw that there were buildings along the line of sky, taller than she had expected buildings to be here, wherever here was. The sunlight hung over them, dazzling her eyes. That was because she was used to being under the hat, the safe safe hat, and she lowered her head again and walked on, looking down at her feet. One foot, two foot, one Gemini, two Gemini.

No, only one now.

When she came to a sidewalk, a curbstone, a traffic light, she knew that she must be in a large town. There were cars going past on humming tires. There were people crossing the wide street—not many people, but too many and all strangers. She wanted to run and hide, but she was too far away from the cave or the lions, too far away from the solitude of the hat. Holding the bags in front of her, she locked her hands and pressed her lips together, and she managed not to run.

The red eye of the traffic light turned green, then red, then green again. When she looked down from the light, she saw people without wanting to see them—a stout woman in a shrill print dress, a tiny man as grubby as a garbage can and blowing his nose into a dirty handkerchief, a black baby being pushed in a go-cart by a young girl with long hair, strawberry color. She ought to stop one of them and ask where she was, in what large town, but it would be quite impossible to stop people who were so plainly going where they were going, who would know so precisely where they had been.

The bag lady would have stopped them. The bag lady was sometimes very brave, but only sometimes. She had not been brave in the terrible storm, crying Save me, I don't want to die, crying like a child. Infant crying in the night.

There, she told herself. If I can remember lines of poetry, I can remember that there is no bag lady, there never was one. I will have to go across this street alone, past all these people, past the red eyes and the green eyes. If I could only find a bus somewhere, I could ask the bus driver where I am. Bus drivers expect questions, they are paid to answer questions, they used to let me ride free....

I have money, she thought. I will find a bus, any bus, and it will join with another bus and then another and another, and I will travel and travel until I find my way home. Millicent will be worried. Janet will be worried. I am Mrs. Florence Butler, and I am going home.

Under her breath, she kept saying it. I am Mrs. Florence

Butler, I am going home. Somewhere on that hill behind her, there was a hat, and a cape and a lost bag lady, and none of the three had come through the storm. But *I* came through, she thought, and I am Mrs. Florence Butler and I am going home and I will find a bus to take me there.

Another street, and another red eye. She turned right, staying on the solid sidewalk, staying close to the buildings without letting herself look at them. She looked at people instead, wanting to find a face that could be trusted to answer questions: Can you tell me where I can find a bus that will take me home? a cave that will take me home? She shook her mind free of its foolishness. There was a street sign high up at the corner ahead of her. She would be able to read its pointing fingers and to take the words off them and to know where she was.

She looked up, firmly. The sign said *Broadway*.

2

It was impossible. The tail of the city she had left could not have turned in its tracks and come back here to find her, to wrap itself around her once more, curl about her body and hold her rigid on a curbstone in the city she had thought she had left—the tail of the city she had thought she had left, the tail of the lion, the growl of the lion. . . .

She caught herself in time. Her mind steadied, and then her body began to tremble, but she caught that in time too. The small nerves stopped fluttering, and the anxiety of her anxious blood subsided. She curled her hands and uncurled them, one at a time so as not to lose her sensible grip on her sensible bags. She could feel the balls of her feet securely under her, and her heels on the curbstone, and the arches that sprang between. There were no lions.

She gave a small sigh, not altogether despairing, and then she drew a deeper sigh that became a long breath. She was able to contemplate the word Broadway without any emotion at all. It was not the city that had turned in its tracks to come back and hunt her down; it was herself. She was now back at her source, without having been able to escape it in spite of all the traveling.

Not source. Only rivers had sources. People sprang from cells, any kind of cell—biological cells or prison cells, they were all one. She could stand on this corner forever and nothing would change. She could stand here—so emotionless, so unsurprised—and admit the simple fact that she was in New York City, and still nothing would change. This was the city she had left, with the bag lady; the city where her apartment-home now awaited her; the city from which she could no longer be protected by the brim of the hat she had bought in the thrift shop.

She could see all around her now, up and down this avenue called Broadway which was a part of what she had meant to escape, up and down this long street, down to cars going, up to cars coming. There was a car coming, a yellow car, a taxicab.

I'm in luck, she thought formally, still unsurprised, accepting a yellow taxi as if it were a marble lion. If she was surprised by anything about it, she was surprised by its yellowness—a dandelion, a sunburst, a ridiculous chariot.

The chariot almost sped past her; she had perhaps committed a danger by thinking about its color before she raised her hand. But her fingers and palm and wrist were already protruding themselves from her sleeve, almost without her instruction, and the taxi flourished its tires in a sudden yellow maneuver and came to a stop in front of her.

She placed a careful hand on the door handle, and opened the door. She inserted herself into the cab and arranged herself on the brown leather seat, her shopping bag beside her and her handbag on her lap. Then she leaned forward to pull the door shut, closing herself inside.

In the front seat, there was the driver. The top of his head was somewhat bald. His shoulders were hunched under a flabby sweater-jacket. His ears, she noticed, though large, were placed flat against his head like a suspicious animal's and when he turned sideways, she saw that his nose was pointed, again like an animal's on a scent.

Between this animal and herself was the glass partition, but it was opened halfway and, through the open space, his voice came, quite audible, gritty with some kind of accent. He was saying, "Where to, lady?" and he sounded as if he had been saying it for some time.

She was simply not used to seeing people's heads, front or back. The hat brim had preserved her from all that. Now she would have to adjust her vision like someone peering through new eyeglasses—bifocals, always difficult. When he said "Where to?" again, she heard her own voice answering competently with the address of her apartment building. That was a relief. She might so easily have forgotten, or lost, the important sequence of those numbers.

The driver grunted and turned his sharp nose and the nose of the taxi out into the street. It was going to be all right, after all, and she felt calm and almost clever. When she said to the driver, "Do you happen to have the time?" her voice was not even rusty, and she had phrased the question well. She might have said "What time is it?" or "Please, could you tell me the time?" but the sentence she had selected seemed

more—not more mannerly, perhaps, but more communica-
tive, though it was (when one thought about it) an odd cir-
cumlocution. Do you have the time?

I have always had the time, she thought. It was not knowing what to do with the time that had, finally, driven her into
a cave. A cave which could certainly not have existed in the
City of New York and which, therefore, she must have
dreamed? Perhaps she had dreamed the whole thing, had
never been away, had never journeyed beyond those Library
lions. Perhaps she had dreamed the lions....

No, the lions were real, they were outside the Library.
And the cave was real, the boys knew about it and even knew
that there was more than one. Everything was plural, lions
and caves, she thought, and then she had to stop because the
thoughts were tumbling inside her head like small round
stones.

The taxi driver must have answered her question about
the time, but she had not heard him, not his words anyway,
only an echo of his voice. No matter. They were engaged in
conversation, which was what she had intended. "Thank you,"
said her careful voice. "Could you tell me—" She hesitated,
went on. "—where we are?"

He did not take this as an odd question, and he turned
his head. She wished he would not do that while he was driv-
ing, but the taxi seemed steady enough on its unguided course.
"You mean where'd I pick you up?" he said and jerked his
thumb backwards over his shoulder (right hand off the wheel,
left hand the only pilot, but still nothing swerved). "Broadway.
Hundred and ninety-first street. You get on the wrong subway?"

She nodded, although the back of his head could not see
her nod, but he must have heard it. "Sure, yeah," he agreed.
"You from out of town or something?"

Or something. She nodded again, and the back of his head heard her as before. "Good thing you got off the subway when you did," he said. "Wrong subway, you could've sailed right into the Bronx."

Sailing to the Bronx, she thought. Sailing to Byzantium. She folded her hands in her lap. The driver went on talking. The city slid past them. She was going home, nothing stormy here. She had only to wait and she would be home, home safe. Safe as houses. Houses were safe, were they not? Safe as caves.

3

When the taxi pulled to a curbstone and came to a stop, she was not prepared, and her heart gave a sudden jerk of recognition. She was Home, she was at Safe Houses. She would have to pay this man, get out of this taxi....

One thing at a time, she cautioned herself, one thing at a time. First, the money. She lifted her handbag so that it stood upright on her knees and reached into it. There was the wallet, the coin purse, the bills and the loose change. She had not opened the wallet for a long, long time. The bag lady had not wanted it. She said aloud, "There never was a bag lady," and the driver said "Huh?" but he had not really heard her.

The doorman was coming out of the building, briskly, appearing under the canopy. Her hands began to shake, but she managed to pull out several of the bills and to hand them to the driver. She had no idea whether it was five dollars or twenty-five, but he started making change in a businesslike manner. When she could remember the spendthrift words, she said, "Keep it, keep the change," and he gave an astonished grunt so perhaps she had given him a great deal. "Have a good day," he said, sounding mellow, and she nodded at him and said, "You, too" automatically.

The door of the taxi was open. The doorman stood beside it. She got out. For a moment, the sight of her clumsy shoes appalled her, but it was not the time to think about them and the doorman was already reaching for her shopping bag.

But that's all that's left of her! she thought, horrified, and she snatched it back. Her voice said, as it should, "Thank you, I'll take that, it's not heavy," and the doorman (Joe? Thomas? Peter? oh, who are you?) said something in reply. She guessed at what he had said and answered him politely. "Yes, a very nice trip," and "I'll pick up my mail later," and then, when he rang for the elevator, "Thank you very much." The door opened, and he held it while she got in and he even pushed the button for her floor. Most considerate, certainly most considerate. This must be a nice apartment building.

When the door shut behind her, she leaned against the wall and closed her eyes. Perhaps they would let her stay here, the walls crowding like the walls of a cave. She pushed her shoulders back against the walls and hung there, clinging, like a bat at noonday. A curious simile, she thought rather pedantically, but of course it was the cave that had made her think of bats, and the cave was still near to her mind.

When the elevator stopped and the door opened, she got out quite calmly, no longer a bat but a tenant, and she turned right and walked down the corridor straight to the door of her own apartment. She felt sober and sane as she studied the doorknob and the locks (there were two of them) and then the peephole in the door. There, for a moment, she felt less sane, because she was suddenly certain that an eye was looking out at her, but sanity took over again and she knew the apartment would be empty. So much for caves, which had eyes in their deepest shadows, which had lions, heavy lions made of rocks. At least, now, she knew that the cave lions were only rocks.

She put the shopping bag down on the floor beside her, upright against her knee, and sanely, soberly, she found her keys at the bottom of the handbag. First, the top lock; next, the bottom lock. She heard the click, exactly as she had heard it when she had gone out of the apartment, however long ago that was, and had double-locked the door behind her—Years, months, weeks, days?

She dropped the keys back into her handbag, leaned over stiffly as if she were very old, and picked up the shopping bag. Then she opened the door and came (she supposed) home.

She closed the door behind her as quietly as if she might wake someone, and she stood still, looking around. Nothing had changed. She put both bags on the table near the door, and then she picked them up again and carried them into the bedroom. When she left, she must have forgotten to close the blinds, and there was a pool of sunlight on the blue rug. The rug will fade, she thought, not that it matters. The sunlight had reached into the room far enough to touch the edge of the blue counterpane, and that would fade too, perhaps. Next to the bed, at easy hand reach, was the telephone. She averted her eyes. It might ring if she looked at it, and she was not ready for its voice.

In due time, she would call Millicent. She would call Janet. In due time. Where had she told them she was going? What would she say to them?

Nothing. Say nothing.

There was a smudge of dirt on her blue rug, and she

looked down at her dirty shoes, cause and effect. She bent over to untie the laces, and when they resisted, she kicked them off, heel at toe, picked them up and carried them with some feeling of severity into the bathroom. There she made use of its amenities (a word the bag lady would never know now), and then she glanced quickly into the mirror above the washbasin. Her hair was flat, her eyes had a brambly look, but her face was not as dirty as she had supposed it would be. She looked away from it, shrugged, and, leaving it behind her, there in the mirror, she went back into her bedroom.

On the night table by the bed, the gold hands of the little gold alarm clock pointed almost to twelve. It must be noon, not midnight. Even in a strange world, midnight would not dye the blue rug with sunshine. But when she crossed over and picked the little clock up, it was silent. So, it had died waiting for her to come back, and it might have been at midnight after all when it had stopped ticking and died, not at noon. She wound it carefully and held it to her ear like a seashell, and she would have liked to set the little hands at the right hours and minutes but there was no way to find out what the real time was.

She could use the telephone and find out the time from the operator, but she did not know the number to call, and, once she had dialed a number, she believed she would go on dialing. Calling up anyone she knew (Millicent first, and then Janet, and then anyone), trying to fill the space with their voices in this enormous room in this enormous apartment. The apartment was much larger than she had remembered it. The walls that had always enclosed her before now stood away from her, the ceiling was infinitely high. I don't want to be alone here, she thought, I don't want to be alone with myself.

If I lie down on the bed...

241

There it was again, exactly as before. Lie, lying, lying, lie, lie, lying.

She put the knuckles of her hand against her mouth. If the bed rejected her, offering nothing, where would she go? The bed was not a refuge any longer, the cave had not been a refuge. The cave was not a brain. What had happened? Where was I?

What had *happened?*

She let the knuckles of her hand drop. Nothing had happened. She had been away for a while, and now she was back. She had gone to all kinds of places, but in the end the City of New York was still coiled around her. She had never left it at all—that strange, giant city that held Byzantium and the Bronx, the cave and the subway, the churches and the houses and the dogs, and the lions—all the world that had belonged to the bag lady and to her.

It was an obsession, she told herself. I had an obsession. Whatever it was, it's over. Whoever *she* was, she's gone. I won't die of loneliness, she thought, not really. I can always telephone someone, visit, talk. No one, except *her,* knows all about my lies, and now she's gone.

The silence in the room began to take shape, like moss growing over walls and ceiling, over blue counterpane and blue rug, over telephone and ticking gold clock. The patch of sunlight was growing too and becoming a flood. It would be better to drown in sunlight than in darkness, but not to drown alone. Not alone, please, not *alone.*

This is an obsession too, she told herself, this drowning is an obsession. She stepped deliberately into the patch of sunlight, and the silence followed her into it. There was no sound anywhere. If the telephone rang, there would still be no sound.

I want her back, she heard her mind crying desperately.

I want her back, it cried. She was vulgar, common, trash, but she kept me awake. She made me tell the truth. She made me feel real, whatever real is. Human. I'd forgotten that I could feel that way.

She moved her head from side to side, against the pain. The flood of silence threatened to drown the sunlight. She crossed her arms over her breasts and put her hands on her shoulders and held herself tightly, trying not to tremble. Only, the silence...

"It's quiet, isn't it?" said the bag lady.

4

Very slowly, almost tenderly, her hands relaxed their grip and dropped to her sides. She turned her head, but to listen not to look. The familiar voice was not out there any more, but somewhere else, closer.

"You're back," she said to it. "I thought you'd gone. I thought you left me, there in the cave, left me alone."

"I didn't leave you," said the bag lady in her reasonable voice.

She said, "I'm glad. I looked for you, but I couldn't find you," and then she added, swiftly before she could deny the words, "I didn't want you to leave me. I wanted you here. I wanted you."

"About time," said the bag lady, very unsentimentally.

"About time what?"

"About time you admitted it." There was a pause, not a silence. The drowning tide had receded, the room was no longer cold; her shoulders did not miss the reassurance of her gripping hands. The bag lady went on, as imperturbable as a minor god. "You've been dodging long enough," she said.

Florence nodded. "Yes."

"Yes," the bag lady echoed, but not mimicking, and then she added almost casually, "You know who I am, don't you?"

"I—think so. Yes, I know."

"Who am I?" the bag lady said relentlessly.

"You're me," she said, and then, seeking support from grammar, she added, "You're myself."

"That's right." The bag lady sounded satisfied.

There was something more to be said, and they both seemed to hover on the edge of it. If either one could make the move toward the other, they would both be safe. But I don't know how, Florence thought hopelessly. I can't lie to her, that's gone. But I can't tell the truth either.

Do so, said the bag lady, no longer outside but certainly no longer in any cave.

I can't, she said.

Then I will, said the bag lady. I love you. Do you love me?

I love you, said Florence and accepted the burden and the freedom at last.